BELINDA MISSEN is a reader, author, and sometimes blogger. When she's not busy writing or reading, she can be found travelling the Great Ocean Road and beyond looking for inspire. She lives with her husband, cats, and collection of books in regional Victoria, Australia.

Also by Belinda Missen

A Recipe for Disaster

An Impossible Thing Called love

BELINDA MISSEN

ONE PLACE. MANY STORIES

HQ
An imprint of HarperCollins*Publishers* Ltd
1 London Bridge Street
London SE1 9GF

This paperback edition 2019

First published in Great Britain by
HQ, an imprint of HarperCollins*Publishers* Ltd 2018

ISBN: 978-0-00-832302-8

MIX
Paper from
responsible sources
FSC™ C007454

This book is produced from independently certified FSC™ paper
to ensure responsible forest management.

For more information visit: www.harpercollins.co.uk/green

Typeset by Palimpsest Book Production Ltd, Falkirk, Stirlingshire
Printed and bound in Great Britain by
CPI Group (UK) Ltd, Melksham, SN12 6TR

For Belinda.
That's me, btw.
Twelve-year-old you is thrilled.

Chapter 1

Hogmanay, 2010

Flames danced towards the night sky, slowly snaking their way along the cobblestoned street like a slow-moving river of fire. At the front of the procession, Viking warriors chanted to the steady rhythm of a beating drum, blending with the sound of bagpipes.

It all sounded so medieval, but it wasn't anything like that — not by half. Positioned near St Giles Cathedral on Edinburgh's famous Royal Mile, our tour group huddled tightly near the end of the spiralling mass of people taking part in the traditional Torchlight Procession.

Tonight officially kicked off Hogmanay, one of the most spectacular — and exciting — ways to ring in the New Year. And I was there to experience it all.

An icy wind sprang up, causing the flames of our torches to wobble excitedly. I tugged my jacket tighter, warding off the chill that blasted my face, and pulled my beanie further over my dark brown hair. Somewhere nearby, a bagpipe started another frenzied rendition of a Proclaimers song. This wouldn't have been a problem normally, but it felt like the same song had been on repeat for the last two days while we'd wound our way up from

London, after already hitting a dozen European cities. Hearing the song again caused raucous groans and laughter from our group.

'You know what this reminds me of?' My best friend Heather leaned in. 'It reminds me of that time in primary school where we had to practice those Beatles songs over and over.'

For months, our class of ten-year-olds spent day after day rehearsing the same four songs, all from the *Yellow Submarine* album, the culmination of which was being crammed on a tiny stage in the town hall to sing for the masses – mostly other schools and mums, but it was our five minutes of fame. One misplaced step saw Heather, the periscope of the submarine, fall off the edge of the stage.

I smiled at the memory. 'I was a bright pink octopus.'

A crackly loudspeaker and the shuffle of feet announced the beginning of the procession and, just like the song, we were on our way. My breath formed small cloudy bursts in front of me and, not for the first time this trip, I was thankful that I'd packed another layer of clothing. Even though we'd been in Europe almost three weeks already, the cold took some getting used to, especially as we were more acclimatised to roasting under the Australian sun at this time of year.

'Josh was seaweed,' I said, the memories of our gone too soon childhood flashing before my eyes. A small child bounced off my leg and collapsed onto the muddy ground, before getting up and running off again. Her exasperated mother was hot on her heels, a puff of fringe and muttered words under her breath.

'Actually…' Heather looked around. 'Where is he?'

Along with half of our tour group, Josh had dispersed as soon as the procession began, blending in with the hundreds of other people joining us for the traditional Scottish event. He was weaving in and out, looking for new, unsuspecting girls to charm with stories of Australian urban legends. Lanky and a little bit standout-ish, I managed to identify him by his *Where's Wally* beanie over by a group of girls. One on each arm, he looked more than happy with how his night was progressing. He turned the corner with the crowd and disappeared towards Princes Street.

Wet roads glistened under street lights, and grass glowed an iridescent shade of green. Everything here just seemed so … vibrant. From the architecture, to the history, the people, and the fiery shade of red hair over by a first aid station. I couldn't help the small smile that spread across my face as I realised that I was *finally* here.

For almost eighteen months, Edinburgh had been circled on our calendars as the pinnacle of our trip. Heather, Josh and I – friends for most of our remembered lives – had decided we would embark on a European bus tour at the end of our gap year. When one year became two, it only afforded us more time to save, adding more destinations to our trip.

We worked jobs we hated, took late-night shifts, skipped parties, felt soggy food floating in filthy dishwater, and I'd forgone volunteer shifts at our local hospital (the plan was medicine, if they ever let me into university) in favour of forcing smiles at retail customers in the Christmas rush. It was all in the pursuit of adventure. It had paid off.

So far, our trip had been a whirlwind experience in the best of ways. In just ten short days, we'd had a Christmas feast of buttery pastries underneath the Eiffel Tower and battled cheesy woodfired pizza after tossing coins in the Trevi Fountain. Salzburg revived our senses with sweet cinnamon-y apple strudel after shopping the *Getreidegasse*, and hoppy beer in Berlin kept us warm against biting temperatures. I ran my fingers along all the old stone buildings and dunked my toes in all the freezing waters. I wanted to feel it all. The moment we arrived back in London, we boarded another bus for Edinburgh, ready for the biggest street party and New Year's celebration this side of the Atlantic.

The procession came to a quick stop along Princes Street, a neat mixture of Georgian and Renaissance architecture. I wouldn't have known that fact if I hadn't spent three hours battling drizzling rain in a thin plastic poncho on a walking tour this morning. Ornate windows from tall buildings looked down on the street and, while I was busy marvelling at that, a scuffle broke my train of thought and drew my attention back to the here and now.

Josh jogged towards us, nattering nervously about something happening further up the road. Despite the cold, a bead of sweat rolled down his temple. His brown eyes were wide with … was that fear?

'This dude thinks I grabbed his girlfriend. He's looking for me.' A jittery hand rested over his mouth as he surveyed the scene before us. Heads turned towards him. Everyone could see what was coming before he could.

'What?' Now my eyes widened. 'What have you done?'

Heather did what she does best and gave him a shove. 'You idiot.'

'No, no, it's not like that. I thought she was single.'

He *always* thought they were single.

A scowling boyfriend emerged from the crowd, his own Moses parting the sea moment, complete with hot-pink beanie and clenched fists. He glared at me only briefly, long enough to acknowledge that I was there, before reaching around me for Josh, who was swearing like a stand-up comedian combating a heckler. My pulse began racing.

Heather pulled me out of the way but, I wasn't prepared to spend the night tending to Josh's wounds. I was on holiday, not working, and I wasn't about to let him ruin all our fun. I handed her my torch and made a beeline for the scrum. Both he and Burly Man were very shouty, shoving each other in the tiny boxing ring that had formed around them.

'Josh!' I shouted.

He held a palm out to stop. 'It's alright, Em, just don't worry about it, okay?'

'That's your girlfriend is it?' Burly Man tipped an oversized chin in my direction. 'Some boyfriend you are.'

Grabbing Josh, I muttered something about men and women still being able to be friends in this day and age without having to get naked with each other. I think I might have been louder than expected because, before I could so much as clutch at Josh's jacket, they were jostling again. A rustle of fabric, a flash of dancing footsteps, and I felt a blunt sting across my face. All at once, everything was dark and far too bright, like a child was flickering a light switch. My sinuses were connected to a trip switch in my heart, and each beat offered a sulphuric burn. I was disoriented and, as my eyes watered, I took a wobbly seat on the ground. It may have been cold and wet, but it was better than swaying about.

I knew how these moments played out, I'd seen it a million times before when volunteering with the ambulance. Music concerts were especially healthy for face to fist experiences. Heather was screaming at someone, probably Josh, who was apologising profusely. Her voice was soon joined by the polyester swish of a hi-vis bomber jacket. I blinked away tears, hoping to get a proper look at the face that swam in my vision.

Touching my nose only made my face burn and eyes water all over again. Through damp eyes, he looked like a watercolour painting. Street lights shimmered in one corner, and his hair a wispy flame-red cloud with sideburns that reached down and hugged his face. His blurred lopsided smile was the most beautiful thing I'd seen all night. As he came into focus, so did Josh over his shoulder.

'Oh, Em, I am … fuck … so sorry. Are you okay?'

Heather slapped at him again. 'What do you think, idiot?'

She barely touched five-feet-tall in a line-up. Despite that, she was full of energy and, right now, looked like a mother about to grab at naughty earlobes. Josh inched away from her and, in all this, it occurred to me just how many people were happy to watch what was happening, to whisper among themselves instead of help. I lolled about, steadying myself with a palm on the cold wet asphalt. Dropping on his haunches, the first-aider snapped his fingers in front of me.

'You okay?' he asked. 'Is there any blood?'

I frowned, confused. 'Huh?'

'Are you bleeding?' He flashed a torchlight across my eyes and offered a fistful of tissues.

Squinting away from the brightness, I dabbed at my eyes. Anything near my nose made me want to vomit, but there was a small trickle of blood. 'Thank you.'

'At least it's not broken,' we said in unison.

His mouth twitched, a smile that threatened to widen as he offered me a cold pack. Under the light, his eyes were, in one moment, bottle-green. The next, they were ocean blue. 'What makes you say that?'

'It's not all bent up and I can still breathe.' Through squinting eyes, I waggled a finger at his jacket, complete with reflective patches and a blank space for a name badge. 'It looks just as good on you as it does on me.'

'Is that so?'

My nose burned, and I rolled forward, tissue to my nose. 'At least it's warm, right?'

'You do a bit of first aid, too?'

I nodded, looking about for my friends. Burly Man had disappeared, and Josh was still being reprimanded by Heather. He looked like a small child, hands up around his chest as if he'd physically shrunk against her anger, which was par for their friendship.

Heather and I met in Grade Two, when my family moved to the area. On the first day of school, while I stood the back of the crowd waiting for something to happen, she strode across the quadrangle, shook my hand, and introduced herself as my new best friend. Who could possibly argue with that?

We met Josh a few months later when he started at the school. He came prepacked with a face full of freckles, crooked teeth, and milk bottle glasses. When the other boys picked on him, Heather went into battle for him, and he's never forgotten it. Since then, it had been the three of us. Josh slotted into our lives as if he'd always been there and, when I got my first period in the middle of gym class, he whipped out a small make-up bag from his backpack. Inside: pads, tampons, and Panadol. His mum had given it to him, so he could, 'be a good friend'.

He still carried that make-up bag but, now, it also contained condoms, Berocca, and anything else needed for a quick hangover fix. That was essentially our friendship.

I dabbed at my nose again, resisting the urge to vomit. 'A little. Mostly concerts.'

'Why don't you come across to the first aid station and tell me more about that.' He held out a hand and pulled me to my feet. Did I mention he had wonderfully strong hands? 'My name is William.'

I brushed myself down – anything to avoid touching my face. 'Emmy.'

I followed his jacket through the crowd, the state of my face more of a bemusement and free sideshow attraction to anyone who walked past.

'So, first aid?' he asked.

'Oh, I did get a call up for the tennis in Melbourne last year.' I followed along with pointed finger and stories at the ready. As often as I could explain the goings on to friends, they didn't quite get it. This guy? He spoke my language.

'I am so jealous of you right now.' William ushered me into the first aid station. 'I've often thought of packing up for a summer and heading down for the tennis.'

The first aid station, which probably doubled as a marquee at family barbecues and sports club days, wasn't much warmer than the street, but an industrial heater in the corner at least took the chill off the air. That's more than I could say for the wet patch on my backside. My friends lingered outside, like students waiting outside a principal's office. Our torches had been handed off to others in the heat of the moment. Occasionally, Heather peered inside, her face wrought with concern.

'Jealous of me?' I said with a disbelieving laugh. 'Please, I've just taken a fist to the face.'

'Well—' he shrugged '—besides that.'

'How about you?' I asked, sitting on a chair by the entrance.

He took the seat next to me, bringing water bottles and paracetamol. 'I did Wimbledon last year. Roland Garros the year before.'

'You did not.' Speaking of jealousy.

'Okay, so, Roland Garros was as a spectator but, you know, always on duty.' He swung about in his seat and looked at me. 'Any drugs tonight, Emmy?'

A bright light flashed into my eyes again. God, he was checking my pupils. 'What? No.'

'Alcohol?'

'Too broke for that,' I said.

William gave me a hard stare, eyebrows reaching for the sky. He was having none of my shit tonight.

'Alright, maybe a swig of vodka and a schooner from the cheap bar at the hostel, but nothing to get drunk on.'

He scoffed. 'You and me both. Tonight has been a bottle of raspberry cordial and far too much water.'

'Doesn't pay well, does it?'

'Can't say it does, but I do love it.' For a second, it looked like he'd folded in on himself. He popped a blister pack of painkillers. 'No allergies?'

I shook my head. His fingers grazed my palm as he dropped the tablets in my hand. My toes curled, and breath hitched. 'No, and thank you.'

'You want to hang about for a while, so I can keep an eye on you?'

Heather's eyebrows disappeared up into her hairline and her mouth rounded into a scandalised 'O'. When Josh suggested they leave me, I didn't try and stop them; I was happy where I was. There was a quick agreement that it would be easier if I just met them back at the hostel instead of arranging a meeting point. Before leaving, Heather snapped off a quick Polaroid.

I scowled at her. 'What do you want to do that for?'

'For posterity's sake. Maybe prove to people you got into a scrap.' She grinned, disappearing into the throng of people.

Josh held a steadying hand on her shoulder. I looked back at William, chin buried in the neck of his jacket and wild hair everywhere. I pulled my beanie off, forcing it into an already bulging pocket.

'I sure you'll be fine, but just be mindful of it, will you?' he said, eyes glued to the crowd wandering past. 'If you have a lot of swelling—'

'Or trouble breathing, go to the A&E?' I flashed a stubborn smile. 'I will.'

'You know, it's you who's supposed to be listening to *me*,' he teased. 'And it's definitely not broken if you're laughing at me.'

'Yeah, well. Call me a bitter med school reject.' My nose had settled into a dull throb, the kind I knew would still be around in the morning. But at least the bleeding had stopped.

'Reject? No. They let me in, they should have definitely let you in.'

'You're a doctor?'

'Yup, a junior doctor,' he said. 'And in a couple of years, I'll be a GP.'

'What an effort.' I sighed. 'You love it?'

'Adore it. It's the best job.' He smiled. 'I mean, it's got its moments but…'

I grinned. My nose ached. 'Yeah, I get it.'

My plan, thwarted as it might have been, was to train as a doctor, because how good is it to do things that feel good for other people? Even volunteering, seeing people off into an ambulance, at least I'd been able to help, or make them more comfortable for a few moments in time. Recently, I'd had a call up from the local hospital, allowing me to volunteer in the maternity ward. There was nothing better than my few hours a week spent in there. But I didn't need to explain this to William, he understood.

Instead, we sat quietly beside each other and watched the crowd shift and change. They moved up and back along the street, A bright orange light filtered down the street, highlighting the faces of young and old alike.

Whether we'd been joined by anyone else in the first aid station was beyond my comprehension. There'd been no call to attention, and no one had approached for anything more than paracetamol and water. We huddled in our jackets, watching, waiting.

Fireworks exploded above our heads with a loud crack, ripping through the night sky, and sending rainbow-coloured sparks back down to earth. Conversations stopped mid-sentence as crowds gasped as marvelled. It didn't matter how old you were, fireworks were still a thing of wonder. I looked up in time for another *thunk, whistle, crack, sparkle, fizzle.*

When the last one sizzled into memory, I stood and brushed myself off again. William looked up at me, his face expressionless.

'William.' I held my hand out to him. 'Thank you for your help tonight.'

'Pleasure's all mine.'

For a moment, I wasn't sure what I was supposed to do, even though I'd been in this same situation myself time and time again. So, I went with what was … normal and totally not creepy.

'Well, goodnight.'

His smile reached his piercing blue eyes. 'Goodnight, Emmy.'

With that, I walked away. People were moving back down the hill towards the station, the crowd noticeably thinner and torches snuffed one by one. A haze of grey smoke had settled above the street. I chanced a glimpse back at the first aid station, not knowing what to expect. There he was, hair aflame and smile wide, chatting excitedly and handing out bottles of water.

Smiling to myself despite the throbbing pain in my nose, I turned and walked away.

Chapter 2

I'd been a little relieved when I finally clapped eyes on the bouncing kangaroo held aloft above the Ceilidh crowd. That stuffed toy was the signpost of our tour guide, for meeting, for lunch, and for relative safety as we travelled. Given most our group were Australian, it seemed fitting. There'd been a moment of panic earlier when I'd traipsed past a Ferris wheel and between rainbow-coloured show rides and couldn't see it. My brain began running through a thousand different Emmy Has Got Herself Lost Overseas on New Year's Eve scenarios. My heart slowed to a steady rhythm when I saw Josh's lanky arm waving over everyone's head. The consulate would not be dealing with me on this trip.

'Emmy!' Heather appeared from the throng, arms outstretched for a hug. I made sure to keep my still sore nose clear of any squashing.

'Hey, you,' I said. 'What'd you get up to today?'

I'd woken to a note pinned on the underside of the bunk above me. Today was a free day, a keep yourself entertained type day, and my friends had disappeared early, along with everyone else. After my efforts last night, I was happy to enjoy the solitary sleep in, especially if I got the bathroom to myself without fighting anyone. Checking that I was mostly bruise-free, if a little sore still, I spent the day alone – something refreshing after weeks cooped up in the constant presence of other travellers.

Heather rattled off her day's itinerary, the old monuments, museums, and back alley adventures. Josh, the avid walker he was, had trekked them up Arthur's Seat before taking her out for a haggis lunch afterwards.

A traditional Scottish band soared to life on the stage ahead.

I'd spent my day meandering around the city centre, taking the stroll from our hostel into the city, and stopping at a chocolate shop for a rich hot chocolate topped with chocolate whipped cream. It was the perfect refresher as I made my way through cobblestone streets and uber green parks.

Cheap souvenirs were about all I could afford, and that was fine, because they were a sight to behold. Kilted sheep, ashtrays, and miles of thistle themed items kept even the most astute traveller happy judging by the sheer swarm of people in each of the stores dotted along the Royal Mile. My sister was getting a thistle stamped coffee cup, just because she could be a bit prickly when she wanted to.

'What about your friend from last night?' Heather asked.

I shot her a surprised look. 'My who?'

'That guy from last night. The first aider,' she said. 'Looked like you were getting along alright when we saw you.'

'William?' I smiled. The truth was, my heart skipped each time he'd worked his way into my thoughts, which had been often enough that I'd thought I'd seen him strolling over Waverley Bridge earlier in the afternoon. It wasn't him but, for a brief second, I was prepared to give chase. 'He was lovely, wasn't he?'

'Oh.' She smiled knowingly, looking to Josh. His face mirrored hers in the sweet mockery of friendship. 'His name is *William*. Josh, Joshua, he has a name.'

'Be quiet. He was lovely, and he helped me when I needed it.

13

'I'm sure he was just doing his job.' Though, even as I said those words, a part of me hoped that wasn't solely the case.

Underneath Edinburgh Castle, bathed in soft purple light, traditional Scottish music rang out across the parish gardens. Our guide attempted shouting instructions over the top of it all, but he was easily drowned out. It needn't have mattered; friends and strangers broke off into small groups as the dancing began in earnest.

Half the fun lay in trying to work it all out. Arms were linked, hands were held and, through a bit of spinning and something that looked a little like a jig, we figured the rest out through tears of laughter, and a whole lot of trial and error. Finding an ounce confidence, things got quicker, and the night fast became a kaleidoscope of beats and colour.

And red hair.

I came to a breathless, unfit stop, lungs burning in protest at the sudden burst of exercise, joyous as it might have been. Leaning against an artificially green tree, William nursed a drink. Hi-vis had been swapped in favour of a warmer woollen pullover, a long coat, dark jeans and scarf, but it was definitely him. While the girl in front of him spoke like he was the only person in her room, he looked about distractedly. A brief smile or nod was all he could afford her.

I wondered – would it be okay to say hello? After all, he was only doing his job. Maybe it would be a bit weird. Hang it, I thought, I could at least say thank you. Edging forward, I half-expected him to have no recollection whatsoever. But, when his gaze landed on me and he smiled, my heart squeezed and the Rolodex inside my mind came to a screaming halt at W. W for William. Willy. Will. Wedding? Stop.

'Emmy!' He straightened and pushed himself away from the trunk. Taking the few unsure steps towards me, he left his companion with a handshake and a smile.

I smiled. 'William, hello.'

'Hey,' he said. 'How's the … how's the face?'

'Face is good.' I took a step closer, tipping my nose down so he could get a better look. 'Not so bad at all.'

'Good.'

'I just wanted to say thank you for last night,' I said, nervously placing my hands in, and then out of my pockets. 'You know, for the help.'

'You're more than welcome.'

'Anyway…'

His focus switched to the group behind me, and then back again. 'You're out of breath.'

'Dancing.' I threw a wave towards what was left of my tour group. 'As it turns out, I'm not as fit as I thought I was.'

'As it also turns out,' he began, placing his bottled water on the ground by his feet, 'I am no Dashing White Sergeant, so all I can offer you is White Guy at Wedding dancing.'

There was that W word again. It felt like a trail of ants were dancing up my arm.

'Dashing what? White guy at wedding?' I laughed, slightly confused, then winced.

'Here.' William closed the last gap between us, hand held high in readiness. 'Let me show you.'

His touch burned into my skin as he slipped gentle fingers between mine and pulled me closer, flush against his body and exposed to his warmth. I closed my eyes and let my body do the rest, my hand on his shoulder, his across my back, my cheek dipped against his and just … felt. Stubbly skin against mine, soft breath against my cheek, and the smell of wool wash that lingered on clothing. We swayed slowly, removed from the pounding background beat, as if nothing and nobody else in the world mattered because there, in this moment, they didn't.

'You know, if this is White Guy at Wedding dancing, you hereby have a standing invite to any wedding I'm ever invited to.'

William shook with laughter. 'You know what else happens at weddings?'

'You shag bridesmaids?' I said.

'Can't say I've had that dishonour, yet.'

'No?' I asked. 'What is it, then?'

'Alcohol.' He moved away only slightly. Cold air rushed to fill the space. 'Want to get out of here before the fireworks start, grab a drink?

I glanced back at my friends, who were lost in the revelry of their own night. I held a finger up between us. 'Let me just go tell some people I'm leaving.'

'I'll wait here.' He smiled softly.

I pointed to the ground, determined not to lose him again. 'Right here.'

William jumped to his left. 'Not here?'

'Right here.' I held his shoulders as we laughed.

'Alright.' His eyes widened. 'I'm waiting. Scurry.'

Heather spun like a slow-motion film scene. In the time since I'd seen her last, which was not long at all, she'd had her hair sprayed pink, green, and blue; a perfect representation of her personality. She swung around to a new dance partner, Josh keeping an eagle eye on her, returning to her side at the earliest possible opportunity. Not for the first time, I wondered if there was something more going on. If that were true, it would make me the happiest third wheel on earth.

'Hey.' I tapped her shoulder.

'Oh!' She peered about excitedly. 'Emmy! Where have you been?'

'Just over there.' I pointed. 'I ran into William. We've been talking.'

'Who?'

'William, the first aid guy from last night.'

'He's here? You know what this is, Emmy? Kismet.' She stopped and drew back with a look of smug satisfaction. 'Oh, sweetie, your face.'

16

I opened my mouth to protest, but she cut me off.

'You like him.'

I rolled my eyes. It wasn't a lie, but I didn't want to get ahead of myself. After all, we were disappearing in a day or two, no need to get out the calligraphy pens yet.

'We're only going for a drink, not picking rings. I just want to let you know in case you came looking for me.'

Like a mother looking for a child, her arm flew out into open space, grappling for Josh. She caught him mid-twirl and dragged him into the discussion. He bounced across and came to a stop with his hand on Heather's shoulder again.

'Hey.' His chest heaved. 'What's up?'

'Emmy's going to get drinks with *William*,' Heather explained, before turning her attention back to me. 'Do you need money? I've got some money. What about condoms. Josh, have you got any spare?'

'Spare? What? No, I don't really carry them just for fun.' He shook his hands about in front of him while Heather performed a pat-down.

His wallet was held aloft like contraband. 'But you've got money. And a condom, you liar.'

'Oh, no, no.' I waved my hands. 'No, I don't need money, it's fine. And I certainly don't need Josh's contraceptives.'

He tutted. 'It's not like it's been used, Em.'

'Yes, money.' Heather dug about in the wallet, scolding Josh for earlier saying he was broke. 'In case you need to get home or call one of us.'

'No, really, it's okay.'

'Emmy.' She shoved a few small notes in my hand. 'Take it.'

I accepted her offer with a reluctant sigh. 'Alright, okay. Are you sure, Josh?'

'Yeah, it's fine.' He shrugged. 'Go for it.'

'Call or message every half hour, or hour, or something.' Her eyes were wide, the space between her brows wrinkled. 'Please? Just let me know you're alright.'

I nodded. 'I will, thank you. I'll see you both later. You guys call if you need me, too.'

'Alright, Miss Medicine, what gives?' William slid a glass across the table. Condensation rolled over itself, forming a ring on the small wooden table. He dropped into the chair opposite and clutched his hands in his lap.

After squeezing our way out of the Ceilidh, chins buried in necklines and hands deep in pockets, we'd strolled past Princes Street and its rainbow coloured carnival to a tiny laneway. Greeted by foggy leadlight windows and a swinging light, it looked like the best option for keeping warm. A spare table by the window was a bonus.

'Flunked the interview.'

He winced. 'Tough.'

'Other pathways, right?' I said, drawing back quickly from the drink, hands across my mouth. 'What the … is that chilli?'

'Cayenne pepper.'

'In a drink?'

'I'll have you know it's a cocktail named The Fighter.'

'The what?' I laughed. 'I was not fighting.'

'Eh, I don't know, Emmy.' He narrowed his eyes. 'You might've been.'

'I wasn't,' I stressed. 'I was trying to get Josh out of the way.'

'Yeah, you should've left him alone.'

I sighed. 'I know that now.'

'So, you love blood and gore, do you?' William's eyes widened. 'You bloodthirsty woman, you.'

'What is it with that question?' I asked, almost pleading. 'Oh, you want to do medicine, Emmy, very noble. Must love guts and gore, huh, girlie?'

'Yes, yes, you're quite right,' William played. 'It's not that I want to do something good in the world. It's actually that I love nothing more than stuffing someone's intestines back into them. Quite like black pudding, really.'

'Or—' I shucked my jacket off and held my hand up '—or, or, why don't you just be a nurse, that'd be a nice job for a girl.'

William gasped. 'They did not.'

'That was my very un-PC grandma,' I said. 'Right before she told me I should just marry and have some children before I fill out too much.'

'Grandma, get back to the home.'

'Funny you should say that, she went into one this year.'

'Oh, shit, talk about foot in mouth. I am *so* sorry.' Even as he said it, he struggled to contain a wicked laugh.

'No, it's fine,' I assured him. 'She's, like, four hundred and seventy-three. It was time. It was that or let her burn her house down with her still inside it. This is the lesser of two evils.'

'Maybe you can go work in the nursing home. Make Nana a cup of tea.'

'I did think about it,' I said. 'I might yet, but I have submitted to the nagging of my parents and enrolled in a Bachelor of Arts, so let's see if I can segue into medicine that way.'

'A degree earned in eight years instead of four is still a degree. Remember that,' he said with pointed finger.

'The disappointment from my parents was palpable when I told them I hadn't made it.' I leant forward into the table, chin in the palm of my hand. 'How could you get this far, Emmy? How could you?'

'We're not angry.' William took a large sip and frowned so hard I thought his eyebrows would slip off onto pouted lips. 'We're just disappointed.'

'Oh my God, yes.' I threw my head back. 'Does that come in the parental starter pack? Like, here's your new baby, and here's the phrases you can use for life. Maximum impact, minimal responsibility.'

'If it makes you feel better, my parents' disappointment lay in the fact I skipped architecture in favour of medicine. "William, your father and grandfather have a long legacy in architecture.

We were so hoping you would carry that into the next generation."' William screwed his face up. 'The extent of my architectural ambition lies in the bottom of a box of Lego. I can't even draw a potato without fucking it up.'

I laughed loudly and freely, glad for the company and quick wit. Soon, our smiles grew wider, as if we'd received confirmation of something special. Around us, tables emptied and filled up over again, the clash of cutlery and loud chatter eventually dying out to a late-night dull murmur.

'So, I've just bought a place in London.' William glanced around for the barkeep. Business had been slow enough for the last little while that he'd taken to bringing drinks to us.

'I thought you lived here?' I stabbed the table with a finger.

'Here? No. My grandparents on Dad's side are Scottish,' he said. 'I'm afraid I'm only as exotic as central London.'

For the first time tonight, I reached out and touched him, tugging at hair by his ear. 'I was wondering where this came from.'

'And it's not even some weird genetic throwback. My father has also been touched with the ginger tinge. My sister got out of it by being blonde like Mum.' He gathered his phone and wallet. 'But I did study here. Actually, do you want to get out of here? I can show you some of the sights if you like?'

'Oh! Yes! That would be amazing. You know the area well?' I was up and ready before he had so much as a chance to continue.

'I know where to get hot coffee and jam doughnuts on New Year's Eve.' He stood. 'Welcome to William's Rad Edinburgh Tours.'

'Are they rated five-star? I'll have you know I cannot possibly lower my standards after the holiday I've had. Farting boys and vomit-stained shoes, infidelity-inspired fights, and cheap souvenirs are nothing to sniff at.'

'Well, then, aren't you in for a surprise?' He held the door open for me and we slipped out into the night.

Traipsing bitterly cold streets, I was ushered around to ancient buildings and seedy looking alleys. Each cobblestoned street unearthed pieces of Edinburgh's medically related history and, through it all, I got to watch this incredible man shine like a beacon of unwavering knowledge. Not only did he talk with passion, he was completely unabashed about it. He was wonky, angular, and his smile was lopsided, but I'd raced so far down the rabbit hole I couldn't see sunlight anymore.

'So, this is the Royal College of Physicians.' William gave his best game show wave. 'Unfortunately, we can't get in. I think it's a little like Hogwarts, you need a special letter or some shit, but this was established in the late 1600s. Not on this site, somewhere else. This one has been here since—'

'Where do you store all this information?' I asked.

'Hey?'

'Where do you keep it all?'

'I did my undergrad in Edinburgh, so ... a bit of time to ponder this stuff. Also, I just love it.' He ended with a wiggle of his head.

'I love that you love it.'

'Oh!' He snapped his fingers excitedly. 'Let me take you to the School of Medicine for Women. You'll like that, it's back near the castle.'

Moments later, just as we'd turned into the next street, popping sounds filled the air. The same kind of popping sounds you would expect when you were on the wrong side of the best view of the fireworks. William pushed his sleeve back, face wrought with concern.

'Shit. We're late.' He looked at me. 'Emmy, I am *so* sorry.'

'Why are you sorry?' I asked.

William's face fell. He sputtered something about me spending money on a trip, and airfares, time versus money and, well, he thought he'd ruined it all. In the distance, ripples of colour reflected in the sky above buildings.

'So, I missed some fireworks.' I shrugged. 'Know what the best part about that is?'

21

'What?' he asked.

'You.'

'Me?'

'I can see fireworks anywhere. I can even come back for Hogmanay any time. I'm here for an experience and this, this is an experience.'

My phone buzzed. Not for the first time tonight, Heather was urging me to get down there, down to the front of the queue, and enjoy what we'd come for: the castle, the fireworks, the party atmosphere. I had it all here, and I told her so in my text back. I'd meet them back at the hostel. I slipped my phone back into my pocket and focused my attention on William again.

We did make it back to the castle, eventually, going by way of more old buildings and stories. It was late, but we ran on nothing more than the excitement of finding someone who picked up on small cues, banter, and that unmistakable wild humour. I kept him entertained with stories accumulated on my travels, while he filled me in on his trip up here. We laughed at the shared frustration of trying to find the best pastry in Paris, and how he had more of a chance to search now his parents had moved to the city so his father could teach at some fancy design school.

It kept us going all the way back to my hostel, somewhere in the wee hours of the morning.

My stomach sank like a boulder in a river. In the back of my mind, this moment had been coming all night, but I was not ready to let go. Outside my hostel, we stood about at odds for a moment, until I reached for him.

I drew my hands up into his hair and pulled his head towards me. I brushed wayward curls from his forehead and kissed him gently. He smelt of beer, chilled air, and the best night I had ever had.

'You are incredible. Don't let anyone ever tell you any different.' My voice choked up. 'Thank you for the most amazing time.'

His hands curled around my wrists, his nose rubbing against

mine. It still panged a little, but I couldn't care. 'Likewise. Don't go getting into any more fights.'

'Promise.' I smiled. 'You are the best holiday souvenir ever,' I whispered as he leant in and kissed the side of my mouth. Innocent enough to say thank you, close enough to make me want more. I took a shaking breath in.

'Even better, I fulfil the cheap and tacky criteria, too.' He grinned proudly.

A snotty laugh rose to the surface as I let go of his jacket and of him. He skipped off into the night, stopping on the opposite kerb to curtsey and blow a kiss. I rubbed stray tears away as I laughed and waved hopelessly.

It didn't matter that I'd known him for no more than a single day. In my heart, I'd known him forever. The fact he was now gone only left an aching hollow in its place. A dark, rattly space only he could fill. I could bite back tears all I liked but, when it hit me that I'd not so much as got a phone number, I took off in pursuit.

I crossed the street and disappeared into the small alley that had stolen him from me. Nothing but the echo of my footsteps and a rolling fog followed me. It had barely been minutes, but he'd vanished into the night.

'William!' I called. My heart gave a panicked throb.

Nothing.

A misty hotel sign at the opposite end of the street beckoned me closer. My steps got quicker the closer I got. A lone motorcycle was parked up by the front door, and the waiting area was still strikingly busy. If I'd raced to the reception desk any quicker, I'd have got an Olympic medal for walking.

'Did you…' I heaved breathlessly and clutched at the counter. 'Did a lanky guy just walk in here? About yay high? Fiery red hair?'

The bored concierge looked up from her magazine and threw me a smug look. 'A guy with red hair in Edinburgh. What are the odds?'

23

'Please?' I pleaded. 'My height, beautiful blue eyes, dark coat a, ah, a scarf. Did you see him?'

'Miss, there have been about fifty people walk in here in the last ten minutes alone.'

'His name is William.' I reached across the counter, pointing at the archaic paper booking system. 'Is he here? Can you call him? I need to see him.'

With a heavy sigh, my not-so-friendly concierge scrolled down the name of bookings. 'There's no one here by that name. He might be staying with another guest. I don't know.'

I could feel my body shrink back into itself and the heels of my feet sank to the floor. He was long gone, and she wasn't checking again. Accepting defeat, I nodded, rubbed away a frustrated tear, and saw myself out.

Finding him was tantamount to finding a needle in a haystack.

And with that, William was just another memory.

Chapter 3

As I stared aimlessly at the shelves of books before me, I couldn't decide if I wanted a biography, some new-fangled self-help title from a washed-up celebrity, or the 'hottest' novel of the month. I placed all three options back on the shelf and continue browsing.

The thought of leaving had my stomach all twisted in knots, and it wasn't just because I'd fallen head over heels in love with Europe, but more to do with a certain redhead with piercing blue eyes and a lopsided smile I'd left back in Edinburgh. It'd been almost a full week since we'd said goodbye to the Scottish capital via the rugged Highlands, and it had all passed in a blur of castles and lochs.

'Have you got what you want?' Heather idled up beside me, the colours washed out of her hair in favour of her natural mousy brown. She sipped slowly at a can of soft drink and twisted her foot around. 'There's a pub down the other end. Want a drink? Josh's saved us a table.'

'Sure, sounds great,' I replied distractedly, flicking through a copy of *Empire*. With a sigh, Heather took the magazine from my hands, replaced it on the stacks and lead me out of the shop.

'Come on misery guts, you can pine for him over a drink.' We skirted past more souvenir shops, Heather stopping me to marvel at suits in the window of a menswear shop, and found Josh breaking off another row of Galaxy and lamenting that we couldn't get it back home.

'My shout.' I pulled my purse out, aware that I had been a wee bit of a Debbie Downer lately. 'What do you want?'

'Cider,' they answered in unison.

'You two,' I teased, making my way over to the bar, my gaze wandering around the terminal as I waited for someone to serve me.

Airport terminals were funny places. Time seemed to stand still; ten o'clock in the morning was deemed a respectable hour to drink, mostly because clocks seemed to be hidden. Businesswomen in Ugg boots shopped for perfume and businessmen for alcohol and overpriced shirts. I smiled to myself as a man in the café across the way, with a shock of red hair, fumbled to organise a clothes hanger, carry on suitcase and a coffee cup all at the same time.

I straightened. My head spun so fast I could have been in a Seventies horror film.

'William!' I all but shouted his name across the bar. He looked up, head cocked to the side in that way when someone calls your name but you're not entirely sure that you've heard. Though I could see him through the angles of the bar, he clearly couldn't see me.

I darted towards him, a sense of elation building up in my chest. 'William!'

He turned again, this time his eyes catching mine. They widened with surprise as he put two and two together, connected the dots, and coloured between the lines.

'Emmy!' That wild, cheeky grin that I fell for on Hogmanay spread across his face as I reached up, throwing my arms around him in a hug. With a laugh, he awkwardly hugged me back with just the one arm, before setting me before him.

'Well, hello to you too, stranger. Of all the gin joints, hey?' He fiddled with the last of his belongings.

26

I let out a breathy laugh. My body felt loose with relief, almost like I was floating. I couldn't feel my legs. 'What are you doing here?'

He held up the arm with the suit hanger wrapped around it. 'Heading to France for a late family Christmas-slash-New-Year-slash-I've-been-a-terrible-workaholic-son-all-year type of party.'

His eyes narrowed on my clothes, and I suddenly felt self-conscious of the activewear leggings and I HEART SCOTLAND hoodie I'd chosen as my plane outfit, especially when he looked handsome as hell in a buttoned-up navy blue sweater and matching pea coat.

'Is this it then?' he asked.

I felt my heart tug a little at his words. *Is this it?* They stung, and the realisation that I was so close to leaving sat in my stomach like a pit of post-meal acid.

'This is it.' I nodded. 'A thirty-hour flight in two metal tubes forty thousand feet in the air and I'll be back in Sydney.'

'God, and here I am internally moaning about my forty-minute flight across the channel.' He stared at me with those piercing blue eyes. 'Want to grab a coffee then? How long have you got?'

I angled for a view of the departures board nearby. 'About an hour or so. You?'

'A little more than an hour or so. I thought the tube would be busier, so I came early. Just as well.' He gave me a wink as we slid into a couple of empty chairs facing the window. Outside, planes took off, while others bounced and skidded to a stop, ferrying people to and from all corners of the world. It seemed like, here in our own little bubble, time had stood still.

'How goes work?' It was so unfair to be this excited at the mere sight of someone.

'Good!' He nodded. 'Great. Lots of impotence, not me, of course.' A lanky finger pointed back at himself. 'Thrush, colds, disease incubators.'

'Still not you, right?' I teased.

He crossed his fingers before taking a sip of coffee. 'Promise.'

'Busy?'

'Just the way I like it, keeps me out of trouble.'

I laughed, enjoying the way we fall back into the banter of Hogmanay. He asked about the rest of my trip, quizzing me on favourite landmarks and dropping random factual titbits here and there. I asked about his work and training, and went back and forth as we outlined where we'd like to be in five years.

Slowly, without realising it, I noticed William's hand on mine, closing his hand around my fingers. 'Where do you want to go first?'

'Hey?' I smiled, distracted by the fact that he was actually here in front of me, *holding my hand.* This sort of thing did not happen in my life.

He grinned. 'When we travel the world together – where are we going?'

'Well.' I huffed and relaxed back into my seat, almost leaning on him. 'I thought maybe I'd just take you home first.'

'Good. Great. I've always wanted to go to Sydney. Where's the first place you're taking me?'

If I had any doubt about him at all, the fact that he remembered so much detail told me everything I needed to know: that he felt the same.

'Right. I guess the first place we'd go is the sandwich place near the train station. It's about ten minutes' walk from home, in this little huddle of shops, and they make the best roast pork rolls. And breakfast, they do a great breakfast, too.'

'Brown sauce?'

'As much as you want.'

'Excellent.' He squeezed my fingers gently. 'I would take you … for a stroll through Soho. There are heaps of bookshops there. Cafés, obviously. We could drink coffee, read books, and duck into the small jazz bars that you don't know are there until you're ready for an espresso martini.'

'Or…' I poked at his chest. 'A Fighter.'

'No, no, no.' He chuckled. 'You need to not do that.'

'After breakfast, we could head to Bondi Beach. We could fail miserably at surfing together.'

'Ooh.' William winced. 'In the summer? Might end up a bit lobster-fied.' He reached across and pinched at my face with pincer hands.

I angled my face away from his grip, laughing hysterically. 'Sunscreen is a thing.'

'All the sunscreen in the world can't protect this pale English skin, baby. Look at it, it's…'

'… alabaster?' I tried.

'Well, I was going to say porcelain, but alabaster sounds less like a toilet, doesn't it?'

I looked away, covering my mouth with the palm of my hand. 'You are not a toilet.'

He tipped the empty coffee cup in the bin next to us and looked at me. 'You hungry?'

'I could eat something.'

Still in a comedic mood, William began prattling on randomly again. I just knew I was about to turn into the human equivalent of a beetroot. My comment might have been a slip of the tongue, but my mind went wandering and my body ached in all the right places.

We wandered the terminal until we snared the last table left in a Lebanese restaurant. No wonder it was full, with the smells wafting from the kitchen. It was brightly decorated with lots of reds, yellows, and mosaic tiles. We ordered a sharing plate of tapas and very responsible pre-flight sodas.

'You sure you don't want your own meal? I'm happy to pay.' William dropped a tattered backpack by his feet.

'No, it's fine,' I said through a yawn. 'We're about to be over-stuffed with bad aeroplane food anyway.'

'Speaking of "we", where is everyone? You were travelling with friends, weren't you?'

I pointed to some spot in the distance, in the same way a supermarket employee would tell you sugar was in aisle three, while waving in that general direction. 'They're back at the pub..'

'You didn't want to join them? I don't want to keep you from them, you know, if you're all travelling together.'

'We're about to spend the next thirty hours together. I'm good.'

'Okay. Good.'

We spent our remaining time nibbling at tapas and chatting about books, arguing over what we believed was the perfect plane read. He argued thrillers, as long as they weren't medical in nature, and I was keen on beach romance. When those options were exhausted, we launched into a discussion about what films might be showing on the plane. It was a beautifully easy, rolling conversation. My phone buzzed a few times – Heather, wondering if I'd walked off with their cider. I whipped out a quick response saying I'd meet her at the gate.

Just as a discussion about the universe and godly beings was getting underway, the departures board clicked over to *Boarding* beside my flight number. It was accompanied with the familiar *ding* and the professional voiceover of a flight attendant inviting all first-class and frequent flyers to board first.

Reluctantly, and with a shared look of disgust, we gathered our belongings, William slipping my backpack across one shoulder. When he reached out, I gladly took his hand. So comfortable was it that I didn't let go until we reached the gate, where everyone was waiting, as wide-eyed as they had been that night almost a week ago. I introduced William again, and asked Heather to take a photo. A Polaroid was the one piece of him that I could take home with me. Then William asked for one. Behind us, a stewardess announced our rows were ready for boarding.

'This is me, I guess.' I reached for my backpack, our hands grazing at the switchover.

'Go on and leave me, then,' he joked. 'Go.'

'Do you think we'll meet again?' I asked, wondering if this would be it. How often could you say you met the same person three different times? How often does lightning strike the same spot? 'We will, won't we?'

'I should hope so,' he enthused, his forehead wrinkled as he nodded.

'Me, too.' There was a mad rush for tickets and passports and, as I pulled mine from my bag, William took my hand again. He rolled a knuckle between his thumb and forefinger. I would have paid good money to know what he was thinking.

One last time, I checked my ticket and passport; in my hand and ready to go. I looked up to William, ready to impart some final words, but he yanked me into a hug.

'Em, come on.' Behind me, Heather was growing impatient.

I wanted to stay, tucked safely inside his jacket, the light scrub of five o'clock shadow against my temple. His aftershave clung to his jacket, and I wanted that scent to hang around, to breathe it in every day, to have it so ingrained in me that I carried it everywhere I went. While I was busy overthinking, he kissed me. What began on my forehead soon travelled to my cheek, and then my mouth. It was warm and solid and turned my poor unforgiving brain to mush as he brushed his fingers against my neck, heavy enough to feel but light enough to tickle like a spring breeze.

One last boarding call rattled from the tannoy.

'You'd better go.' William pulled back. I started to turn, but he pulled me back one last time, my heart giddy. Between his lips – lips that had just kissed me – was a pen, and he pulled up the sleeve of my hoodie before writing an email address on the curve of my wrist. The way his fingers grazed that soft spot sent shivers down my spine. I bit down on my bottom lip.

'Let me know that you get home safe?' His forehead wrinkled again.

I nodded, grabbing the pen and scribbling my own email on

31

the top of his hand. 'In case you get bored in France.' I looked up, giving him one last smile. 'See you soon?'

'Speaking of the universe, when you get home, I want you to look up the invisible thread theory. I'm a firm believer, especially after today. Keep in touch.'

'You, too.' I pointed at him, voice shaking.

He kissed me again, once more for good luck, before I walked away. He waited until I disappeared down the gantry, my last glimpse of him a lanky ginger with arms waving above his head.

I gave the flight attendant a tight smile as she inspected my ticket, pointing me in the direction of my seat at the rear of the plane. My backpack only just squeezed into the small space beside Heather's, who was talking to Josh. He'd lucked out with the seat in front of us. I shuffled awkwardly into my seat, fiddling with the straps and unwrapping the small blanket before arranging it around my legs.

It wasn't until we pushed off the gate, the captain welcoming us on the PA system, that the first uncertain tear fell down my cheek. Next to me, Heather passed over a packet of tissues and squeezed my hand.

I'd been so unsure of myself since I received my rejection letter to study medicine. I hadn't known what I wanted, past the experience of university, of travelling.

Now I knew what I wanted, and it wasn't possible.

I wanted to stay.

Chapter 4

8th January 2011

Hi Emmy,
I'm bored.
William.

9th January 2011

Hello Bored,
I'm so glad to hear from you! How are you? And how can you possibly be bored in Paris? Please, go eat some pastries for me.
A very jealous Emmy xo

12th January 2011

Hey yourself,
*   It goes a little like this, Ems. There's only so much firewood I can chop before I'm a little sore and achy. I could really go for a massage right now, so I've been sitting in front of the fire, reading up on some medical journals, getting some naps*

in and – when it stops snowing – looking out for pastry. How's it been settling back into real life? Are you okay?

I have a wee confession to make, if I may, in the way that English people apparently don't talk about their feelings. So, New Year's Day? I woke up with the awful realisation that I hadn't got your details. I pulled my pants up and raced over to the hostel, only to be told your bus had already left. Needless to say, I'm glad you found me at the airport. Really glad.

How was the flight home? What did you say – thirty hours? How the hell do you cope? And what do you do for thirty hours of sitting still? That would drive me spare (though I would absolutely not hesitate to visit).

William.

P.S. Let's switch to good, old-fashioned letters? My address is below.

2nd February 2011

Lovely William,

Oh, you have no idea how thrilled I was to see you, too. Did you know I ran after you on New Year's Eve? You'd disappeared around the corner and I thought, 'Oh, shit!'. So, I tried to follow, like Alice down the rabbit hole, but you'd disappeared. I walked into the first hotel I saw to ask if they'd seen you and was told trying to find a red-head in a Scottish city was a long shot, but good luck with that.

As for the flight home, there were a lot of films on the inflight entertainment. The cabin crew kept us all well fed on starchy foods (sleep inducers that they are), and I read a book that Josh had packed with him. So lucky for that book – it filled Dubai to Sydney nicely.

Do come and visit, you'll love it. I'm thinking sometime around October when I may or may not have a birthday? The weather will be just nice, and we can hire a car to explore some.

I'm off to the beach this afternoon, after bypassing the bookshop and picking up some textbooks. How's work going? When does it start? School starts for me in exactly one month. Kind of looking forward to getting it over and done with.

Ready when you are,

Emmy x

28th February 2011

Emsy,

How are you feeling about school today? I know what you mean about getting it done. I'm in this GP office for eighteen months before I move on to the very last stage of my training. They're a nice bunch. If it keeps going like this, I wouldn't be offended by returning to this practice as a legit GP. You know, one of those people with a thousand letters after their name that sound all so important? It feels like it's so close, but so very far. I mean, I can look at how far I've come of course, but ... well, I'm sure you know what I mean.

I Googled Sydney today. Can we get a ferry ride? I love that you're so close to the beach. The trusty Thames just doesn't cut it in terms of bikinis and sun-drenched umbrellas – although, we do try.

I bought a couch over the weekend. To most people that's not terribly exciting but, for me, it means I no longer have to sit on the floor and watch telly. It's a comfy little second-hand number from a vintage shop not far from here. I had a friend help carry it home. If you're ever feeling a little stressed, just imagine two lads walking down the Harrow Road, ancient couch sagging between them, and they happen to prop it up against the wall for a drink at the local – good times!

You'll be well chuffed to know I delivered a baby today. Well, not technically mine. I didn't birth it, nor did it come out of me, but I happened to be in the right place at the right time and, if I didn't know what I was doing beforehand, I do now. The poor woman was in the clinic and, well, there I was. Hats off to any woman that ever wants to put their body through that because I am completely okay with being a boy right now. If I kept a gratitude journal, it might read something like this:

Today I am grateful for: my penis.

W

19th March 2011

Dear William,

I don't even know where to begin with that statement. Good? I'm glad? Did they not teach you what happens in school? Seriously, congrats on the first birth – in the practice, that is. Your first time is always special, and a time to be cherished, don't you think? Mine was at the tennis – birth, that is. Get your head out of the gutter. It was spectacularly beautiful, if a little messy.

I've just been pulled up in class for laughing at your penis comment. My classmate Craig covered for me – said it was his fault, so I live to see another day of Introduction to Australian Literature. Well done to you for that. The lecturer even asked if we'd both like to leave – whether I wanted to or not, I didn't want to in front of 200 other people. No thanks. Instead of leave, I figure I'd just sit here and write you a letter.

Do you remember my friends Heather and Josh? Josh of the New Year's Eve face punch spectacular? About thirty seconds after he'd knocked me to the ground, and Heather found out he'd been hitting on another girl, she realised she was jealous. They're now dating – and I'm thrilled. How could I not be? The three of us have been friends for years but, now, they're just … a bit more. I am seriously excited for them. What kind of a shit friend would I be if I wasn't?

Fun fact: we're currently reading My Brilliant Career by Miles Franklin. What's your idea of a brilliant career?

E x

1st April 2011

Hey Fighter,

It's 11 p.m. – I've just opened my mail after a long day, having had a microwave meal and a shower. Not at the same time, of course – chicken cordon bleu (or what bares a slight resemblance to it) doesn't play well with water.

Thank you for making me laugh – I needed it today. Right now, my idea of a brilliant career is to get out of this GP placement unscathed. I'm exhausted. Off to bed.

First Aid Extraordinaire

14th April 2011

My Favourite First Aid-er,
Get some rest. Lots if you need it.
Come back when you're feeling up to it.
Emmy xo
P.S. I wasn't fighting.

3rd May 2011

My Emmy,

You're officially mine now. I have claimed you, and I'm keeping you. Okay? Okay. Good.

Why do we begin a letter with 'Dear'? All my bills begin with, 'Dear William', and I could swear they don't actually mean it as a term of endearment.

Thank you so, so much for sending the box of treats. Biscuits, tea bags, a kitschy coffee cup and an ugly tourist magnet – I love it.

You are something else, you know that? I am so sorry I've been shit at the letters this month. You'll be pleased to know you're at the top of my list with a red star for URGENT.

I was thrilled to get your parcel – both because it kicked me in the backside and reminded me of what I think of about five minutes after leaving work each day, and for the fact that it is amazing and thoughtful. Clippy Koala has found a home above my desk at work – along with one of your photos. I'll leave you to guess which one.

Mum, Dad, and Jen came to stay last weekend, which was lovely and meant that Mum did all my washing and cooked way more food than I'll need for the next month (spoilt, I know). Dad helped with a bit of painting, and Jen stole my Wi-Fi and watched telly – so all's right with the world.

I'm so glad I met you. Have I told you that today?
William. xo

28th May 2011

Lovely William,

Hello! This letter is brought to you by my university library which, sadly, is nothing like Hogwarts. I'm here with Craig working on an essay for Political History. I'm quite sure neither of us know what we're doing, but we're going to give it a go anyway.

I'm glad you enjoyed your parcel. They were just some little things I collected along the way.

Last weekend, I did my first volunteer stint since I got home. It was a rock concert, and not a band that I love, but it was nice to get out and about. It made me think of you – have you done any volunteering since Edinburgh? It felt good to get back into it, if I'm honest, so I've put my hand up for some more.

Emmy xo

27th June 2011

My Emmy,

Quick catch up – I'm off the grid for a week or so now. Heading up to the Peak District for some camping (drinking), unwinding (not reading textbooks), and doing nothing (true). I hope you're keeping warm. Enjoy this box of goodies. The teapot reminded me of you. I'm not sure why, but it did, so I thought you should have it. I was shopping with my mum at the time, and she did question why I'd bought it.

Never fear, I'll be on the lookout for cheap and tacky souvenirs while I camp. Enjoy your care package.

W.

P.S. It's a negative on the volunteering – too tired/busy/ circle appropriate answer.

24th July 2011

You beautiful man,

Thank you – a thousand times, thank you. It's not every day a girl is spoilt with a Fortnum & Mason tea set. (did you take out a second mortgage for this? It's so delicate!) You're way too thoughtful and beautiful and now I need to think of something to send you in return.

It was my last exam today, so this has come at the perfect moment. I have tea steeping as I write this.

And I'll use the voucher to take my sister out this weekend. Frankie is twelve years older than me, though it sometimes feels like there's one hundred years between us. She doesn't live at home, but she's just broken up with another boyfriend (and I say 'another' in the nicest possible way). So, a night out for the both of us will be great, I think. I hope. Maybe I'll see if Ezra wants to join us, too. He's the lucky middle child – nine years older than me, but I think he might be busy with his girlfriend and her daughter.

Have the best time while you're away. I'll wait for your next mail to arrive – oh, and I'll send you one, too.

Love,

Emmy x

16th August 2011

Em,

I thought I'd wait until I posted this stuff to send you a letter. Recently, I've found I quite enjoy getting things in the mail that aren't bills. I hope you feel the same.

Great weekend away – brain feels a little recharged, and I got a decent amount of sleep. If I'm honest, all I did on the first day was sleep. Everyone else went hiking and climbing. I stayed back at camp and slept – it was glorious. I ate lots of baked potatoes, drank too much beer, and pondered a few things that are a story for another day.

One of the best parts of our trips is the people we meet. What started as four friends getting away for the weekend has become somewhat of a choose your own adventure. It started when Hamish invited another friend along. Now it's friends, girlfriends, people I've never met before and others who float in and out as occasion needs – and it's fun. For example, there were fifteen of us this time. The only people I hadn't met before were Owen, Claire, Angela, and Pip. Pip is a boy, mind you.

Slipped into Sheffield on the way through to pick up a small gift for you. Enjoy.

What are your plans this weekend? Can't wait to hear from you.

Will x

27th August 2011

My Emmy,

It's your birthday soon, right? I thought I might try and fly out for it. I'd love to see you again, and I've often wondered if our meeting was pure chance, or if there was something more to it. Anyway, I'm going to stop rambling – we can talk about all that when I arrive. I've found a hotel, and flights are currently cheap enough. If you have any objections, speak now or forever hold your peace...

W x

5th September 2011

My Favourite William,

YES, PLEASE VERY MUCH THANK YOU OKAY

Now that I've breathed into a paper bag and calmed the hell down – yes! I would absolutely love to see you this side of the equator. And for my 21st birthday of all things. That would be an incredibly sweet gesture. I'll blow off life for a little while and we'll go exploring.

Oh, and I've picked up some work at the local hospital. It's admin work, but it's great fun. I think I'll do a short course on medical terminology. Currently investigating options. It seems more fun than my BA at the moment.

E x

29th September 2011

Lovely Emmy,

So, don't I feel like an idiot right now. Leave declined. Couldn't even wrangle a few weeks later in the year. I am so sorry. I'll just sit in the corner and lick my wounds.

William.

16th October 2011

William,

Please don't feel the need to apologise. It's out of your control. We will catch up again, somewhere on this earth. It's just a matter of things aligning. Hey, maybe if I get punched in the nose again, you'll appear. I can't say I'm keen to repeat that experience though.

Off to a party tonight, wish me luck!

E x

12th November 2011

My Emmy,

It feels a little strange to say it's been so long since we've talked. One thing I did notice? I've missed it – and I know that it's my fault. I've been working and socialising, got a bit of late autumn camping in, and have been studying until it feels like my eyes are about to drop out of my head.

The end of first year is fast approaching for you – how do you think you've fared? And are you enjoying it? I know we talked about moving sideways into medicine (despite how tired I am, I do love it – please don't let that put you off). Have you had any leads on night school? I'm keen to hear about that – please keep me updated. I'll send you a book if you like. I'm going to send it to you anyway. It was a great help to me, so I'm sure you'll find it useful.

Recently, someone's asked to rent one of my spare rooms. They'll be working in London soon and will need a place to stay. Problem is, I don't mind the peace and quiet when I get home. Upside is I can charge rent, I suppose, and that'll help with the mortgage. What do you think?

I found this great little eatery nearby that I'm going to take you to one day. Best pho ever. It's just off the Harrow Road, near home. Have you been to your favourite sandwich shop lately? I look forward to the day I can (finally) get there and shout you lunch.

I'm off to bed for the night, but look out for the postcard I sent you from our camping trip.

Yours,
William x

1st December 2011

My William,

Corn-wall. It's been ten minutes and I haven't stopped laughing. My mum snatched the postcard from me and wanted to know who sends postcards like that. Ha!

So, what would you say if I came to visit instead? I have a job now (because that doesn't make me sound like a bum at all), so I could grab a cheap ticket, stay in a hostel. Maybe we could meet in Edinburgh for New Year's? Or, maybe after New Year's? I think it's a bit late to organise a New Year's trip now.

Let me know,
E x

10th January 2012

Ems,

Yes, to all the above except the hostel. I have plenty of room here. It's staggering how big this place is for just me. Now, I did buy it with the future in mind, and I do have a lodger now, but there is still plenty of room here. I'll make up one of the spare rooms, and we can work out what happens from there. Just buy the ticket and let me know when you've booked for. I'll meet you at Heathrow.

Gotta run, but wanted to let you know that it's a very big yes from me.

Will x

27th February 2012

William!

I am laughing so much right now. I squealed so loudly at your email that Craig and I got kicked out of a lecture. For real, this time. In front of everyone, and I laughed all the way out the door and into the halls. Don't care, too busy being excited. Let's make this happen! I'm going to put together my London Bucket List. I know, I know, bucket list makes it sound morbid, but it's a list of places I want to see and things I want to eat.

So, shoot me some recommendations.

Much love,

Emmy.

15th March 2012

My lovely Emmy,

I love the idea of the bucket list. If you get it through to me early enough, I'll work out a rough itinerary. How long are you thinking of staying for? A week? Two? A month? Let me know all of that and I'll work around it. I'll show you all my favourite 'outside London' spots, too.

William.

31st March 2012

Dear Mr Tour Guide,

I've attached a mini-list of everywhere I think I should go. I want all the kitschy, flag-waving tourist experiences. I want high teas and night-time cocktails, fancy theatres and bus tours. Buckingham Palace is open in the summer, right? Let's go there, too. Have you been?

What do you think of my list?

Emmy.

20th April 2012

Hey there,

Just checking in to see if you got my last email? I'm guessing you're run off your feet now, so that's why you've been quiet. It's okay. I've been dealing with some stuff here, too.

Dad's not well. The idiot went and had a heart attack, so we're all sitting in the hospital waiting room at the moment. The doctors think he'll be okay, so that's a good thing, right?

Can I ask you something? I know we've always emailed or posted, but can I call you? I need someone to talk to about this, and I think you're the only one who'd make sense. You know, being a doctor and all.

Looking forward to hearing your voice.

E xo

15th May 2012

William,

Okay. I'm getting worried now. I have no other way of contacting you. Heather checked Facebook and can't find you. Are you okay?

Emmy.

21st June 2012

William,

I'm not sure what's going on. I hope it's that you're busy and you're kicking ass at your job. Saving lives and taking names, right?

I have some news. Heather and Josh are moving to London in January. They've both picked up work, and they're flying high. I'm a little jealous, and a whole lot of sad but, more than anything, I'm excited for them. Her career is kicking along nicely, and I'm so proud of her. I'll miss them both terribly, but it's a good excuse to visit, right?

Are you okay?

Emmy.

3rd August 2012

William,
Where are you?
Emmy.

I tried one last time to send an email.

This message was created automatically by mail delivery software.
A message that you sent could not be delivered to one or more

of its recipients. This is a permanent error. The following address(es) failed:

william.scott@southlandclinic.co.uk
No Such User Here

***

When Dad was sick, William was the one person I would have trusted over anecdotal websites, misinformed family, or sanitised for the public doctors. Talking to him, though we hadn't physically spoken to each other in almost eighteen months at the time, would have put my mind at ease and pointed me in the right direction. And when my two best friends decided to pack up and move to London, he was the one person I thought I could count on for … something. What I hadn't counted on was this. This was cold, and it hurt.

I tried to email from another address, but that one bounced back, too. Good to know it wasn't just me, then. I went so far as to check the local phone directory. The results page was blank. Facebook offered me a whole heap of blonds and brunettes, but no flame-haired Londoners. I was shit out of luck.

Thinking about it constantly only turned sadness to anger, and when I finally got past that point, I wanted to be done with the reminders of that holiday and the months afterward that were tacked to walls of my bedroom. I removed the photos, postcards, and notes, and placed them in a box along with all the trinkets, toys, mugs, and books he'd sent. William had been relegated to a box underneath my bed.

Chapter 5

New Year's Eve 2012

The post office smelt of sunscreen and agitation. A fly buzzed about my head, and I could feel sweat making a beeline from my neck right down to, well, where the sun didn't shine. My backpack was laden with books, photos postcards, dog-eared envelopes, and a tea set. They were all memories I needed to give back.

I stepped forward, said all the right things, signed the customs declaration, and forced the last few years of my life into the nondescript brown cardboard box. Behind the counter, a woman with a weathered face tapped her artificial nails and suggested maybe I needed a bigger box.

Forcing a smile, I bent the lid over the contents and taped it shut. 'My box is perfectly big enough, thanks.'

Behind me, someone sniggered.

I tossed the roll of packing tape back at her, along with my parcel, and hoped for the best.

'I really don't care if it breaks.'

As far as I knew, William hadn't moved, he'd simply vanished. I'd never found a 'Return to Sender' in the letterbox, and his emails or letters never indicated that I'd done or said something untoward. He'd obviously lost interest, moved on to a girl closer to home, maybe. Probably. I couldn't imagine he'd be single for long, as much as that thought irked me, irrationally, a little.

Stepping outside, away from the confines of a barely-there air-conditioner, I slipped my sunglasses on and, feeling a little lighter, made my way out into the street. The sunny glint of an old steel bumper and front wheel caught my eye.

'Hey, you.' I smiled.

'Hey yourself.' Craig waved an arm at his car in a flourish. 'You like?'

The same Craig who'd saved my skin in class – when I'd been caught more than once laughing at a letter – was slumped against the pillar of a car that was probably older than both of us combined. After that very first class, we began searching for each other before lectures. Our buddy system soon extended to study blocks in the school library and coordinating subjects, because what's better than having someone to pinch notes from? It was especially helpful when one of us didn't feel up to going to class or needed an extra shift at work. It helped that we were both considered mature-aged students; two old souls looking out for each other. He became one of my closest friends.

Now, he stood in the street looking like a retiree floating the wave of a mid-life crisis. All he needed was a set of golf clubs to go with his wide-brimmed hat, popped-collar polo, and salmon-pink shorts.

'I'm not diametrically opposed,' I said through a chuckle. 'Not sure about the outfit though.'

'Funny.' Craig threw his head back in a mocking laugh. 'Picked her up this morning. Want to go for a ride?'

'Got air-con?'

'It's got windows.'

'No!' I gawped, bending down to peer through the window. 'And eye-bleedingly beige seats.'

'I know. It's great, isn't it?' Craig's hand hung limp over the top of the steering wheel. 'Used to belong to my cousin's mate.'

A reliable purchase, if ever there'd been one. I peeled the tin can door open and took my place on the blistering hot, third-degree burns vinyl that we all know and love in the Australian summer. 'I'm surprised by the lack of pink, going by your very fancy shorts.'

'They're for the party tonight.' He pouted. 'There'll be a pool, right?'

'Definitely a pool,' I said.

'Good.' Gears crunched underneath us. 'All I need now are my lambswool seat covers and I'll be set.'

'Oh, please don't.' I laughed. 'Please.'

'What? You don't like a little wool in winter?'

'Only if my clothes are made of it.'

Craig grinned to himself as he pulled the car into the street. I reached across and turned the radio dial on and up. While the road shimmered and my hair stuck to the back of my neck, at least the windows blew a bit of air around, even if it did feel like being caught in a low speed hair dryer.

'What's happening in the post office? Anything exciting?' he asked, throwing a quick glance my way.

I shook my head. 'Just bills. Nothing fancy.'

'Are you okay?' His voice was almost drowned out by the rhythmic *thwap* of air coming from both windows.

I nodded and looked at him. 'I am.'

'Really? Because you're doing that thing.'

'What thing?' I looked at him curiously.

He reached across and pinched my chin between his thumb and forefinger. It wasn't the first time he'd touched me, but it was the first time I'd noticed the wobble of energy – one I'd perhaps been keeping at arm's length.

'Dimpled chin. It's your go-to when you're worried or upset.'

'Really? You noticed that?' I angled myself towards him a little more. What the hell else had he noticed? I suddenly found myself recounting things, non-specific things, but still wondering what they said about me.

'It tends to come out.' He unwound the sunroof by hand. 'The night before essays are due, and about an hour before exams. Afterwards, of course, you bound out of the room like you've had the weight of the world removed.'

'I'll be okay.' I thrust my hands through the sunroof and felt the wind wrapping itself around my fingers and tugging on my hair. 'How about you? Are you ready to party?'

When Heather first told me she and Josh were packing up and moving to London, I was like a spinning top of emotions. I rode the wave of their success, celebrating Josh's internal and international promotion at the marketing company he worked for. I popped streamers for Heather who, after winning Young Real Estate Agent of the Year had been poached to head up the new London branch for Coglin Real Estate.

Then, I cried. A lot.

As excited as I was that my two best friends were in love and starting a new life together, because how absolutely thrilling for them, I was also a teensy bit devastated that I would be without them. It was fitting that their farewell party was a New Year's celebration, too. New year, new life, new beginnings.

Heather's parents still lived in the same beachfront property they'd bought when they married. A pebble-mix footpath reflected nightlights, and candles glinted and threw tall reflections across tables. A catering team dithered about in the far corner, and the vibration of late sixties music filled the air.

I looked out across their tightly manicured backyard, the scene of countless afternoons during high school. Part of me wondered how often I'd see it in the future, if at all. The palm trees that waved wildly during storms, the tennis court we used despite having no idea what we were doing, or the pool we'd throw ourselves into at the first breath of summer each year. Would Heather be back often, or would it mean I'd finally get off my backside and get back to London, albeit to visit her? I hoped so, on both counts.

'Do I look okay?' Craig leant in.

Hand on front door, I turned to look at him. 'Why wouldn't you?'

'Oh, you know … wasn't sure, that's all. I haven't met your friends before, so, you know.'

After winding the car around the beach roads, admiring white foamy waves, scorching white sand, and everyone who wasn't us out in the surf, Craig had insisted on a drive-by past his place to change into something more 'party appropriate'. The trendy salmon shorts were replaced with light pants and a thin sports coat.

'Are you kidding? You look great?'

'I do?' He smiled with relief. 'Thank you. I wasn't sure.'

'You've met my friends before,' I said. 'Surely?'

'I promise I haven't.'

Heather was floating about in a sea of guests, under trees dripping with twinkle lights, and around tables adorned with more food than any of us would ever eat. From a young age, it was easy to tell she'd be a master networker and, even now, was treating the crowd like an industry event, making sure to leave no one behind as she made her way around the yard and thanked everyone for coming.

When I introduced Craig, Heather embraced him like an old friend. Questions spilled out like a pop-up video, before he was drawn off to meet Josh and absorbed by the crowd. I went in the opposite direction, catching up with her family, many of whom I hadn't seen for a while. I caught sight of him again when the party made its way across to the beach.

A large driftwood fire licked the sky, the larger logs saved for seating a handful of us around it. Heather did the sandshoe wobble across the beach and sat herself next to me. Josh had taken it upon himself to, 'hook Craig up with some contacts', so we watched in wonder as a group of business buddies slapped backs and regaled each other with stories of last-minute economic heroism.

Heather shouldered me. 'He's lovely.'

I took a deep, shuddering breath. 'He is.'

'Josh wants to adopt him.'

'I like him,' I said.

'What are you worried about?' she asked. 'That he won't live up to the Great Edinburgh Hype? You know why they're called holiday flings, right?'

I turned to her. 'Why? I mean, of course I do, but remind me.'

'Because they're just that: flings. We get so caught up in the unrealistic expectation of what could be that we build it up in our heads as something that would never exist in the realm of normal, day-to-day stuff. This? Him? He's the real deal.'

I scratched my forehead. 'Yeah, yeah, yes, of course.'

'You can't put him in a holding pattern because of someone else.' She circled her finger above her head.

We were interrupted by Craig, who approached with Josh.

'You okay, Ems?' he asked.

I nodded. 'I'm just asking Heather if she's all ready to leave.'

'Visas, man, who needs them?' She wiggled sand through her toes and took a sip of her drink. 'You know, if anyone should be packing up and leaving, it's you.'

'Me?' I scoffed. 'No.'

'Why not? You've got the British passport. We all do, thanks Dad, but you could walk into a job. Look at what you've done at the hospital.'

From my intrepid beginnings as a volunteer, I'd quickly found a place in the administration team. It started with getting to know the staff as we circled the kettle in the staff room. Soon, I was taking mail to them as I skipped past reception each afternoon. When one of the team left, I was first in line to be offered the job. It was perfect chemistry. While not technical, it gave me a wonderful companion to the night schooling I'd been doing in the hope of furthering my chances of getting into the medical field.

'You know, I would.' Craig said with a loose shrug.

I lifted my eyes to him. 'You would?'

'Absolutely. What have you got to lose?' he asked. 'Why not give it a year, finish school, and go?'

'I could.'

'You really should.' Heather bounced up. 'And, while you ponder that, I have to go check out these people who've just arrived. Think about it, then tell me yes. It's the only answer, really.'

We watched my friends disappear into silhouettes as they skipped across the road to meet their newest guests. The log wobbled under the weight of another body on it: Craig.

'Are you sure you're okay?' He tugged on the skirt of my floral dress, dark blue with shimmering reds and silvers. 'You've been a bit down all afternoon.'

'I am.' I rested my elbows on my knees. 'This is good.'

'You can go visit them,' he said. 'This is not goodbye, just see you soon.'

I grinned. 'You're not the first man to use that line on me.'

'I'll bet the other guy wasn't as much fun as me, though. I mean, accounting, phwoar.'

'Did you mean what you said?' I asked. 'About going?'

'Absolutely. It's a great opportunity, and you'd have plenty of scope within health to do something.'

'If I asked, would you come with me?'

A slow smile spread across his face. 'I would, yeah.'

'Let's do it, then.'

'Really?'

'Absolutely.' I shrugged as if this was the easiest decision ever. 'Once we've finished our degrees, we'll get the worst cheap flights ever ...'

54

'... eat amazing airline food...' he added.

I pointed at him. '... And you'll get caught at customs...'

'I'd love to come with you,' he said.

With quick breaths and the slow lean of hesitation, Craig leaned in and kissed me. It was gentle and sleepy, his fingers curling through my hair. His lips were warm and red wine wet but, for a moment, all my what ifs, buts, and worries slipped away into the ocean before us. My heart didn't skip or murmur its disagreement. Instead, it kept a steady, happy rhythm, and urged me to pull him closer.

Chapter 6

January 2014

I took the stairs at St James' station two at a time, up into the open air, and past the throngs of school holiday tourists vying for a perfect photo near the Archibald fountain. I shook my wrist to check my watch again. The pedometer part of my New Year, New Emmy project had about another week of half-life left.

The summer air was thick and smelled of sunscreen and sausage sizzles. Almost all the shade around the park had been swallowed up by families and children playing with their Christmas-gifted water pistols. Across Park Street and near the Pool of Reflection was Craig, waiting with a light blanket and wicker basket.

'I'm so sorry.' I puffed. 'I was late out of work.'

He peered up with a gentle smile, eyes shielded from the dappled sun stabbing through the trees. 'That's okay.'

'Yeah, but it's not, is it? I've kept you waiting again.' I dropped to my knees and crossed my ankles beneath me. 'This is gorgeous, thank you.'

Craig stilled me with a finger as I leant across and kissed him. 'You haven't seen the food on offer yet.'

It was a hearty spread of crackers, fresh shop-bought dips, and some smelly cheese which broke every plastic knife we tried cutting it with. In the end, nibbling at the block was the only way.

'Alright, so, I have a question for you.' Craig settled himself opposite me and poured soft drink into plastic wine glasses. This was the state of our student lunches – cheap and cheerful, but still very lovely and fun experiences.

'Sounds serious.'

Craig narrowed his eyes. 'A little?'

'Shoot.'

'London. How serious are you about going?' he asked.

'I'd like to go,' I said slowly. 'I love listening to Heather talk about it. How about you?'

Honestly, it had been all I'd thought about for weeks. Heather and Josh had settled in with ease. Facebook accounts full of smiling faces and location shots were testament to that. Weekends at country clubs in Bath, towering white cliffs of Dover, or the Titanic trail of Southampton were coupled with freshly painted bedrooms and new furniture, exotic takeaway dinners, and the excited exploration that comes with discovering your new city through fresh eyes.

'Had you asked me on New Year's Day, I would've said it wasn't a great idea. Maybe just a knee-jerk reaction to your friends leaving.'

'But?' I asked, curious as to how he'd changed his mind in the weeks since.

'Well, this week at work hasn't been so great. I'm not really cut out for the family firm.' He looked about nervously. 'At the end of the year, with school over, it wouldn't be such a bad idea.'

'So, you want to go then?'

'I think we should start planning, yeah.'

Planning felt like a ten-thousand-piece Ravensburger jigsaw puzzle and looking for the edge pieces one by one. Most people were of the opinion I should just 'get a job and get over there' which, I suppose, was correct. Financially though, it meant having a safety net before stepping on that plane.

Money, that magical thing that makes the world go around, became easier to come by when I switched to distance education. By the time lecture theatres opened their doors for the school year, I was already curled up on the couch reading final year subjects and bashing away at the keyboard in the hope an essay might pop out somewhere near the end.

As much as he hated it, Craig took extra shifts at the family business. He made coffee, swept floors, and shredded old files just to make himself useful. And, when he was finally allowed to take on clients, he worked night and day to prove that he was not only worthy of their accounts, but that he was capable. It astounded me that he got any of his university work done at all, but he did.

In June, while I was busy picking up volunteer work with the ambulance again and getting back into the groove of things, Craig moved us into a spare bedroom at a friend's house. The paint was a little peely, and I spent a weekend watching my fingers wrinkle up under sugar soap and water, but it gave us the opportunity to be proper adults. No longer were we under our parents' roofs, but in our own space, being adults, doing very adult things in the privacy of our own place.

'I suppose at least it'll give us an idea of London.' Craig stood by the door, hands on hips, and surveyed our new room, which smelled like a not so delicious blend of chemical cleaner and lavender carpet powder.

'Are you still keen?' I patted the space on the bed beside me.

'We only have this place for twelve months, so, I do hope so!'

The idea of returning to the UK made me jittery with excitement, it lit a fire inside me all over again – just when I thought those feelings may have disappeared under the rubble of adult life. The opportunities for advancement were endless. I mean, they were at home, too, but something about London felt a little more … special.

Heather and I stayed in contact with a constant game of tag across time zones and inbox messages. We sent each other what we'd called care packages. Where she wanted Tim Tams, Vegemite, and local chocolate, all I wanted were tea bags and the ugliest souvenirs she could find. I was beyond thrilled at my Will and Kate wedding ashtray. It didn't matter that I didn't smoke or that the printed image was misaligned, it did a wonderful enough job on the top shelf of my bedroom. It was a regular talking point.

As the year wore on, Heather was happy to remind me that she'd been in London almost twelve months, and that I must be due to join her soon enough. Right on their twelve-month anniversary, she rang. I moved away from the ruckus that was family dinner, and sat in a spare room.

'You'll get the biggest bedroom,' she opened with.

'And?' I asked.

'And,' she drawled, 'it's very lovely. I'll paint and buy you some new linen and get everything ready for when you arrive. That way, you won't have to worry about a thing.'

I laughed. 'Why? What's the catch?'

'The room's downstairs. We sleep upstairs, which makes us closer to the toilet.'

'Lazy,' I teased. 'So lazy.'

'So,' she said. I could imagine her twirling a phone cord around her finger. 'When are you coming?'

* * *

Job applications began a few months before we planned to leave. It became a constant waiting game, hoping for the familial ding of an email notification. It was the old Did I, or Didn't I Get the Job? game. There might be a polite rejection coupled with best wishes or, maybe, an appointment request. Come hither and talk to us, always near enough to the midnight hour, always over delayed phone lines or pixelated Skype conferences. I jumped on every opportunity that sprang up, kind of like whack-a-mole.

Craig's employment process was a little easier. He'd managed the first job he applied for, helping a start-up company, and his visa sponsorship was sorted in under a fortnight. Luckily for us, his start date would be determined by mine. He simply began taking on work remotely we got there. Hooray for late nights in front of the television and crawling into bed nearer to sunrise than usual.

But it didn't matter. We were thriving, effervescent with excitement and just counting down until the moment it was my turn.

When my call finally came, early one Friday morning, I was in the middle of balancing a piping hot coffee cup, while swiping into the building at work, and trying to answer my phone, all without spilling a precious caffeinated drop.

'Emmy, it's Brian Ward.'

'Hello, Brian Ward.' I ground the toe of my shoe into the ground, pulverising a dry leaf. 'How are you?'

'I'm great. I mean, it's late here, but I figured I'd get you at a good time.'

'You have, yeah. I'm just heading in for the day.' I stopped. 'What is it for you? Midnight?'

'Not quite,' he said. 'I'm just catching up on some paperwork. Have you got a moment to chat?'

'Of course,' I said. 'Absolutely.'

'That's what I like to hear,' he said. 'I'm just wondering how you're placed for flights? When's the earliest you can start?'

'Are you saying I got the job?' I squeaked. When the lid popped off my coffee, splashing hot liquid over my hands and threatening my canvas shoes, I finally loosened my grip. Anything but the shoes, they were my favourites.

'It's only a six-month contract at this stage, but I'm saying that you should book a flight.' Hearing the smile in his voice was the most amazing feeling. 'You're going to be a great fit for the team.'

'Oh boy, oh boy, I've just … oh, I spilled my coffee. Again.'

'Yep, definitely a good fit.' He laughed. 'Ideally, I'd like you to start as soon as possible. Pam's a little snowed under right now. I'm going to email you with some details, just let me know when you can get here.'

Chapter 7

June 2014

As the plane bumped and skidded to a stop along the runway at Heathrow, a niggling doubt came knocking, asking if we'd made the right decision. A brief panic set in, and all the things that could go wrong flipped through my head like one of Dad's old holiday slideshows.

'I'm sure it'll be fine.' Craig yawned and stretched out sleepily. He gave my hand a gentle squeeze. 'People change jobs all the time.'

'But we changed countries, too.'

'That's because we are the best.' He winked at me. 'You'll be fine once you get a bit of sleep.'

After taking enough sleeping pills that I swore I could smell colours, and still not managing a useful rest, I chose to put my worries down to a lack of sleep. I was exhausted, aching from being cramped, and very much looking forward to a regular bed and a hot shower.

Customs made me nervous. It didn't matter that I wasn't smuggling small animals or drugs into the country, I still felt like I'd done something wrong. The snaking queues and conversation that never rose above a murmur didn't help.

'Is everything okay?' I peered over the counter while Craig's visa paperwork was pored over.

'I wouldn't be here without my first work visa. Enjoy your stay,' the customs agent said with a smile.

Before anyone could change their minds and call us back, we scuttled through arrivals and towards the train terminal. That old familiar smell of brake dust and cramped spaces welcomed me like an old friend with an arm around the shoulder. The moment I boarded the train, luggage pushed against the carriage wall, I let out a heavy sigh.

'This is amazing.' Clutching at a stanchion grip, Craig ran a finger along the bottom of the tube map. 'So, we're getting off where?'

'Paddington. Then we get the Bakerloo to Queen's Park.' I yawned and cuddled into him. I loved how solid he felt, my head resting in the nook of his neck. 'You smell awful.'

'You don't smell so great yourself.' He smoothed a hand over my hair and kissed the top of my head.

Swapping from the train to the tube at Paddington, I made it a priority to pick myself up a blue-coated bear, all the while trying to avoid getting weepy at the sales counter. Somewhere between the passport stamp and trying to push three suitcases through a bustling train station, I realised that I hadn't simply caught the train to the next city. I'd flown to the other side of the world. Sure, I'd done it before, but this time felt different, like I'd hardly been away at all.

Heather was waiting on the front doorstep with streamers, helium balloons, and a Welcome Home sign. She bounced excitedly on the spot, apologising over again for not being at the airport on account of an open inspection. With her long hair pulled into a loose bun, she looked more relaxed than I'd ever seen her. There was a renewed happiness to her that she hadn't had in Sydney.

'You look *so* good.' I wrapped my arms around her and squeezed. 'I'm so glad to see you.'

'And you, my love, look like hell.' She held me at arms' length. I nodded, breaking into laughter. 'I really do.'

'When are you starting work again?' she asked, eyes narrowed.

'Tomorrow.'

She cringed. 'Come on upstairs, get some rest.'

Josh and Craig were already climbing the stairs to our apartment on the second and third floor of a terraced house just off Harrow Road. Our scratched-up suitcases banged against the polished wood banister with each misplaced step. Inwardly, I cringed. Please don't let me be here five minutes and be breaking things already.

'Here we are…' Heather pushed the front door open with an excited flourish and dragged me inside.

The apartment was bright and airy, full of white paint and gloss-white kitchen fittings. A grey couch and aqua cushions added blobs of homely colour, and red placemats clung to a lightly stained wooden dining table. Light breezy curtains hung in rooms with dark drapes, and the single bathroom in the upper storey was shared by all. For all the photos I'd seen, it hadn't prepared me for how I'd feel.

This was, despite the exhaustion, sheer exhilaration. I flopped down on the couch, a foot stool soon adorned with a tray full of homemade biscuits. A pot of tea appeared shortly after, as an excited Heather told me about her latest baking adventures and fresh interest in all things tea. We caught up on the last week spent running around and preparing to leave, all the scandals and drunk uncle stories from our farewell party, and the boring details of our flight. While I moaned about the smelly guy next to Craig and laughed about the toddler who came to say hello and high-five every forty minutes, Josh busied himself hanging comic prints on the wall.

After the hammering had ceased, the biscuits were eaten, and my mind finally began to slow, we relaxed with showers and began putting personal touches on our bedroom. Lace curtains,

63

bookended by heavy drapes, blew in the breeze. Just as she'd promised, Heather had organised a new duvet, spare blankets and pillows, and a few stackable blocks I'd already earmarked as potential bookshelves.

Our bed was a cloud soft and, as I lay back for a moment, the pillows hugged in all the right places. I curled onto my side and closed my eyes.

Chapter 8

I was awake.

I pushed the covers aside and wandered around our new bedroom. My suitcase still bulged by the window, and my passport had been placed on the bedside table next to me. Fresh clothes for work had been arranged over the back of a chair, shoes on the floor. Craig slept quietly, dark tufts of hair poking out above the duvet he'd cocooned himself in.

The world outside was still asleep, blanketed in the glow of orange street lights. Cars were parked any which way they landed, and the occasional wheelie bin had taken a drunken stumble across the footpath.

The world around me had changed so much in the last forty-eight hours and, while I could see, feel, hear, smell, and taste, my brain was still buzzing at what was happening. I wanted to get out and explore our new city. I didn't care that it was too early, or that I had promised anyone I'd start work, I just wanted out.

Except life and her responsibilities didn't work like that. I showered, arranged toiletries on our allocated bathroom shelf, and pushed a few books into my shelves. In the kitchen, I poured a coffee and enjoyed a few moments of peace.

'Craig.' I rubbed his shoulder gently. He barely stirred. 'I'm going to work.'

'Already? We just went to bed.'

'It's just gone seven-thirty.'

'Explains why my bladder feels like a water balloon.' He rolled onto his back and blinked up at me a few times. 'You look so pretty.'

'Thank you. Are we still treating our landlords to dinner out tonight?'

He nodded, yawned, rubbed at his eyes.

I kissed him, and his awful morning breath. 'Okay. I'm going to work now. I'll message when I'm on my way home.'

'Good luck.' He yawned. 'I love you.'

'Love you, too.'

As the sun tried desperately to peek from behind thick clouds, I pulled on a light coat and started my trip to work. Today had a nervous energy about it that swung from buildings like Spiderman and made you believe something incredible was about to happen. Or maybe that was the jetlag talking.

My walk to work was longer than it needed to be, not because I got lost, but because I was purposely slow. I was too busy drinking everything in as I went, making mental notes of what I saw. Rows of almost identical redbrick terraced houses, their tiny yards that were all so similar, but so distinct, each of them a personal expression of their owners. Last time I was in London, I'd barely scratched the surface, stuck to tourist attractions and sightseeing buses, so it felt a little unfair that I'd agreed to throw myself straight into work again. But there I was, standing outside Moyes Medical, a coffee in one hand, and a nervous heart full of hope.

Faded blue concrete walls met a gated carpark with zero signs of a garden. Well, there was one, but it was apparent it hadn't been tended to in months. A letterbox slot sat in a front door of toughened glass, which was adorned with a reminder that drugs were not kept on the premises. Despite the fact the place looked empty, I tugged on the door. Locked. I knocked, this time rattling the door for full effect.

Still, there was no one here.

The email said eight o'clock. I checked it for the fourth time, but then gave up and leant against the wall. Each person that walked past could have been a colleague, but none of them made eye contact for long enough to make conversation. Just when I started getting jittery at the notion that maybe I'd screwed up, the shuffle of footsteps got closer.

'Emmy! Hello.'

Turning towards the voice, I was met with salt and pepper hair and a gentle smile. My new boss. My shoulders slackened as tension unwound itself from around me. Shame about the early morning nervous sweating though.

'Brian, hi.' I shook his hand.

'It's good to meet you in person. Welcome.'

'Finally. Thank you. Sorry, I think I'm a bit early.'

'Better than being a bit late, right?' he said. 'Let's get you inside and sorted out.'

One bay at a time, lights flickered on throughout the building, which smelled of pine floor cleaner and fresh carpet. I followed nervously, trying to take in all the little details: the empty rubbish bins, neat rows of seats that presented in the waiting room, and my new workstation. It greeted me with a scuffed laminate benchtop, a computer pre-covered in Post-its, a telephone and file stand. Like my job in Sydney, they seemed the essential ingredients of a medical receptionist.

'How was the flight over?' Brian hung his coat just inside his office door. 'Not too awful, I hope?'

'Ah … long?' I said with a weak laugh.

'I haven't been your way in about five years, I think.' He squinted. 'Wedding anniversary trip. We were there thirty years before that for our honeymoon'

I covered my mouth and laughed. 'I wasn't even born then.'

'Don't say that out loud,' he teased. 'Ever again.'

'Sorry.'

'You landed yesterday, didn't you?'

'I did,' I said, following when he motioned for me to join him. 'That's crazy, I can't imagine doing that. Thank you.' Another light switch revealed a staff room.

I expected the sink to be stacked with old coffee cups, a sugar encrusted counter, and the fridge to be filled with green food. Instead, surfaces were wiped down, bins were empty, mugs hung on hooks above the sink, and the refrigerator smelled of bicarb.

'Can't very well operate a surgery and be filthy.'

'Sure.'

'I had the girls organise a welcome pack for you.' Brian grabbed a cellophane-wrapped basket from the bench. 'It's nothing big, but you've made a huge trip, so welcome aboard.' He wrinkled his nose. 'Or is that abroad?'

'I'll take either.' I grinned.

'Pam should be here in about twenty minutes. She'll sort you out with passwords and whatnot.'

'I'll just—' I gestured to the kettle '—grab a coffee, then?'

'Absolutely.'

***

Trying to make myself familiar with anything on the first day felt like a bit of a lost cause. I looked at the notes stuck to my computer screen. They made no sense. I scrolled through the numbers stored in the phone. Still, nothing. There were IN trays and OUT trays, drawers had been relieved of their belongings – maybe by the last receptionist, or maybe they were just particularly neat about everything around here. I sat at my desk and adjusted my chair to height. Up and down, spin it around.

It was a good view from here. The dead little garden by the

window, a small handful of chairs in a waiting room that stretched around the corner and into a larger pool room, and the front door, which was rattling in frustration.

'Oomph!' A tall blonde with a curly bob tripped through the front door.

Having absolutely no idea what else I should do, I stood and waved nervously.

'Ah, fucking useless door,' she sputtered in a thick Irish accent before an excited smile popped to the surface. 'Oh, Emmy, it's Emmy. I'm Pam as in ham. Hello.'

'Hello.' I bit back a nervous laugh. 'Would you like some help?'

'Oh, no. I am perfectly good now I'm in the door. Thank you.' She snipped the lock back in place and grinned at me. 'It's so good to have you here.'

'Thank you.'

'Just let me caffeinate, and we can get the ball rolling.' She dropped a bag by her seat and offered me a hug. 'Have you had breakfast? I've got some bread, I can make toast.'

'Oh ... no ... no, I'm good. Thank you.'

'You know Red won't be in until around lunch time, don't you?' Brian's voice caught her as she strolled back to our desk.

'Aye. I called him last night, the crazy cat. He said he'd be in by midday, but I told him to just take his time, have a bit of lunch and then come in. His first patient isn't until one o'clock, but you know what he's like.'

'That I do.'

Pam turned to me, eyebrows aloft. 'You are going to *love* Red.'

'I am?'

'Bloody beautiful soul. Patients love him. By that I mean they'll wait a week or two to see him before going to some of the others we have here. He's ridiculously funny. I mean, I like to think of myself as the office comedian, but he—'

'No, no.' I held up a hand. 'Don't tell me anymore; you'll ruin the surprise.'

A slow smile spread across her face. 'Oh, I do like you. Brian, I like her. You picked good.'

'I do my best,' his voice rang out.

When my computer login failed to appear in Pam's inbox, and my swipe card didn't fall out of the mail bag, I was pushed onto the admin team. Piles of paperwork, filing, and account reconciliations kept me busy in a small office that thrived on gossip and stained teacups. I fiddled, cleaned, and shredded, made drinks and small-talk, and shuffled out of the building at lunchtime, content that things were settling nicely. That buzzy Sunday feeling of not being sure? I'd wiped the floor with it.

* * *

'I'm so glad you're enjoying it,' Heather enthused. 'Really, I was worried about the whole straight into work thing, but I'm glad. I really am.'

I yawned. 'I am exhausted though.'

'Where are you? It sounds loud.'

It was almost riotous. A portafilter banged against the counter every thirty seconds to let thirsty patrons know coffee was on its way. Exhausted staff offered apologetic looks to the woman in front of me over the fact that no, that was absolutely their last lemon jam tart and, no, there weren't any 'hiding out the back'.

'Just in a café, grabbing a sandwich.' I peered over and around shoulders, trying to pick my first London lunch. 'I want to eat everything.'

'Hoki's?'

'That's the one.'

'Good. That's the best one.' She took a deep breath. 'Speaking of best ones, I've booked a table for dinner tonight, figured you'd be excited enough to brave a trip into the city.'

'Absolutely. Can't wait.' I slipped a twenty over the counter, put the change in my pocket, and nestled the sandwich bag under my arm as I slipped out into the blowy street. 'How's your day?'

'About to go try sell a high-rise to some dude with more dollars, sorry, pounds, than I'll ever see. Speaking of which, I gotta go, see you when you get home.'

I shouldered the front door open and spilled into the practice, Pam nattering away on her headpiece. She waved her hands around, urging me closer with each flick of the wrist. I checked my watch.

'You're not late, just come here.' She pulled me behind the counter. 'Red! Get out here. I have a present for you.' Pam winked at me.

'A present, for me?' His voice sang through the hall from his office. Patients didn't even try to stifle their laughter. 'Well, isn't this just …'

Shit.

With his wispy flame-red hair and striking blue eyes, William stood in front of me. Over two years of silence had been squeezed shut in the blink of an eye. His face mirrored the same shock that felt like a million electric pins against my skin.

'… Christmas.' He glanced over my shoulder at Pam, who pushed me closer.

'Remember Brian said he was getting me some help? This is Emmy, fresh off the plane from Sydney. Don't mind her accent though, she does speak English, and you'll get used to it.'

My heart raced out of the gate before I could so much as even think about yanking on the reins. He'd been out of my life and off my radar for long enough to not matter so much anymore. But in that moment, I was a twenty-year-old girl standing under an Edinburgh street light all over again. I was thrilled and thrown all at once, like he'd reached across the room and physically pulled the air from my lungs. For a split second, his chin dimpled, and bottom lip twitched, before it was replaced by a mask of professionality.

'Hello.' He held out a hand and took a steadying breath. 'I'm William. It's lovely to meet you.'

'William.' I swallowed. Hard. 'I'm Emmy.'

With that, he'd established how we were about to operate under the same roof together: as strangers.

'Here's your next patient.' Pam pressed a manila folder into his chest.

When I turned to move, it felt like I had every person in the building watching, waiting for a reaction. Two other doctors, Bob and Trevor were looking on silently, waiting for us both to move away from their trays. I gathered my coffee and broken pride and took five minutes to work through my thoughts in the staff room.

We didn't speak for the rest of the day.

* * *

Heather shouldered me. 'You've been ridiculously quiet over dinner. What gives?'

At a table by the window, the view of the Thames outside soon became a twinkling mass of office lights and street lamps. Suited staff polished glasses behind a mahogany bar, and waiters refilled wine like the bill was never going to arrive. Josh and Craig had lamented their decision to walk through Greenwich and up the hill to the Meridian Line, and I … well, I filled in the gaps.

It wasn't that I'd been particularly quiet. Alright, maybe I had been. I'd mentioned the good stuff: the great staff, the easy environment, and my new friend, Pam. I showed photos of my welcome hamper and declared I was happy for decent office coffee. By the time I'd left for the afternoon, Pam had crowned me her new best friend. She'd confided in me about her projectile vomiting cat named Victor, her commitment-phobe boyfriend, and her overbearing but emotionally distant mother who thought Pam, at thirty-nine, needed to be put out to pasture if 'that lad won't put a ring on it'.

Now, with tummies full and the bill settled, the tipsy warmth of wine propelled us along the riverbank towards Westminster station. The boys pushed on ahead, nattering about all things business and leaving us well alone to chatter about all the things you can only ever say to your best friend.

'The job's good, right? That part wasn't a lie?' she asked.

'No, the job's great. I mean, by lunchtime? I was glad I'd made the move. I felt at home, everyone is so lovely. There's my boss, Brian. He's very sweet. Bob is like this forty-something Beatnik obsessed with concerts. Trevor has something like one hundred kids and a wallet slideshow to prove it. The admin team are lovely, very welcoming.'

'By lunchtime tells me that after lunch—'

'So, all morning, everyone was like, "Oh, Red's in later, you're gonna love Red, Red is amazing."'

'Who names their kid Red? What are the other two called? Blue and Yellow?'

'Right?' I laughed. 'Anyway, I just nod and play along because, well, I don't know any differently. And they're still on and on, Red this, Red that, Red is apparently the saviour of the universe. Patients love him, old ladies love him.'

'Rescues kittens from trees and brings women to orgasm with the snap of a finger?'

'I didn't hear that one, but I *will* ask.' I laughed.

'And when he finally walked into the office?'

'You are going to shit yourself.'

'Not in public, no.' Heather stood on the spot, hands on hips, looking every bit the member of a serious discussion. 'Quite sure of that.'

'Red is William. As in, Edinburgh William. As in, I missed the fireworks for you, and wrote you letters, but you can't be bothered telling me if you died or just don't want to speak to me anymore. That William.'

Her mouth popped like I'd slapped her on the face. 'No.'

'Yes.'

Heather roared with laughter. 'Fuck off.'

73

'I wish that was the case.'

'Do you not see the humour in this? Because this is hilarious.'

'Oh, it's great.' Eyes wide, I laughed sarcastically with her. 'It's wonderful. Not only is he still unfairly beautiful, he now refuses to speak to me. The same man who once sent handwritten letters, drawings, boxes of tea, and silly little gifts, is now refusing to so much as hold conversation with me.'

'Are you sure it's him?'

'Unless he has an identical twin somewhere, with the same name, then yeah. I think it's a solid thing that it's him.'

'Well, shit.'

'Does he know?' Heather pointed further along the path to where Josh and Craig had sat on a park bench, their faces phone screen bright.

'No.'

'Is he going to know?'

'No.'

'And we're taking this path because?'

'Because we haven't spoken in over two years. He obviously doesn't want to be my friend, otherwise he'd make some kind of concerted effort to do something other than ignore me, and nothing *really* happened, did it? We kissed one night and wrote each other a couple of letters. Does that even make us anything?' I threw my arms about, exasperated. 'I don't know. I don't even know how to handle it, so I can't ask Craig to yet.'

Heather winced. 'Maybe? Maybe not? I mean, nothing physical. It *was* just one kiss.'

'Exactly. We're nothing. Not really, right?'

'In that case, my only suggestion is to go to work each day and kick ass. You're good at your job, you know what you're doing. Right now, it's just a matter of getting into the groove of that office, which I think you'll be able to do easily enough. I suspect, like you, he's also a little bit shocked.'

'I suspect that might be part of it,' I said. 'But, also, I'm a little excited to see him again, is that wrong?'

Heather's brow furrowed, her eyes squinted. 'I don't know if it's bad, but I don't think it's great. Maybe give him a few days, you know what boys are like. He'll come around.'

'You think?'

She shrugged. 'Sure. If not, I'll waltz on in there and sell him a house.'

I snorted. 'Things are going that well?'

Things weren't great in the land of real estate. It had been a frustratingly slow week, and she'd failed to close on a few deals that had seemed like a sure bet. Her boss had given her the stink-eye more than once when she'd delivered the news that the Hawes property in Chelsea was a no-go, and that the buyers in Kensington had backed out quicker than a one-night stand running for the bus.

'I'm sure it'll pick up shortly. Early summer gets people moving around. It'll be fine. I'll sell a few extra properties and it'll be fine.'

'Do you still enjoy it?' I asked.

'Enjoy it? I love it. It's what my failed architect's heart gets off on.' Heather had always aspired to be an architect but, life being life, she hadn't quite made it to that point. Until then, I'd forgotten William came from a family of architects.

'Failed? Please. Why don't you study again?' I asked. 'I've seen your drawings. If I know one thing, it's that you're designing my house for me.'

Heather scribbled for days at a time, always had. Her old flat had been full of drawings, musings, and re-imaginings of local buildings. Half the trouble she had moving was deciding what works she was going to take with her. The rest were rolled up in tubes in her parents' attic.

'Out in the hills of the English countryside, with sprawling views, sheep, and an afternoon sun room, while the cherubs blob around gleefully in the golden rays of contentment?'

We burst into laughter.

'Something like that,' I said. In that moment, my brain was awash with possibilities. 'Hey, what if we both went back to school? We can study together, online study is a thing, we can get qualified. I can do my nursing thing. That's the bottom rung of the ladder, isn't it? Getting the paper.'

'We could.' Judging by the scowl on her face, she didn't look convinced.

'But you're not convinced.' I snapped my fingers.

'I think the plan for this week should be you holding a conversation with William without spontaneously combusting.'

Chapter 9

As I sat on the edge of the bed, picking through what was left of my clothes, I did my best to feel enthused about the day ahead. My first week had raced ahead of me like a dog on a leash, while I felt like I was jogging along behind it. I walked a different route to work each morning, exploring side streets and cafés until I knew the area well enough to not get lost. On Thursday morning, I was sure I'd found my favourite coffee shop. Their apple turnovers met my 'Are They Apple-y Enough' criteria, so I decided I'd keep going back.

'Hey.' Craig rolled over and pinched at my hip.

'Hey, you.' I reached back and grabbed his hand.

He wriggled across the bed a little. 'You okay?'

'I'm good.' I nodded. 'Just exhausted.'

'Friday today.' He smiled sleepily, his large brown eyes squinted contently. 'Weekend tomorrow.'

'Then *you* start work.' I leaned down and peppered the top of his head with kisses. 'Are you excited?'

'Can I say no?' His laughter was softened by burying his face in the pillow. 'I'm enjoying this tourist life.'

'I'm so jealous of you.' I zipped up my pants and kissed him again. 'See you tonight.'

77

'I love you,' he grumbled.

'Love you too, slacker.'

All week, I'd been itching to get William alone for some sort of discussion. I wasn't sure exactly what I wanted, but I didn't like the stilted, stale feeling that hung about the air. We didn't talk. At all. It was more a series of pointed directives and the bare minimum in work-related chatter. It was if the last few years did not exist in this universe. Any chance of changing that was dashed when I arrived at work. At the end of the hall, his office door was shut, his muted voice the only way to tell he was in.

To broker a peace deal, because I felt for some reason I'd done something wrong, I'd spent Wednesday night not exploring my new city and playing tourist, but baking something for morning tea. A hummingbird cake with cream cheese frosting. The slice I'd cut for him now sat limply in the kitchen sink, along with the coffee I'd delivered with it. The milk had skinned over, and the cake was crusty on the outside.

I breathed a huge sigh of relief when Pam strolled through the front door. Being stuck in here alone with William was fast becoming my idea of a nightmare.

* * *

'Do you know how to address envelopes?'

Was he talking to me? I peered up at William as he stood on the opposite side of the counter, a bundle of papers and their envelopes in a hand that dangled over the counter. Yes, he was, and it took everything in me to not snap back. My jaw clenched, and fingers curled over the keyboard.

'Why wouldn't I?' I asked.

'I need these sent out. Today. Make sure you put the letters in the envelopes, write the address on the front—'

Pam cupped her phone receiver and glared at him. 'William, what is up your bum this week? Stop being so rude to Emmy.

78

She's perfectly capable of doing the mail. Unlike you, she can answer her own phone.'

Warmth pinched his cheeks, but he didn't waver. 'The addresses go on the front of the envelope, stamps too, and then you put them in the mail so as people actually receive them.'

I shrank back into my chair. 'I guess you're giving that job to me because you don't understand how to do it yourself?'

Beside me, Pam punched the sky and snapped her finger at William, whose jaw dropped just enough to be noticeable. He scowled, announced he was out to lunch, dropped the mail on my desk and shot through the door like a dog with the gate left open.

'Jerk,' I mumbled.

'He's *never* like that.' Pam leant across. 'Ever. Honestly, it's like your being here has brought something out in him. 'He certainly seems to have a stick up his you-know-where since you arrived.'"

'Who'd have guessed?' I sighed.

Never like that or not, it was unacceptable. He'd been an ass from the minute I stepped through the door. I'd barely got a full sentence in on Wednesday before he walked from the room without saying a word. On Thursday, I'd asked him to pass the milk, only for him to walk straight past me and place it back in the fridge. And he was yet to dial my extension if he needed anything from the front desk, despite the fact Brian had assigned me his patient list. Because what could go right this week?

'Emmy.' Brian appeared around the door of his office like a vaudeville mime. 'Do you drink?'

'Quite an unhealthy amount lately, yes,' I joked.

'Good. Team drinks tonight at the local, it's this great little pub just off the High Street, you'll love it.'

'Sounds great.' After this week, a drink (or five) sounded just what I needed. The William thing had left me in knots.

'Be a love and send out an email asking everyone to confirm?' he suggested, disappearing again.

One by one, everyone replied.

Except William.

* * *

London evenings were quickly earning a place in my heart. Even in the suburbs, she had a special kind of shimmer about her. The smell of barbecue wafted down streets full of children out playing late in the longer evenings. In my reverie, I may have wandered too far in the opposite direction, but I still managed to double back into the pub on time. Last to arrive, and after a quick wander of the building, I found everyone seated at a long table near the bar.

'Emmy!' A collective cheer rose from the table, glasses thrust in the air. There were party hats, streamers, and a clip-on koala that looked suspiciously like one I would have sent to William, except I was sure the one I'd sent was draped in the Australian flag. It was soon attached to my collar.

'Thank you, I feel like I'm a little late.' I rested my coat on the back of my chair and looked around. 'Still getting used to finding my way around.'

'No, no, not late. There's no time limit.' Brian stood, motioning to a free chair. 'Sit, sit, what do you want to drink?'

'Surprise me.' I clapped my hands together and briefly glanced over to see William who, down the other end of the table, was managing to enjoy a lively conversation with Trevor. I tried, but couldn't make out what was being said.

'You are going to fit in just perfectly.' Pam stretched across the table and snapped a party hat on my head. 'This is why I like you so much already.'

There was a shuffle of the drinks menu and a quick show of hands, and Brian disappeared to collect drinks. He returned with a rattling tray and a joke about a second career waiting for him. When he was satisfied everyone was comfortable and had a drink of some sort, he raised a toast.

'Emmy, may your hours fly by, your days be fun, and your tenure long. It's only been a week, but it's already been great.'

'And, hey, five days in and she can still remember the practice's address.' William held his drink up. 'That's commitment for you.'

With that, he'd successfully managed to induce a pregnant pause.

'Now the formalities are out of the way, tell us all a little bit about the Emmy that arrives at home every night.' With his coal-dark eyes and floppy hair, Trevor leant into the table and clutched at bony elbows.

'Is Emmy short for anything? Emily? Emmeline?' Bob asked. 'Maybe your parents were fans of Emmylou Harris?'

I chewed on my bottom lip. 'I don't think so, no. I mean, it's not short for anything, and I don't think Emmylou Harris is my dad's jam. He's more a Beatles fan.'

Pam clutched at my arm. 'I want to know about your boyfriend. Why didn't you bring him tonight?'

'Oh, I didn't think it was a boyfriend type occasion,' I said nervously, looking around at exactly zero other spouses while I fumbled for the phone in my pocket. 'But I do have some photos.' I skimmed through a couple, glad that Craig was not partial to a nude. 'Oh, this here. Was one of our first dates, I think.' I thrust the phone out to the centre of the table. 'Sunset, Sydney Opera House, wine and cheese picnic. It was all very romantic, a cruise ship leaving the bay, dance music thumping all the way down past the Heads'

'Oh, look at that.' Bob clutched at the phone. 'I really think we should have a team building trip to Sydney. Is that Luna Park in the next shot?'

I walked around the table, squatting between Bob and William, the rustle of fabric testament to the fact I'd knocked William. 'Right, yeah, that's one of the ferries out to Manly ... and that is—' I scrolled through '—the view from the bridge.'

'You can climb the Harbour Bridge?' Bob was so excited he

almost squeaked. He slapped William excitedly, who had barely raised a brow at what he was being shown.

'Isn't it great, Emmy?' Brian asked. 'I did that a few years ago with my wife. Phenomenal.'

'Emmy can be our tour guide,' Pam volunteered. 'She can drive the minivan around, with her boyfriend.'

I laughed. 'He'd probably be drinking wine with you lot, he's a total lush.'

'Wedding bells soon?' Brian asked.

When I grimaced, everyone laughed. William didn't budge, a regular stick in the mud.

'No, nothing like that,' I said. 'At least, I don't think so. Not entirely my decision, I suppose.'

Even through his silence, the invisible thread that had held us together all those years ago was still there. It wound past us, through the table, under and around the legs of chairs to trip us up, and knotted itself around my brain. The only thing that pulled me out of this confusion, because that's what it was – total, utter confusion – was a question about spiders the size of dinner plates.

'I promise you, if I took you around the country, you wouldn't be eaten by spiders.'

Trevor thrust his hand in the air. 'I'm going to second Sydney for a team trip, Bri, just saying.'

'Harbour Bridge, Bondi, wineries.' William offered a saccharine smile that steadfastly refused to touch his eyes.

'I would take you there.' I lifted my glass to my mouth. 'All you would need to do is show up, William.'

'I'm not sure we'd all be allowed to take holiday at once, somehow,' Brian said. 'But let's eat. I am starving.'

As knives and forks gnashed at dirtied plates, wine glasses refilled without asking, empty schooners disappeared as if by magic, and I shared my first meal with my new team. With each fresh question that tumbled out, it felt like a job interview all over again, but it was fun and loud, with laughter and well-meaning advice about everyone's favourite regular patients.

'Alright.' William stood and stretched. 'My shout. Who wants what?'

'Tell him you want a cocktail.' Pam leant in. 'He's a good shout.'

So, I did. All without response. Watching him melt into the crowded bar area, he felt like a distant memory, someone who was there, but wasn't, and it made me question everything. I wondered whether I'd simply imagined Hogmanay and the days after. Maybe it *was* all just me.

'I asked the guy at the bar what he thought you might like, based on the completely useless fact that you've never been here before.' William placed a glass in front of me. 'He likes to call this one The Vanishing Act.'

'Just don't do that to us.' Bob held his drink up and I was toasted all over again, all the while feeling as small as an ant.

The issue of William notwithstanding, it was a fun night. We laughed, we joked and, instead of leaving of our own accord, the owners asked politely if we wouldn't mind vacating the premises as they were keen to go to bed.

Outside in the cold, we stood awkwardly around a street lamp, making small talk before Pam made the first move. She crushed me in a vice-like hug, thanking me for my help during the week. Trevor mumbled something about a football team, while Bob shook my hand and wished me the best as he slipped off into the night. Brian wandered off to the nearest bus stop, politely discussing procedural changes with Pam as they went.

Suddenly, it was just William and me.

Under the streetlight, his hair was a voracious shade of red, made worse by his choice of clothing: dark jeans, sky-blue shirt, and a navy coat. I thought about walking away in silence, but I turned back to find him, head bowed and peering at me from underneath his giraffe length lashes. I walked over to him and poked his cheek.

He chuckled, standing taller. 'What was that for?'

'Just checking to see if you were real,' I said. 'I thought you might be a post-jetlag, sleeping-pill-induced hallucination that had been following me around all week like the ghost of winters past.'

'Why? You're planning on coming back to work on Monday, are you?'

My heart sank somewhere down around my feet. It was entirely possible I was piercing it with my heels. I glanced around the street, at the couple leaving arm in arm, up at the old gaslight lamps that now held light bulbs, and then at William. How was it so easy for someone to break my heart just by being there?

'Are you done?' My bottom lip quivered.

'Done with what?'

'I have tried all week to get something out of you. Anything. I have brought you coffee, only to find it cold in the staff room an hour later. I baked a cake on Wednesday night. Do you know why I did that? And it's sure as shit not because I'm a great cook, because I'm not.'

He shrugged. 'Because you're busy sucking up.'

'Because I just wanted you to talk to me. That's all it was meant as – a conversation starter, but you didn't even have the heart to look at me when I handed it to you. Even then, I found it stale the next morning. I have said good morning and good night, I have asked specifically if I can help you, and I have nothing to show for it, but a shitty cocktail designed to upset me.'

William shifted about uncomfortably, glancing around and looking for an exit.

'You hurt me,' I said. 'But I suppose you think you were being funny?'

He drew his wobbly lip through his teeth, and his chin dimpled the same way it had the day I arrived.

'I have gone out of my way to ask you for help, to try and engage you. Even today you couldn't reply to a blasted email

84

about a group dinner.' I rubbed tears away. 'You make me feel like I don't exist, like I'm invisible.'

'Oh.' His eyes widened. 'You feel like *you* don't exist? See, I thought that's what we were doing. You stop responding to me, so I stop responding to you. That's fair isn't it, Emmy? Ems. My lovely, beautiful Emmy.'

'What?' I sputtered. 'I have never, ever ignored you. I went out of my way to try and contact you.'

'Really? And that's why we've not spoken in, what is it—' he checked the date on his phone '—over two years? Is that what you call going out of your way? Because I'd hate to see what you're like if you don't want to be found. There was so much I tried to share with you, and you didn't have the bloody heart to respond.'

'William, I wrote to you constantly. Every month. Where are you, William? Have I said something wrong, William? Are you okay, William? Are you even still alive, William? I'll let you go now, William. I'm not going to try anymore, William.' I was so worked up that I yelled, 'Every month! And when that didn't work, I took to the phone book, to Facebook, anything I could think of short of turning up on your doorstep, though … surprise!'

'Yeah? And I wrote to you every other week,' he shouted. Late-night revellers walked past and glared at us, two idiots standing on the sidewalk arguing about writing letters. Because who would write letters anymore? 'And I never got a single reply, so explain to me how that works?'

'You know what? I'm not doing this with you.' I checked my pockets to make sure I had all my belongings. The last thing I needed was to walk back inside, tail between legs, and announce I'd left my phone behind. 'Not you.'

'Not me?'

'No, not you.' I checked for traffic. 'Of all people, not you.'

'So, what, you're just going to walk away again? Vanish into the night?'

'You know, I was so excited to see you again, I really was, but not like this. If this is the William I get now, you can bugger off. I don't want you, us, like this.'

Before he had a chance to respond, I skipped across the road, ignoring the oncoming van that honked its displeasure. As I disappeared around the first corner that offered itself up, the first angry tear slipped out.

Chapter 10

As far as I was concerned, I could see the lights of Piccadilly Circus a thousand times over, and they would still be just as wonderful as the first time I'd seen them as a ten-year-old on a trip to visit family. It was an odd realisation to know that I was here again. As if he sensed it too, Craig leant down and pressed a kiss to the top of my head.

'Pretty incredible, isn't it?' he asked.

I lined my camera up and snapped off a few random shots as pedestrians moved around us like water circumventing rocks in a stream. 'It really is.'

'Hey, so, last night.' Craig nuzzled my hair. 'And this morning.'

'Hmm?' I twisted out of his grip, so I could capture the famous water fountain at a different angle.

'That was nice,' he said quietly. 'Good to reconnect with you after this week.'

I frowned a little. I hadn't noticed any disconnection and felt pangs of guilt that he had. In fact, after getting in late last night, he was the only person I wanted. I woke him up to tell him as much and, when we'd worked out we were home alone this morning, we'd taken advantage of that, too.

'It's been a little busy.' I took him by the hand and pulled him into the next café we walked past. It had brown awnings, gold lettering, and promised the best coffee in London. That was enough to be going on.

We were sat in a little table by the window, cherry-red with a Gingham tablecloth. A slow breeze blew in each time someone walked through the door. Was it the perfect morning? Just about. All I needed was a hot coffee and a decent meal.

'So, tell me about your first week. I feel like we haven't really delved into it much.' Craig leant across the table and held the tips of my fingers. I teased at his fingers and drew him into a play of grabbing at hands. He won when he reached under the table and pinched at my inner thigh.

'Well.' Stray hairs tickled my forehead as I let out a deep breath. 'Where would you like me to begin?'

'Are you happy? I feel that's important. I want you to be happy.'

I smiled. 'I am. It's been a little stressful, first week and all, but I'm here, aren't I? How amazing is that?'

'You know, I've spent the week running around and playing tourist, but I don't think it's sunk in yet that I'm not going home?'

'Right?' I bounced excitedly. 'Tell me about your week again. I'm going to live vicariously through you.'

'We haven't really talked this week, have we?' Craig pouted, as a milkshake was placed in front of him. 'We just kind of ate and slept. Well, you have.'

I pouted. 'Sorry, that's my fault.'

'It's not your fault, you've had a big first week, anyone would be tired. It's okay.'

Somewhere, somehow in the conversation, I was eclipsed by stories of Churchill's War Rooms, the rabbit warren of bunkers and secret rooms, and the walk along the Mall towards Buckingham Palace. The street art at Shoreditch and decommissioned warships sitting in the Thames were one of the highlights of the week. I was thrilled that he was excited, but when my description of work was limited to filing, sorting, taking calls, and not the adventures

Craig had been having, I was almost relieved when my phone rang.

While I was busy trying to race through international departures, my sister Frankie had been in the throes of a minor meltdown. If she couldn't come with me, she reasoned, we must be in constant contact. Social media or email was Satisfactory, text was rated Very Good, and a phone call was classed as Excellent with bonus gold stars for effort. A week into my trip, she was already winning on the contact stakes.

'Hey, you,' she said as I fumbled with getting my phone to my ear.

'Frankie? What are you doing? Isn't it early?'

'It is exactly five o'clock in the morning. On a Saturday.'

'Why are you up so early?' I shuffled from the table and excused myself, giving Craig a smile and whispering, *it's Frankie*. When I got outside, I realised I'd missed her last rambled sentence. 'You're what?'

I listened for the crackle on the other end of the line to stop, and then realised it was just an overly patriotic sidewalk salesman shoving a flag in my ear. Piccadilly Circus was so hectic it felt like elbow room only, yet it seemed salesmen outnumbered tourists. With bus tours, cheap merchandise, theatre tickets, if there was something to sell, it could be bought at any of the numerous stalls dotted around a fountain that turned tourists into human pigeons.

'I said I'm pregnant!'

'Get out!' I shouted, jumping, laughing, waving my hands about, much to the amusement of the people around me 'No! Yes! I mean, amazing, but what?'

'Crazy, right?'

'I didn't even know you were seeing anyone!' I squeaked. 'How did I not know this?'

'Well, it's kind of not serious, and we've barely spoken since.'

'Ah!' I struck a hand out to stop me falling completely as I sat

89

on the steps around the fountain. 'You naughty thing. What are you going to do? Do Mum and Dad know? What about Ezra? What did he say?'

'Mum and Dad are being super chill about it. Ezra says he's surprised you weren't first. In the words of Madonna, I'm gonna keep my baby. I'm not getting any younger, Em, I'm thirty-six. I might be a bit of a hot mess and all but, if I get rid of it...' Her voice drifted off. 'I mean, what if I never get another chance?'

'You don't owe me an explanation,' I soothed. 'I promise, if you're excited, so am I.'

'There is one more thing though.'

'You've moved back home, haven't you?' I asked. 'And you've stolen my bedroom.'

'I think commandeered is the right word.' She snorted her little giggle. 'Caretaking? Mum and Dad are going to help until we get into a routine, and we'll go from there.'

'And the father?'

'He's not so keen to be involved, and I'm okay with that.' She stopped. 'I think.'

'Okay, well, that's only my business in that I will help you as much as I can from here. I can't judge any of that.' Already, I was mentally preparing a list of things to buy and deciding I was going to be *the* coolest aunty ever. 'Can I do anything for you? Do you need anything?'

'I'd really like you there at the birth.'

'Me?' Well, that would certainly mean getting to know my sister in a whole new light.

'Yes, you, dummy. Is that possible? I'm not sure if that works with your dates or anything, but I'd love it if you could be. You can watch all the fun stuff, catch the baby as it flies out.'

I didn't quite have the heart to tell her that wasn't exactly how it worked, but I was sure she was aware. 'You know what. You text me all *your* dates, and I will see how the stars align. I'm not going to promise you anything though.'

'And now that I've bombarded you with my news, please tell me you're settling in and not at all homesick? Because I am so jealous of you right now.'

There was only so much I was ready to impart on anyone, at least until I got my head around everything that was happening. Even so, Frankie listened intently, asked her usual thoughtful questions, peppered her sentences with advice, and then excused herself to be sick again. The last thing she left me with was my James Bond mission: to find the most hideous baby clothes I could. It would earn me some serious aunty credibility. Challenge accepted.

I raced back into the café, my breakfast now a limp reminder of what it used to be. It didn't matter. I was beyond thrilled, and my mind raced ahead of me, trying to calculate if and when I could get time off. Would I be lucky enough to manage a week around the birth? Oh, my heart. This was better than anything that had happened during the week. When I told Craig, his nose wrinkled like someone had farted on him.

'You don't want kids?' I asked. 'I thought you did? You love your nieces.'

Craig snorted. 'In ten years, maybe.'

'Oh.' My shoulders dropped. It wasn't like I was ready for kids either, but I couldn't help but be disappointed in Craig's reaction.

'Eat your breakfast, Em.' He poked at one of my strawberries. 'It'll go cold.'

Chapter 11

'So, Emmy. Your first weekend in town. What delights did it bring to thee?' Pam leant back in her chair, fingers madly trying to untangle her headset from her hair. 'Rest? Relaxation? A trip to the local Tesco? That's always a joyous experience.'

I placed my coffee mug down in time for William to hand me a file. 'This might sound a little odd, but I wrote a bit of a bucket list before we flew out.'

'What?' For the first time in a week, I had William's undivided attention. Shirt sleeves rolled up and tie hanging limp, he'd barely been in the office fifteen minutes and was readying himself for his first patient. 'What did you just say?'

'I started working through my bucket list?'

'A what?' William's face fell. 'No ... Em.'

'You're not planning on dying on us, are you? I just got your bloody login sorted.' Pam steadied William as he half-sat, half-fell between us onto the desk. 'At least give it a month or two.'

'What?' I baulked. 'No. Nothing like that. Stop being so bloody morbid. It's just that if this job doesn't pan out, and I really do hope it does, I want to be able to say that I've seen everything I want to before I go home. It's just the usual kind of touristy things, nothing unusual.'

'Like what?' Pam asked. 'What did you do this weekend?'

'Breakfast near Piccadilly Circus followed by shopping on Regent Street. My sister called, I'm going to be an aunty, which I'm thrilled about. Oh, and I now own an incredibly chintzy Big Ben pencil sharpener from Hamley's.'

'That sounds bloody awful. Not the baby thing, but the pencil sharpener.' Pam replaced her headset. 'I want to join you. Show me the list.'

William leant across me and stole another pen. 'Send it to me, too.'

'Really?' I asked.

'Oh, yeah. I love that kind of thing.'

Pam's finger hovered over the flashing orange light of her phone. 'Hey, what's the worst souvenir you've ever got, William?'

'Urgh,' he groaned. 'You don't want to know. Is this mine? This is mine.' He snatched a file up, called his patient, and disappeared into his office.

'Mine was crabs,' Pam mumbled. 'Could've have just bought a magnet from the shitty shops, but no, I had to find a fella who taught salsa dancing and clearly thought saltwater … anyway.'

My email pinged.

I want that list.

It was the first of five emails he sent me about sending the list over. In between everything else I needed to do today, I managed to reply to William somewhere near closing time. Why he wanted the list after the debacle of Friday night was beyond me. Pam snatched a copy up from the printer and shoved it into her handbag.

'I'm going to take this home and make sure you've got the full London experience happening. Add some of my favourite places.' The screen of her computer flickered black. 'Now, are you sure you'll be okay for the next hour?'

'It's just Trevor and Red,' I said. 'I should be okay. It's a quiet afternoon.'

She bent over and scribbled her number on my desk pad. 'That's me. Call if you need help closing up. Even if you don't, text me and let me you survived.'

'Thanks.'

When the last patient walked out, I let out a deep breath and raced for the bathroom. I'd reached the end of my first solo afternoon without incident. Everyone was still alive, the computers hadn't melted, and patients had left happy. I started working through the end of day procedure, which had been stepped out in Pam's heavily aggravated scrawl, and high-fived myself when that went off without a hitch. Trevor dropped the last of his files by my computer and disappeared, leaving just William in the building.

My stomach jumbled with nerves. I both did and didn't want to be left alone with him. He'd only occupied the loudest corner of my brain all weekend. By Sunday night, I'd decided I wanted to wipe the slate clean and start fresh. Whatever had happened, had happened. It did nobody any good to dwell on it. I didn't want to end up like Frankie, still moaning about someone who'd stolen her favourite cassette in high school. This morning had given me a small taste of that. I just had to work up the gumption to speak to him.

Dozens of different scenarios had played out in my head. In all of them, I'd been tough and strong, said my piece and got an apology. The second he appeared in the doorway of his office, I felt all those plans pack up and float away like butterflies out the nearest window.

'Emmy, you got a minute?'

'Me?' I pointed back at myself.

He looked up at me, bewildered. 'You are the only Emmy here, aren't you?'

Jelly legs carried me down the hallway and into his office. I slipped past him nervously, hearing the door close softly behind him.

'Take a seat, please.' Busy studying a file, he didn't look up as he crossed the room and sat by his desk.

I didn't dare look around. I don't think I wanted to. Peripheral vision gave me shelves full of trinkets and framed certificates – standard doctor's office fare. An examination bed and light were shoved against the wall behind him, along with anatomical posters that must be sold on special commission to doctors. I'd never seen anyone ever use them, but I'd also never seen a surgery without them. I rubbed sweating palms against my pants and waited.

'You look confused?' I asked.

Without looking up, he flicked through the last few pages, a frown slowly forming. 'For the life of me, I cannot work out what's going on with this guy. His test results have come back clean, but I feel like I'm missing something.' He closed the file and offered an apologetic smile. 'How was your day?'

'It was okay.' My chest tightened, unsure where this was all going. 'Yours?'

'Um, not great.' He scratched at his forehead. 'I just … I keep going over last week and there are about a thousand things I could have done differently.'

I rested my elbow on the edge of his desk and chewed a hang-nail. 'What do you want me to say?'

He shook his head. 'Nothing. For me, personally, sorry doesn't feel like enough. But, I am sorry. I am so sorry, Emmy.'

I took a shaky breath. 'In fairness, we've both been shits.'

'Maybe, but it was my job to make you feel welcome. Judging by the look on your face right now, I didn't do that very well.' He leant forward, elbows on his knees, hands clutched in front of him. 'I'm not going to footnote any of it with an excuse, because I have none.'

Scared I was going to cry if I looked at him directly, I picked at my fingernails and concentrated on my lap instead. 'Thank you.'

'If it's okay with you, I'd like to score a line under last week and start afresh.'

I blubbed about for a moment, the words I was looking for not quite ready to show themselves, though I'm sure my mouth bobbed about like I was holding silent conversation.

'Emmy?' He reached across and flicked at my pinkie finger. 'Please? Friday especially was inexcusable and, like you said … not us.'

I nodded and, finally, lifted my eyes to meet his. God, how I'd missed how they looked at me. 'I'd like that too.'

As I stood, William leapt to his feet. After watching each other for a few stilted moments, he moved. An arm around my shoulder drew me into a hug. He was warm, solid and, best of all, real. My breathing slowed, and that awful, back of the brain tension I'd been carrying all week unknotted itself and slunk out through the window. I wanted to stay there in his embrace, my mind tripping over memories as I did so.

We pulled apart slowly, rubbed arms, and with gentle smiles and quiet thank yous, I made for the door.

'Hey, Emmy.'

'Yeah.' I turned back to him.

'Remember, once upon a time, I said you should work under me?'

I smiled at the memory. 'Something like that.'

'I need to make up some hours. I was thinking of opening Saturday morning. Brian tells me I can do it if you or Pam agree to work. What do you think?' he asked.

I furrowed my brow, trying to think. Craig was working, and so was Heather. So far, my plans consisted of sleeping. 'Sure, why not?"

* * *

I slid the bolt through the front door lock and looked out onto the street. It was all a little wistful, a warm breeze blowing detritus around the street, summer dresses getting their first outing of the season. For some reason, that also meant every second guy over the age of fifty was walking around in little more than shorts.

'What are you doing this afternoon?' William appeared from his office, carrying his usual bevy of paperwork and referral requests. After our discussion earlier in the week, he had been a breeze to work with. He was charming, funny, and he easily reminded me of the man I met on that fateful night. It had been a complete about-face, one that I was glad for.

'Not a lot,' I said, not wanting to admit that I'd been thinking about a sun-drenched river cruise all morning. That, plus a few cocktails and a decent meal would be perfect today.

He cocked his head to the side, eyes squinted. 'Really? Nothing?'

'Really.'

'What is it?' He handed files to me one at a time. I got annoyed and grabbed the pile from his hand. 'Your second Saturday here and you have zero plans?'

'Well, everyone else is at work, so…' My voice drifted.

'Right.' He stood a little straighter. 'Give me your death list.'

'My what?'

'That death list you made.' He waved a hurried hand. 'Come on.'

'It's not a death list, William.'

'Whatever it is. Are you printing it? You'd better be printing it.' He walked towards his office. 'Do you own a hat?'

'Yes. No.' I reached back to the printer, a fresh list falling softly into the tray. 'Why?'

'Because we're going out.'

A tickle of uncertain excitement bloomed. Whether this was a good idea or not remained to be seen, but I thought I was willing to take the chance. If anything, it would be a good opportunity to properly clear the air and kickstart our friendship. William returned with a wide-brimmed hat that was far too big for me, resting heavily on the tips of my ears.

'We are?' I asked. 'Don't you have plans?'

'Only with you.'

One look at my clothes – thick pants and shirt – told me I was not prepared to spend an afternoon in this heat. 'I'm going to need to change first.'

* * *

Ninety minutes and three outfit changes later, we took the steps up and out of Tower Hill station, where a medieval scene unfolded in front of me. A high-walled Tower of London set inside a moat, complete with drawbridge and…

'Beefeaters.' I grinned.

'Yeoman Warders is their correct name' William skipped along backwards. 'Same thing though.'

I scrunched up my nose. 'Hey?'

'It's a history thing.' He stopped and waved his hands like a gameshow host at the masses in an exhausted, sweaty queue. 'Now, we can join the line ride or, if you'll follow me down past the Royal Menagerie, I can show you something else.'

And he was gone, a local who'd seen the sights a thousand times before and was intent on getting to his destination. I passed the wire-framed animals of a long-gone zoo, skipped the tower's entrance, and found myself tugged along by a tight hand. I was sure I looked like an old cartoon where the character gets yanked offstage by a walking stick around the neck.

'Come on.'

It almost took a slow jog to keep up with William, before we came to a crashing halt along the river barrier. A water taxi bobbed up and down like a cork, ready to ferry passengers up and down the Thames.

'Are we getting on the boat?' It was on my list, in the form of water taxi, sightseeing, or dinner cruise. I wasn't fussy. I'd be happy with the three o'clock to Millennium Pier.

'Nope.' He pointed to the imposing structure further down the river. Tower Bridge, its steel structure painted blue, red, and white sat waiting. 'We're going to climb the bridge.'

'Climb?' I looked down at my favourite blue dress, and ballet flats that were barely suitable for walking anymore, let alone scaling heights.

We'd stopped by home on the way to the train station. Silly me had figured a sunny afternoon deserved an equally sunny dress. I'd done a quick sniff test and found one still smelling of fabric softener. When I called Craig to touch base and let him know I wouldn't be home this afternoon, he said he was just glad I was making friends, and that he'd see me sometime that night. Apparently, I'd seemed stressed lately.

'Well, you don't physically climb it with a harness like a rock face. It's just an elevator. You go to the top, take a stroll along the walkways, enjoy the scenic views of London.'

'I have to ask. Have you ever been a tour guide?' I said. 'Because you really should consider it if the medicine thing ever dries up.'

'Funny you should say that.' He looked at me, impressed by my observation. 'I might have moonlighted a bit to pay for university.'

'You did not!' I laughed. 'You never told me that.'

'I think you'll find I did,' he said. 'On both accounts.'

'You didn't.' I shook my head. 'I promise you didn't.'

'Okay.' He held a hand up to stop me. 'Because we've agreed to *not* rehash the how's and whys, let's just take it that I may have run walking tours. I got paid, like, £30 a night to walk about for three hours. What's that in your money?'

'Maybe $60? Close enough.'

'So, do you want to?' he asked.

One final tinny call for the water taxi echoed loudly through a speaker behind our heads and pushed us further along the walkway, past worn out, meandering crowds.

'Yes.' I smiled. 'I do.'

'You really didn't do this last time?' he asked disbelievingly. 'I mean, it's only one of the greatest structures in London.'

'Wait.' I pulled him to a stop. 'You really did walking tours?'

'Yes.' He nodded, eyes wide. 'I really did walking tours.'

'How many other girls did you pick up?'

He made a circle with his thumb and finger. 'Zero.'

'Liar.' I pointed at his cheeks. 'Pink, pink cheeks everywhere.'

'No lies.' He swatted my hand away. 'Between school, family, *you*, and picking up work wherever I could to pay for things, I didn't have a lot of time.' He stopped. 'Anyway, let's climb this bridge.'

I huffed and puffed my way up the stairs towards the bridge pylon, past moss-tinged concrete, stopping to read plaques and notices as I went. William leapt ahead in bounds, that type of fitness reserved for someone who'd lived in London long enough to know better. Couples posed for selfies in time to capture iconic red buses as they rolled past, while families of tourists swapped cameras to ensure they had at least one photo that included everyone. William watched me watching them.

He leant in to my side. 'Do you want one?'

'One what?' I asked. 'A family? No thanks, I already have one. That's enough for now.'

He sighed, eyes rolling skyward. 'A photo. Do you want me to take a photo of you on the bridge?'

'Oh,' I said. 'No. That's quite okay.'

We slipped through the crowd and into a quickly moving queue, before being shunted like cattle into the aforementioned elevator, William raised his eyebrows as if to say, 'Look, see? Nothing to worry about'. I elbowed him and shuffled in closer as the small space filled with bodies. As we were pushed closer together, I turned to face him.

'Better not be any climbing.'

'Why? Worried we can all see up your dress?'

I stifled a laugh and tapped his chest. 'You wish.'

The lift shuddered to a quiet stop and, as I stepped out into the theatre, I felt a guiding hand on my back. Not a heavy hand, but a gentle hover that pushed me in the right direction. Our silence was comfortable without explanation and continued through the short film and out into the first walkway where I wandered about and tried to make sense of the London skyline.

I followed William, who strolled along as casual as if he'd been here a thousand times before. 'You know, I am fascinated with the whole tour guide business. It's a completely different side of William I didn't know existed.'

He threw me an over the shoulder cover model look. 'I'm a regular dodecahedron, Emmy.'

'What else can you tell me?'

'Okay.' William guided me by the shoulders towards a point along the window. 'I can tell you over there at St Mary Axe, colloquially known as The Gherkin, they make some fantastic cocktails in the bar on street level. A lot of these old buildings that butt right up against the waterline were warehouses. Flush with the river for easy trade carriage up and down the Thames.'

'And?'

He leant into my shoulder, a fistful of white knuckles gripping the handrail as he continued pointing. '"The Walkie Talkie" over there is just about to open up some restaurants and what's called Sky Garden. Naturally, we'll be going, because I'm adding it to your Death List.'

'London List.'

'Whatever. We're going to go there and drink and eat, and I'm trying to convince Brian we need a special team meet up away from the local.'

'I'll sign that petition.'

'You know The Shard, don't you?'

'The building, not the drug, sure.'

'We like to name our buildings here, if you haven't noticed. The pickled onion will find you the mayor's office.'

'I quite like that building. It's squat. It looks soft.'

'Some would say dump.' He stood straight. 'And that, Emmy, is the view from the west walkway.'

Even with the promise of better views at other buildings, I wanted to stay. I wanted to photograph everything, so I'd never forget. I caught William mid-phone-call down the other end of the walkway, enough distance that I couldn't hear what was said, but close enough that I could see he was flustered. His brows pinched, and fingers dragged through his hair as he paced back and forth, only barely dodging other visitors. I snapped a barely there smile as he returned.

'You okay?' I asked.

'Me?'

I made a show of peering around him and back again. 'Yeah, you.'

'I'm alright.' He pushed his sleeve back before glancing at the overhead screen. 'We have five minutes. Let's go.'

'Go where?' I asked.

When William disappeared, I followed. Out into the stairwell of fat rivets, sturdy iron, and stairs worn down through generations of use. He raced down the flights, two steps at a time, while I was busy shuffling after him. My shoes were intent on slipping off at the heel each time they so much as got wind of a bit of space around them.

A shrill alarm sounded and, as we popped out into the stifling warmth of late afternoon, William came to a sudden halt. I crashed into his back again. He spat out far too many apologies, all the while herding me a little further along the river.

'Here,' he said. 'This is the best part.'

Almost immediately, life came to a standstill around the bridge. Traffic stopped, barriers went up, and masses of people stood engrossed in the scene unfolding.

'And now,' William leaned in, 'the bascules raise.'

'The what?'

The roadway lifted ever so smoothly. Higher and higher, like breath being held, until a little passenger boat passed underneath, almost comical in size, with its flags waving about wildly in the breeze. Within a few minutes, it was all over. I let out a little laugh.

'What?' William's head followed the boat along the river.

'It's just, look how small that boat is, and it brought an entire corner of the city to a complete halt.'

'There's a lesson in that, Em.' He looked across at me, a wistful smile on his face. 'The smallest thing can make the greatest change.'

We watched until the sailing ship was nothing but a dot upstream and others had lost interest. The bascules had long lowered, and traffic flowed as if nothing had happened. When the sun began dipping behind the tips of skyscrapers, a chill filtered through the air. All the while, we watched the ebb and flow of the river, pedestrians, and red buses over the bridge.

'William?'

'Hmm?' He straightened from where he'd been leaning against a river wall.

'I've really enjoyed today.'

He smiled contently. 'Me, too.'

'Can I buy you dinner to say thank you?'

He grinned. 'You know, I've never had a woman buy me dinner before.'

'That's a yes, then?'

'I know this cosy little place in Bermondsey.' His body turned in that direction. 'Shall we?'

We slipped into a side street of gentrified brownish-yellow brick buildings and public spaces. There were a handful of eligible stops along the way, tables and chairs in the sun and cool drinks at the ready, but we bypassed them all in favour of a pub with a tiled exterior and diamond-button booths.

'Very fancy, Doctor Scott.' I slipped in the door ahead of him, thrilled at his out of the way choice.

'I do my best, Emmy, I do my best.' He slipped up behind me. 'You grab a table, I'll get some drinks to start. What do you want?'

'Please, let me pay.'

'I'll get this first round.' He looked me straight in the eyes. 'Please? I owe you one.'

'Well, if you're paying, I'll let you pick.'

He smiled broadly. 'I can live with that.'

I wriggled my way into the last booth in the back of the building, hidden conveniently between the toilets and the calming breeze of the open back door. William shuffled past with drinks twice, before he found me laughing behind a menu. Until that moment, he looked completely lost.

'I'm sorry, that's cruel.' I watched the fear in his eyes subside as he sat down. 'I wouldn't run away, you know that.'

'I think the fact you got on a bloody plane all those years ago is evidence that yes, yes you would.' He pushed a frosty glass towards me. 'You deserve this. You are an awful woman, Emmy Sumner.'

On closer inspection, the red powder on top of the drink brought memories of Edinburgh flooding back, and I began laughing all over again. 'You didn't. What do they call this one? The Fighter.'

'I really did.' He was so proud of himself. 'And yes. Though, in fairness, I did have to look up the recipe for the bar lady, but hey.'

'Here.' I raised my glass. 'What are we toasting?'

William shrugged. 'Ridiculous chances and impossible things.'

'*You* are an impossible thing.'

'I do my best.' He gave me a smug grin. 'Now, we have some years to catch up on.'

'We do.' I blew my cheeks out.

'Tell me everything. How's your family? Are they all well? Mum, Dad, Frankie?' He narrowed his eyes as if he wasn't recalling entirely correctly but, as usual, he was spot on.

'Everyone's really well. Mum and Dad are doing their thing, Frankie is pregnant, Ezra is doing Ezra things, which I don't always understand.'

'What does he do for work?'

'He is a graphic designer, so very good at art, lots of very nice tattoos that he's designed.'

'Oh, nice.' William snaffled a chip. 'Not my kind of fun, but okay.'

'No, me neither, though he has offered countless times to help me out there,' I chuckled. 'How about you? Is your dad still teaching?'

'He is!' William's eyes lit up. 'I love that you remember that. He loves his job, no plans to retire. Mum loves running up and down the Champs-Élysées and drinking strong coffee and laughing with her new girlfriends. My sister Jen is working in this amazing little café, but is thinking of studying art history, so we'll see what happens there.'

'That's wonderful. I'm glad they're well.'

'Yeah, me too. I don't see them enough, of course, but I try.'

Over one drink, and then two, we swapped stories and tried to match up our timelines. I ran through stories of school, of Craig and the trouble we got ourselves into. There was the holiday to New Zealand my parents paid for, and the downturn of volunteering at events, which seemed to be replaced with volunteer work in the maternity ward of the local hospital.

'But the babies in the hospital.' He pinched my cheek. 'You love it.'

'I did.' I shrugged. 'I really did.'

'We had a lady deliver in the clinic once. You should have seen it, the poor woman. Thankfully, we managed to get her into the staff room, so there was a little bit of privacy there, but still.'

'I remember that story! Everything was okay though?'

'A-OK.' He jabbed his straw into his drink. 'Medical school?'

105

I shook my head. 'I'm looking at nursing though.'

'That's good,' he enthused. 'Really, that's great.'

'But we'll see.'

Even after he disappeared with my credit card to order dinner, our conversation picked up where it had left off. After he got over his fascination of my dress with pockets, we drifted from Edinburgh, to London and back again. It was comfortable, it was stealing food from each other's plates, finishing sentences, and finding common grooves among the plethora of topics we skirted around. As we walking to the station and found the first train heading in our direction, the thread felt like one continuous unravelling of time.

I loved it.

'I've gotta ask.' William held a seat flush as I sat down.

'Ask away.' I crossed my leg over and looked around. It had been close to nine o'clock when we left the pub and, still, the train was particularly busy. A busker set up at the other end of the carriage and started playing something mellow on his accordion. By the sounds of things, we were on an underground gondola ride.

'When you applied for this job...' He scratched at his top lip. 'Did you, like, did you look to see who worked there?'

I shook my head, a slow smile spreading. 'You, Red, were not on the website.'

'What?'

'Sorry to burst your bubble. You do have an ego thing, don't you?' I teased. 'You weren't listed.'

'Am I really not there?' His phone was out and on before he'd so much as got the sentence out. 'I'm not on there. They told me I'd be there months ago.'

'Told you.'

'Would you have applied had I been listed?'

My mouth dried. 'What do you think?'

'I think you would have run a mile.'

I pinched at his leg. 'I would've made like the Von Trapps, over the hills and far away.'

'Yeah.' William tipped his head back against the window. 'Thought as much.'

Chapter 12

Craig pushed the cereal box across the table, eyes seemingly focused on a spot in the back of his mind. When the box gave off a hollow rattle, I opted for toast instead. I poured another coffee, sat back at the table and looked him, face pinched up and studying his bowl intently. Heather and Josh were already out for the day, and their absence only added to the heaviness in the room.

'Are you okay?' I tried to lean into his line of sight, although he avoided my direct gaze like a stargazer at an eclipse. 'Craig?'

'Hey?' He lifted his eyes to meet mine. Finally. 'What?'

'Is everything alright? You seem a bit out of it.'

'No, yes. I mean, I'm fine.' He waved a hand about his head. 'Just thinking about something at work. Just having some trouble with one of the new accounts.'

'Everything okay?' I asked.

'Fine,' he said. 'How about you? Good night?'

After getting off the train last night, William and I had walked home the long way. Despite assurances I could get around on my own, he wanted to introduce me to the idiosyncrasies of our borough. It added another hour to our night, and I heard about the crazy cat lady three houses down from him, who had more money than God, and possibly more years under her belt. Of the three Chinese shops we passed, he rated them out of five, using taste, price, and suspected MSG content on a sliding scale as a comparison system, and the laundromat was to be avoided at all costs. Better to go up to the next borough for that one, he said.

When we'd finally reached my apartment, we stood about in awkward silence before farewelling each other with curt waves and embarrassed smiles. I bounced up the stairs feeling a little light on my feet, as if a little piece of the Emmy puzzle has snapped back into place. But, when I got to bed and Craig rolled as far away as he could, that elation turned to confusion, which lingered as I watched him opposite me.

My brows pinched together, and I was sure a light sweat broke out. 'You're not upset that I went out yesterday?'

'What? No.' He shook his head adamantly. 'No. Like I said, I'm thrilled that you're making friends. Where did you go? Talk to me.'

'Tower Bridge and then out for dinner.'

'Oh, I went there the other week. It's pretty impressive isn't it?'

'I got to see the bascules raise.' I made the hand motions of a bridge rising. 'I think that's what they're called?'

'Bastilles?' He rubbed his face. 'Yeah, I don't know.'

'How's work for you?' I asked. 'Did yesterday go as planned?'

For all the medical things I could do, there were just as many accountancy things that I couldn't make heads or tails of. So, listening to Craig talk about capital surplus, job costings, and amortization kind of slid over my head. Thankfully, his first week had been more about settling in at the office, meeting new clients, and familiarising himself with their accounts.

'… and then the network was down most of the morning. IT had no idea what was going on, I had a client waiting on paperwork, so that was a great look to close out week one. The boss was on the phone screaming blue murder about it last night. He seems to forget that I'm an accountant, not an IT specialist. It's going great, Emmy.'

'I'm sorry.' I reached for his hand and brushed a thumb across his knuckles. 'Small steps, right? In a few weeks, you'll look back and laugh because everything will suddenly be going smoothly.'

'You're right.' He collected our dishes and placed them in the sink. 'Oh, and Heather asked me to talk to you about leaving your washing in the machine yesterday. She said please don't do that, please empty it when you're done.' With a defeated sigh, he shuffled off to the bathroom and closed the door behind him.

From the highs of last night, to the reality of life in a shared house. It reminded me of the time I got in trouble for using Frankie's make-up. I was fourteen, and denied it to the back teeth, even though I still had lipstick smears across my cheek where I'd tried rubbing it off. In my haste to get out and about with William, I'd forgotten my friends. Duly noted.

For the rest of the morning, I cleaned. Mum had always said she knew when I was properly upset, because I would clean my bedroom from head to toe and sell off all the things I decided I didn't need. Today, I hit that level here. I scrubbed benches and toilets, made sure there was nothing left in washing baskets, and rinsed coffee cups the moment they were used, though I didn't get around to listing anything on eBay, so that was good.

* * *

Heather waddled in the front door, her arms laden with enough shopping bags to cut off circulation. I unhooked the first few from each arm and helped her into the kitchen, groceries spilling in all directions. Josh lumbered up the stairs behind her, in charge of the alcohol component of the shop.

'I think we should start getting this delivered.' Heather laughed weakly. 'I didn't think there'd be that much. They do offer delivery. I'm going to look into that.'

'Do I owe you anything?' I grabbed at the bags on her left arm.

'What?' Heather glanced up from where she was hunched over a bag of fruit that had rolled across the kitchen floor. 'Don't be silly. The Community Chest is very … chesty.'

Community Chest started as a joke, something I'd suggested while playing online Monopoly with her in the months before Craig and I moved in. What started as a joke about teaching me street names, 'because you need to learn that Regent Street is expensive, Emmy', became a mini planning device. The Community Chest became the spot I shoved our weekly monetary contributions. Grocery money and emergency funds were all tucked away inside an old Charles & Di biscuit tin. Heather took from that as needed. The only rule was, we needed to have our shopping list tacked to the refrigerator by Friday morning. No list equalled no food.

'Okay. Good.' I grappled for a stray orange that rolled towards me. 'I do owe you an apology though.'

'What?' She grimaced as she straightened up. 'What the hell for?'

'I left my clothes in the machine yesterday. I was just heading out and didn't want to keep people waiting. I should have stayed until it was done, I'm sorry.' I scratched at the back of my neck and waited with baited breath for her response.

'What? God, I wasn't even angry. I just passed comment that you'd forgotten to empty the machine. I think I even laughed, threw everything else on top of it, and hit the go button again.'

'Still, I'm sorry.'

'For goodness' sake, Em. If something's wrong, I'll tell you.' She gave a little laugh. 'It's fine and thank you for cleaning the kitchen. It looks good. Finally.'

'You're welcome.'

'To be fair, I had to touch your lacy undies.' Josh shook his head. 'Yuck.'

'Oh, so you'll touch her lacy undies, but not mine.' I swatted at him with a stick of celery. 'I know where I'm not wanted.'

'Yeah, well, Heather lets me play with hers.' He pressed a kiss into the side of her head. 'Love you.'

'If that's the price, I'd rather not,' I teased.

'Hey, what are you guys doing Friday night? Can we have a family dinner?' Heather asked.

'I'm free,' Craig called from the bathroom.

'How did he hear that?' Heather whispered, top lip curled.

I shrugged. 'I have no idea.'

'Did he tell you I was angry?'

'Ah, yeah.' I nodded, forcing a block of cheese into a spare refrigerator space. I made a mental note that the fridge would be next on the cleaning list. 'Made out like I'd broken the fourth amendment of friendship.'

Heather sighed and shook her head. 'I think the problem is him. He's been pretty touchy with everyone this week. There was one night he got home, walked in and didn't speak to anyone.'

'I'm sorry.' I felt helpless. 'Work has been a bit not so great for him.'

Craig appeared by the kitchen door. 'Everything okay? Need a hand?'

'All good.' Josh squeezed his shoulder. 'Just talking about Friday dinner. I'll get some fancy wine from the cellar in Fenchurch on my way home.'

'Do you want me to cook?' I asked.

'Dumplings?' Heather asked hopefully. 'Because yes, please.'

Chapter 13

Standing in queues waiting for coffee gives you time to ponder life's important things. Like, how much money did I have left in my account? Just how much were two meals, dessert, and drinks on Saturday night, and can I therefore afford that ham and cheese croissant that I'm sure is whispering my name. *Emmy, please eat me. I'll riddle you with guilt all day, but our short, loving embrace will feel oh-so-good.*

There was no charge against my card for Saturday night. Nada. Zip. Not even for drinks.

I checked all my accounts, just in case the money had come out of some random hidey hole, or was sitting in limbo, waiting. But, no. My first thought was that something had gone wrong, that the bank was about to call, and my stomach saddled up for the ride. Rubbing my forehead, I stuttered through my order and stepped out into the street with an oversized coffee and cold croissant.

And then it dawned on me. I had sent William to pay, the sneaky sod.

Pam was busy trying to untwist herself from her jacket when I walked into the clinic. She was flustered and cursing, and William was in the staff room, giggling like a child who'd just set a cherry bomb in a toilet. Following the sound like a trail of crumbs, I pushed the door open and glared at him. His face lit up like a great mystery had been solved and he hooted with laughter once more.

'Right, how much?' I asked.

He glanced around, his face portraying a state of complete cluelessness, hand pressed against his chest. 'Emmy, I honestly have *no* idea what you're talking about.'

'You little shit. I gave you my card so you could pay for dinner. I checked the balance this morning, and there's no charge on my account. So, how much do I owe you?' I could at least breathe easier knowing there was nothing wrong with my card and wouldn't have to explain that one at home.

'I have zero idea what you're saying, Emmy.' He grinned. 'I tapped and go-ed. Went. Whatever. I can't understand your English today, you weird Australian.'

'William,' I complained.

'Emmy, it's fine. Honestly. I haven't had a day like that in a very long time, so consider it a thank you.' He stopped. 'A welcome home gift, even.'

I shook my head. 'William, I wanted to do something nice for *you*.'

'I tell you what.' He shuffled around me, and backwards out of the room, a wobbly coffee in one hand, and a supermarket sandwich in the other. 'You can pay this weekend. Pick somewhere else from your Death List.'

'London List.'

'We'll do what we did on Saturday: work the morning, party in the afternoon.'

'Madame Tussauds,' I said. It was the closest I was ever going to get to the royal family, and I was prepared to put my pride on the line for a photo to send Frankie.

'No.' William shook his head, lips pursed. 'I don't do those creepy-ass dolls. I am out.'

'Really? Aren't they like cadavers?' I asked. 'They're all dead on the inside.'

'Yes, but cadavers don't follow you around the room with their shifty little eyes.' His office door kicked shut in my face. 'Can you get my first file please, Em?'

'I want to go to IMAX, then,' I called through the door.

'No!' He called back. 'We're not going to the movies. You'll probably try and hold my hand, or feel me up, or something romantic like that, before stealing my popcorn.'

I snorted a laugh and walked away.

'I'll go see a movie with you.' A leaf crinkled as Pam drew her fingers through her hair. She'd moved on to battling her headset. 'What are we seeing?'

'Anything, as long as it's in IMAX. I'm not fussed.'

William's door shot open and he hung his body out into the hallway, eyebrow raised. 'Do you have a size thing, Emmy?'

'What?' I baulked, feeling my cheeks warm.

'Why IMAX? Why not just go to the local Odeon or whatever?' he pressed.

'Because, despite what your mother told you, bigger is better, Red.' Pam sauntered past him with a grin.

I turned away and laughed.

'I can see you laughing at me Emmy. I can see you.'

'Alright.' I steadied myself. 'What about St Paul's Cathedral? Can we climb to the top of that?'

'For fuck's sake, are you trying to kill me? Do you have *any* idea how many steps are in that godforsaken place?'

'Actually, it can't be godforsaken. It's a church. Technically, God lives there.'

From the kitchen, I could hear Pam roar with laughter. 'I love you two, just so you know. I'm so glad you got that stick out of his arse, Emmy.'

'Oh, you have no idea.' William closed himself in his office again.

115

'What does he mean by that?' Pam returned, a plate of toast with a small buffet of spreads dotted around the rim. If that's what she ate at work, I was lining up for a weekend breakfast at her place.

'I have no idea,' I said, sifting mail into different pigeonholes. 'Hey, question.'

'Shoot.'

'Know any good gyms around here? I'm thinking of taking a class or two.'

The quick solution to my tightening pants would be to just stop visiting the bakery on the way to work, but I was prepared to work for my baked goods if I had to.

'Ah, the twenty-four-hour gym on the High Street is quite good. I went for a while but, you know, commitment being my strong point and all.' She winked. 'No, seriously, it's a good place. You should try there first.'

'Thanks, I will.'

She crunched on a piece of toast. 'I do have a strong commitment to carbs though.'

* * *

Pushing the doors to a gym open for the first time wasn't exactly my idea of fun, but that's what I did shortly after eight o'clock that night. There had been internet searches and comparisons during lulls in the day and, in the end, Pam's High Street suggestion was still the better option. I'd cooked dinner, got another 'home late' text from Craig, caught up with my friends about their days, and slipped out the door quicker than you could say 'ham and cheese croissant with sweet relish, please.'

It was inviting enough, as far as gyms went. The décor was sharp, and the equipment didn't look one hundred years old, unlike the gym I went to in Sydney. I filled out my new member form and watched as the numbers on the scales chased me down like Jack Nicholson in *The Shining*. A bit of work to do, then.

'What's your aim?' A girl with bubble gum pink hair and lipstick peered up at me from where she was squat by my hips, callipers in one hand, a handful of me in the other.

'Overall fitness, I suppose,' I said quietly. 'I haven't run in a while.'

'Oh, you're a runner?' She stood, scribbling notes on my card. 'You could do with some weights, too, tone it up a little bit.'

Did I mention how much fun first nights at the gym are?

I spent a little over an hour being poked, prodded, and counselled before being let loose in the cardio room, where I could pound the treadmill and watch reruns of *EastEnders* to my heart's content. In a room full of people glued to the screen, one raven-haired woman chanced a waved. When I waved back, she claimed the machine next to me.

She leaned over while setting herself up. 'Hello.'

'Hi.' I gave her my best leave me alone grin and kept up my Thriller-esque zombie shuffle.

'Good to get out of the house, right?' she asked.

I nodded. 'It is.'

'That's why I come.' Her movements had her bobbing about like a chicken. 'Always nice to get a little bit of *me* time.'

I grinned again, hoping to get out of too much discussion. But I did need to make more friends in the area, so kept chatting away for the next little while. It was light and barely broke surface tension, but it was refreshing to add another voice to the mix.

When I left, glowing like a supernova complete with a lake of sheen over my face, I checked the class board by the front door – possibly designed to guilt members into coming back. Thursday night, eight o'clock looked like Pilates o'clock. And, if that didn't suit, Friday night, too.

'The Friday night session is great. Small group, lovely teacher. Everyone else is out on the town, so there's not a lot of us.' Raven-haired lady, whose name I still didn't know, was by my side again.

Maybe she was a Weeping Angel; I was sure she'd still been on the treadmill when I'd switched mine off.

'Slow, sloth-inspired movement is more my speed,' I joked.

'Good for muscle tone,' she said. 'I mean, I won't be there this week, I've got a client meeting at seven, so that's cutting it a bit fine.'

'That's okay, I've got plans, too. Maybe next week, then?' She might've been quick off the mark, but I could always do with a gym buddy.

'Oh,' she pipped, a sudden spring in her step. 'Okay, yes. That'd be great.'

She slung her bag over her shoulder and disappeared into the night. I made a calendar note in my phone and headed in the opposite direction. I was glad that, if nothing else, I'd met another local.

Chapter 14

On Friday afternoon, I dashed out of the office without saying my usual goodbyes. I was running on limited time. Me being me, I'd volunteered to cook something for dinner that was not only fiddly, but would need to be made in a sizeable quantity, else we'd all go hungry. I scrambled around local supermarkets, dashing into one when the other decided chilli jam was far too exotic to stock, and into a grocer for shallots when I couldn't find spring onion. Checking off the last of my dog-eared list, I shoved the paper back in my pocket and hot-footed it home.

'Oh, hello, Emmy.'

Our neighbour, Jim, lived in the two floors below us. He was a carpenter in his late thirties, had beautiful brown eyes, and a face that looked ten years older with a beard. Over the last twelve months, according to Heather, he'd spent a lot of time redecorating the entry to the building. Josh kept him in a steady supply of gin in lieu of paying for any of the work.

'Hey, Jim.' I leaned over the railing. 'How's life?'

'Good.' He smiled warmly. 'Do you need a hand?'

'Oh, no, thanks,' I called, dashing up a few more stairs. 'Got two.'

Gentle laughter filled the stairwell, and for a moment I thought

119

we should maybe invite him to dinner. Maybe another night. That would be nice.

'How are you settling in?' he asked.

'Very well, thank you! I love your city.'

'Glad to hear it.' His door clicked shut behind him, and he was gone for another day.

Still mindful of the Great Washing Faux Pas of 2014, I gathered up every limp, discarded piece of clothing I could find around the apartment, and shoved whatever would fit in the washing machine. As it whirred quietly by my feet, I cracked a bottle of white wine, turned the radio up, and started dinner prep.

Heather arrived home first, cradling a bouquet of flowers like a baby. Full of vivid pink, white, and purple blooms, she danced around the lounge, trying to determine the best place to display her new spray. Settling on the coffee table, she dug about the back of the cupboard for a vase before disappearing to change. When she returned, I handed her a glass of wine.

'How is it we live in the same house and it feels like we barely see each other?' she asked.

'It's not just me, then?' I relaxed against the counter as she refilled my glass. 'How are you?'

'I'm so good. Look at my flowers, he's so lovely.' She scrunched herself up, shoulders around her ears, eyes crinkled. 'I could squeal like an escapee balloon.'

I tried to recall the last time Craig had bought me flowers, and I was sure the answer was buried somewhere in the summer of 2013, about five minutes after we started dating. The realisation pinched at something uncomfortable. I didn't want to think of things as a competition, because they weren't, and every couple was different, but a bit of spontaneity wouldn't hurt. Maybe I should buy him flowers. Yes, I'd do that.

'What about you? How are you?'

'Me?' I turned my concentration back to my mixing bowl, tipping chopped shallots into pork mince, spices and cabbage. It didn't feel great between the fingers but would feel much better in my belly later.

'Yeah, you. How's the work situation?'

'Work's great.' I smiled at the memory of William carrying a small child out of his office. Held way above his head, arms and legs akimbo, both he and the boy laughing like it was the funniest thing to ever happen. 'Everyone is just … it's a great team.'

'And?' she pressed.

'And?' I asked.

Heather pinched at my arm. 'What about William? Is everything sorted there?'

'It's really nice to have my friend back.'

Craig appeared next. His face was bright and open and, when he offered me a hug, I was only too glad to accept. It had been far too long since he'd seemed so relaxed, and he did look particularly lovely with his suit and tie just that little bit loose.

'Hey you.' He peppered my face with kisses.

'Hey you.' I bit back laughter, my hands still sticky with dumpling mixture. 'How are you?'

'Good!'

'Just good?' I asked. 'You look great. Relaxed. It's nice to see.'

'It's just good to get out of work early, innit?' He kissed me again and leant into my ear. 'We can have an early night, maybe?'

'Ooooh.' My lips curled into a delighted 'O'. This was the side of Craig I liked best. 'I'm on board with that. But you smell, go wash up for dinner. I'm almost ready to go.'

'I smell?' He played, sniffing his armpits. 'Yeah, I smell like dank office. I'll be back in a minute.'

When I finally had a small pyramid of dumplings crammed into the fridge, Josh arrived home with even more wine and a spring in his step. Heather poured drinks and set the table, and Craig was just … Craig. For the first time all week, all four of us sat down to dinner together, and we were positively buoyant – living the dream, even. With soft background music and an open

121

window, it was the perfect setting for a warm evening.

'This looks incredible.' Josh leaned in to sniff his dinner. 'Thank you for cooking, Em.'

Craig squeezed my thigh. 'It really does.'

'Can I have a humble brag before we start?' Josh looked at each of us.

'Please,' I said.

'Right, so.' He wriggled in his seat, hands splayed across the table. 'I had lunch with the team at Piccadilly Circus today, because one of my ads made it up to the screens. I mean, it was in a tiny corner, and it was gone in a flash, but it was *there*. *My* work, in glorious technicolour. Me! Of course, we had beers to celebrate before heading back to the office, but it was so exciting.'

Josh pulled his phone from his pocket, fingers gliding across the screen before he passed it around. I watched on excitedly at the small reel of photos he'd taken during his moment of triumph. Heather beamed at him, prouder than I'd ever seen her, and Craig offered his congratulations in the form of a quick handshake.

'Well.' I raised my glass. 'Cheers to you!'

With drinks held high, Josh gave Heather a quick nod, almost unnoticeable if you weren't looking.

'I'm so glad we organised to have dinner together tonight,' Heather began. 'Because I have something, we have something we need to say.'

I gasped loudly and rapped my hands on the table.

'The other night while you were both busy being workers, Josh and I were having a boozy dinner at The Ivy and, over a far too expensive glass of champagne, he asked me to marry him. Naturally, I said yes.'

'Oh my God!' I leapt to my feet. 'Are you serious?'

'We've spent all week making sneaky phone calls back home to let family know.' Josh nodded, downing the last of his glass.

'I am so thrilled.' I wiped my eyes. 'This was always going to happen, but … oh, my heart.' I raced around the table and hugged them tightly.

I was so proud of my friends, for the life they'd made, and the choices that had brought them, and me by extension, here. Excitement rained at the prospect of their wedding, which was not a pairing off of two friends, but a solidifying of the last twenty years we'd spent together. And then, when I watched Craig flinch momentarily, I felt a pang of uncertainty; both for and about him.

'So, big plans for tomorrow then?' I looked around the table as the excitement ebbed, albeit minutely, and we returned to the food in front of us.

'We're going to get away early.' Heather rubbed at Josh's arm. 'Take the train to Southampton. There's this huge new resort open by the bay. We'll spend a few nights there celebrating.'

'That sounds lovely.' I clutched at my chest. 'Craig, have you got much planned for the weekend?'

'I'm, ah, working again tomorrow.' He offered me a quick glance. 'You?'

'I'm working in the morning.' I took another sip of wine. 'After that, I'm going to look at St Paul's Cathedral.'

Craig relaxed back into his chair. 'Right.'

'Is that okay?' Even as I said it, I felt a wave of confusion wash over me. I wasn't sure if that was because I heard myself asking for permission, or because of something deeper I didn't want to touch on.

He placed his glass down. 'I was hoping we might have lunch together tomorrow. There's a nice little café in our building, but if you've already made plans…'

'No, Craig. I can change my plans, it's completely okay.' I grabbed at his leg and forced a smile. 'I can do the other stuff later. I'd love to have lunch with you.'

After the last of the bubbly had bubbled, and the final dumpling disappeared into a grateful stomach, Craig and I retreated to the bedroom. Later that night, he made love to me like he had something to prove. And it wasn't just once, he came back for seconds, then thirds, and I was sure he'd bend me around like a pretzel given half the chance. While it made for a nice change, something still felt a little off-kilter. Finally done, he offered a smile and a chaste kiss, before he rolled away and collapsed into his pillow.

As for me, I lay awake all night watching the clock tick over.

Chapter 15

Nine o'clock, and the waiting room was already full. A baby cried in a corner, an elderly woman was tutting and checking her watch, and I had no doctor to speak for. For every second the clock bounced forward, I was sure it slid three paces backwards. My phone was running off the hook with people desperate to see William on a Saturday, even more so than the people already waiting.

I'd made sure his consulting room was set up, not that that was difficult. All he needed was a working pen, an empty waste paper basket, antibacterial lotion and hand wash, and a clean exam bed. I hadn't been inside his office often but, this time, I chanced a look around. Thank you cards and photos of new babies stood proudly on the shelves above his desk. When they overflowed, there were two noticeboards quickly filling. Holiday trinkets snuck in around the cards, photos of him in shorts and snorkelling gear, and the tiny koala I'd sent him shortly after getting home from my Hogmanay trip.

'I am so sorry!' He blustered through the door. 'The alarm went off, I promise. I might have hit snooze. I might also be a little hungover.' A messenger bag looked like it was trying to choke him, while his shirt hung out of his trousers. His tie was barely knotted, and the jacket of his powder-blue suit folded in on itself. 'Emmy, I'm so sorry.'

I handed him his first three files and a lukewarm coffee. 'Your room is ready. It's okay, I've sorted it out. Welcome to Saturday.'

'God, I love you.' He kissed my cheek. 'Honestly, you're incredible.'

A microsecond after he spoke, he realised what he'd said. My heart thudded to a stop, and then raced to catch up with the world around me. The phone was ringing again, another patient had walked in, and I needed to work. William looked at me, turned away, then turned back to me again.

'Well, you know what I mean.' He offered a nonchalant shrug and called his first patient for the morning.

His admission left me a little skittish, a cat with a rogue laser pointer. Just when I thought I'd brushed his words off as a slip of the tongue, doubt crept in and asked me if I was totally sure, or would I like to phone a friend for another opinion? As patients built up, and the morning dragged on, the sweetest sound I could hope for was the handful of cancellations that came through. When I finally got to switch the phone over to night-mode, there may have been a small celebration.

'William,' I called.

'Emmy,' he replied.

I did the awkward jeans dance in the staff room, trying to change out of work clothes and into something more Saturday afternoon appropriate. Yes, I needed that gym membership.

'St Paul's Cathedral,' I said.

'You don't want to go, do you?' he asked.

'What?' I looked towards the direction of his voice. 'Yes, yes, absolutely I want to go.'

'But? I feel like there's a but coming?'

'Craig wants me to have lunch with him first. Is it okay if we meet there at, say…' I checked the time, 'Three o'clock?'

He was quiet for a moment. 'Three is good.'

'You sure?' I pulled a T-shirt over my head and tossed my shirt into my backpack.

'Absolutely.' He appeared in the doorway. 'I need to look into a few things here anyway. Go and enjoy lunch. I'll meet you on the steps at three.'

'Thank you.' I brushed past him and bolted out the door, aware that I needed to get going if I was going to make it to the café before one o'clock. I wanted to be early.

As it was, after a signal fault at Baker Street, I was twenty minutes late. Constant text updates didn't help the situation, judging by the responses, and I arrived at the Southwark office to find Craig walking out of the café with lunch to go.

'All I wanted was lunch with you, Emmy.' His jaw twitched. 'Is that too much to ask?'

'I was … the train … Craig,' I whined. 'I was on my way. I left work in plenty of time. I can't help the trains.'

'And I've got a meeting to get to now.' He pushed his sleeve back. 'Or I'll be the one who's late.'

'Craig, please?' I said. 'What is going on with you? I want you to talk to me. Just tell me what the issue is.'

He yanked a chair back, and it scratched loudly against the concrete floor. I scrambled into the seat opposite, irrationally worried that I'd be chastised for doing that wrong, too. He checked his watch again.

'I said I was sorry,' I mumbled.

'How was your morning, Emmy?' He sank back and shoved his hands in his pockets.

'It was good, actually. I mean, William was late.' I scratched at my forehead. 'But it all worked out in the end.'

'And William is the tour guide, right?'

'He is.' I reached for my phone. 'Also, I've been talking to Heather this morning. She's so excited, talking about wedding plans.' I swallowed down a hard lump. 'You know, I was thinking, wondering, is that something you could see us doing?'

127

'Doing what?'

'Getting married.' I knew the answer as soon as the words came out. Something flickered across his eyes, and I'm not sure if it was defiance or anger.

'Not right now, no,' he said, his answer so quick, I doubt he even gave himself time to think. 'I might consider it in ten years or so but, no, it's not something I necessarily want to be doing. Like the kids thing. No plans. And is this really what you want to be talking about today?'

'It was just a question,' I said. 'I … I'm confused right now, I don't know what to ask you.'

'How's your day been? What have you done today? What account are you working on?' He raised his brows. 'You know, usual stuff.'

'Oh.' I peered up as he stood and straightened his jacket. With a few curt words, my boyfriend had turned into a complete stranger.

'Anyway, I need to get to a meeting.' He leaned down and kissed my forehead. 'Enjoy your afternoon.'

The last I saw of him through my blurred vision as he melted into a crowd of people, was jacket lapels flapping under force of movement. Wiping my eyes, I walked away from the café and into the heart of Borough Market.

As a consolation prize, I was happy to find my own lunch among the narrow passageways and rustic eateries. My stomach had been growling long before I got on the train. Now, it was just an unhappy symphony of neglect and anger. As I walked across Blackfriars Bridge and picked at a roasted vegetable roll and sipped an orange juice, I tried to dissect what was going on with Craig.

I couldn't come up with anything. At least not something positive. Or maybe I just didn't want to admit anything to myself.

He was constantly working late, most evenings not getting home until nine o'clock, sometimes later. When I questioned him, nothing more than a gentle enquiry, he couldn't come up with anything but a shrug of the shoulders and a, 'that's business, Emmy'. Thinking about him lately, I felt like I was being squeezed. The 'we' was becoming a source of constant agitation. It wasn't the lovely fluttering tummy and sense of togetherness that I once got when we could sit for hours churning out essays and arguing about where to get the cheapest student dinner.

Sitting on the steps of the cathedral, I watched as a bridal party stepped out into the sunshine. The bride and groom were bombarded with well-wishers and mobile phone photography, and had the most beautiful smiles on their faces. In the middle of a crowd of people, they saw only each other. It was perfect. It was exactly what I wanted in life. I clapped along with everyone else lucky enough to be watching, though went back to playing with my phone when they disappeared.

I had a quick catch up with Frankie, who was feeling every minute of her morning sickness, especially at night. She was also indulging in copious amounts of macarons and the chocolate I'd posted her when I first arrived. I scrolled through Facebook and tried doing the obligatory check-in selfie. As I lined the camera up and smiled, a plastic shark on a stick appeared in frame. I put the phone down, and it disappeared. Hold the phone up, and it reappeared. I tried for the quick over the shoulder glance, just to see what was happening, and William was there, biting a knuckle to try and stem his laughing fit.

'What the hell is that thing?' I laughed, getting to my feet.

'This?' The mouth of the shark snapped each time he squeezed the stick's handle. 'This is Steve.'

'Steve Rogers, or Steve Trevor?'

William dragged his bottom lip through his teeth. 'Rogers?'

'Correct answer.'

'Steve used to accompany me on my tour walks.' He nipped at me again. 'I remember you telling me you had to follow a kangaroo on a stick. I used Steve.'

'You remember that? That was Edinburgh we talked about that.'

'I remember.' A lanyard appeared next. 'Now, this is an old London Pass that someone gave me one night. It was their last day of use, or something, and I always kept it. Apparently, because I would need it today. So, you can look like a real tourist with that around your neck.'

I checked the expiry date as he hung it around my neck. Yep, well and truly dead. 'Did you get this from one of your other tourist girlfriends?'

'I can assure you, I was too busy studying anatomy to actually experience it.' He looked me in the eyes. 'Unless, of course, we're referring to my own.'

That was probably an image I didn't need in my head, especially right on top of such a shitty lunch date. I did my best to push any thought of him like *that* from my mind.

'And this, is the *pièce de résistance*.' He handed me a black cap with the word 'TOURIST' stitched across the front. 'You are the tourist, you need to wear this. It'll go great with your I HEART SCOTLAND hoodie.'

'Oh my God,' I groaned, remembering my embarrassment at being caught in it at the airport. That jumper had now been relegated to very cold winter nights. 'This is so awful. I love it.'

'You look great, Ems, really.' He gave me two enthusiastic thumbs up. 'Seriously looking the part right now.'

'I'm so cute.' I brushed myself down. 'But am I Edinburgh cute?'

'I don't know, I'll get someone to punch you in the face and we'll find out.' He nipped at my leg with Steve. 'Let's go see some church.'

Rapt in ornate ceiling paintings, wall carvings, and the tiled floor, I listened to everything the multimedia guide had to offer, including the slightly ironic videos, showing me exactly what I was already looking at. We moved through the Quire, with its dark wood and gothic features, and onto the High Alter where William removed my headset.

'What do you think, Emmy? Want to get married in a church?'

The lump in my throat rose again. Of all the questions I wanted today, that wasn't one of them. I shook my head in quick bursts. 'Nah.'

'No?'

'I'm not religious. There's no doubt it's a gorgeous building. Look at it. But I don't think it's right to stand up in a church if I don't believe in what it's teaching.' I turned the guide map over in my hand. 'Having said that, I wouldn't mind staying for Eucharist.'

'I would only stay until they got to the biscuit part. I'm hungry.'

'Biscuits? They're communion wafers, you idiot.' I slapped at his arm with the guide and unfolded it again. 'Except, we've missed Eucharist for today. Do you want to move?'

'Let's go.'

Stairways twisted, and cold stone walkways narrowed as we embarked on what I thought would be an afternoon stroll up a few flights of stairs. The only problem with that theory were the 530 steps that stood between me, the Golden Gallery, and views of the Greater London skyline. I hunched over, slipped on worn stone, and swore at William more than once before we got to the Whispering Gallery, only halfway up the walk.

'Here's the fun part.' A hand on either shoulder, he pressed me down into the worn wooden bench that snaked around the wall. 'Put your ear to the wall and wait for a moment.'

He shuffled off excitedly, glancing back over his shoulder to make sure I did as instructed. A frown and clicking fingers appeared when he thought I'd moved. Almost directly opposite me, on the other side of the gallery, he stopped, kneeled on the seat, and pressed his cheek to the wall.

'Emmy, can you hear me?' A whispered voice had wrapped around the walls and come back to me like an old tin can telephone, a friendship boomerang.

I cupped my hands over my mouth and laughed. 'Yes. Can you hear me?'

'Yes.' He shuffled about and got comfortable. 'Emmy, I have something to tell you. It's very important that you listen to me, your local friendly GP. Can you do that?'

'I think I can, yes.' I waited with baited breath, expecting a lewd joke which, by default, would be shared with anyone else who caught wind of his voice around the wall.

'I missed you,' he said. 'But I'm so glad you're here now.'

I sank back against the wall and smiled. It was possibly the nicest thing anyone had said to me in weeks, and it made my heart sing and ache all at the same time. I pressed myself back up against the wall. 'I missed you, too.'

'Did you really? Because I'm not feeling it. You don't seem very communicative.'

'What?' I turned to see him hunched over, shoulders shuddering with laughter. 'I'm continuing without you, then.'

There was nothing safe about a quick shuffle to the nearest exit, only two hundred and something steps above ground but, through a giggling fit and watching William trying his best to move an entire family who'd blocked his path, I beat him into the next stairwell. It took him more than his fair share of 'pardon me's to reach me a few flights above him.

There was a moment of peace when he caught up to me, both of us out of breath and words. He tried to splutter a few thoughts out while I wondered if my heart rate was still safe and, somewhere in the middle, we threw each other a dismissive wave and kept climbing. After ducking through low gaps and palming the cool walls, the Stone Gallery, which circled the outside of the dome was phenomenal. We stopped only long enough to recover our breath, shake out our jelly legs, and keep going.

'Come, stand on this step so I don't have to look down at you when I'm talking.' William held a hand out and pulled me up to meet him. It was a tight fit, the stairwell being so narrow, but we squashed up together.

We were only twenty steps short of the Golden Gallery, and the queue to join the tiny space was long and getting longer. Where we had only a few before us, people snaked around the old steel staircases as far as I could see, and I wasn't a fan of glancing down for too long.

'This place is incredible,' I said. 'I just love that each wall has been touched by thousands, millions even, over the course of history. It blows my mind to think of who came before us.'

'And now the tourists—' he tucked a lock of hair behind my ear '—in their silly hats.'

As his fingers grazed my ear, I reached out and brushed my thumb across a nick close to his bottom lip. 'You cut yourself shaving?'

'I did.'

'I didn't think you'd shaved this morning?' Thinking back to how he looked this morning, I'd have been surprised if he'd even showered. 'You looked a fright when you got in.'

'I shaved in the bathroom at work once you'd left.'

'Did it hurt?'

'Hurt? Emmy, it stung like hellfire and vinegar.' He touched it. 'And you know what's worse, is that I can't stop licking it. It's just there, and annoying. You know what I mean?'

'I can't say I do, no. It's been a while since I've shaved my beard.'

'The more you know.' William grinned. 'Hey, you know what would go great with that hat?'

'What's that?'

'One of those old disposable cameras. You know the ones where you have to take the whole unit to the chemist to get developed?'

I laughed. 'You know I still have that photo of us at Heathrow?'

'I should hope so. It's an important historical document.'

We listened for the shuffle of feet on the metal grates as, finally, the queue started to move further towards the rooftop.

'How do you get your sideburns so straight?' I placed a finger at the base of each of them, almost perfectly aligned with each other.

'A template,' he said. 'I wrap it around my face and go for broke.'

I snorted so hard I coughed. 'You do not.'

Twenty steps became ten, five, two and, then, with a helping hand, I stepped out into the late afternoon sun and wraparound views of the city. My hair flickered about in my eyes and my mouth, caught up by the high-up winds. When I finally got it under control, I stopped still. William peered over the edge, a serene smile on his face, like he didn't have a care in the world. Buses looked like Matchbox cars, pedestrians were mere specks of life, and buildings looked like Lego miniatures. It was beautiful and peaceful and, as if I didn't believe it myself, it solidified the view that maybe moving to London was the best thing I'd ever done.

Even if that came at a cost.

Chapter 16

Before I had time to think about it too much, I'd been in London one month, then two, and the weeks were only rolling on quicker. Life was busy. Between full days at work, nights were spent on the couch or dining out in new and exciting restaurants. My gym sessions were jogging along behind me, exhausted, and only hoping I could undo those extra bottles of pinot noir.

Saturdays had become unofficial sightseeing days. Whether William joined me or not, I explored London and her surrounds, zipped around the tube, poked around some of the many museums, joined the British Library, bought poorly made souvenirs, and ate cheap street food.

Eventually, I got William through the doors of Madame Tussaud's, even if he did spend the entire time muttering about 'dirty little cadavers' under his breath. Originally, I'd asked Craig. I'd desperately wanted to spend more time with him, but he had baulked at the idea and told me I'd finally lost the plot. I'm still not sure how serious he was about that.

There was a marked difference in how the two sides of my life were unfolding; a friend who couldn't wait to get out and about on weekends, versus a boyfriend who had little interest in anything unless it suited him. At home, a late day at work meant a six o'clock finish. Here, it was lucky if it was before eight o'clock. Weekends we used to spend together were replaced with text message check-ins just to see if we would be spending any time together. Business meetings had overrun the relationship goals Craig had spent so long sprouting about. A feeling of uncertainty was settling in and making itself comfortable, perhaps unpacking our old picnic basket and rug, the one the was now relegated to the back of someone's cupboard. Sometimes, it made me think that maybe I didn't know him as well as I thought I did. Other times, he'd surprise me.

I knew that my London List specifically listed an IMAX experience, complete with wonky 3D glasses and overstuffed popcorn, but I was just as thrilled when Craig came home with some rooftop cinema tickets from work. His boss had suggested he needed to go home on time and not worry about the business tonight. Whatever reasoning, and whichever cinema, it was going to mean a new experience and spending a Friday night *together*.

'Which one?' I held two dresses in front of me. One green, one blue, neither of them worn before. I'd picked them up a week earlier when Heather and I decided Westfield was a great way to fill the afternoon. I'd picked them up for the bargain basement price of £10 each, a steal in any currency.

Craig gave a perfunctory glance before returning to his phone, where he was engrossed in banging out messages of great import. I was a little miffed. Maybe it was too much to ask him to give me five minutes of his time?

'Craig?' I tried again. 'What one do you like?'

'Honestly, Em, I don't care. Wear whatever you're comfortable in.'

'You don't have a preference?'

'Can you just put one on?' he asked. 'Our tickets are for the seven-thirty session. We need to go.'

Unless the alarm clock was lying, we still had ninety minutes to get there. Surely that gave me at least thirty seconds to ponder my clothing choice. Or, at least, ask my boyfriend for advice. I huffed my annoyance, did the eenie-meenie-miney-mo in my head, and opted for the navy blue with white bird print. I found a pair of matching heels and a light cardigan, and we were out the door before Craig had a chance to finish moaning about his email.

* * *

We barely spoke the entire train trip into the city (more emails to answer), but it was just nice to be with him. A narrow, slippery set of stairs took us to the top of the six-storey building. It was industrial but cosy, a brass-fitted bar was joined by a candy-striped popcorn stand. Blue and white deck chairs looked like something from the set of an Elvis movie, and rope lights only added to the tropical feeling. I did a quick scan to see which seats were available, and happened upon a shock of red hair and a bright laugh that emanated from one of the first few rows. I skipped off in that direction.

'I thought you said you didn't do cinemas.' I peered into the row and was delighted to find that I was right and I wasn't talking to a stranger.

William's face lit up with the excitement of a winning scratch card. He leapt to his feet and greeted me with a quick kiss on the cheek. 'No, I said I don't do cinemas with *you*, because you'll keep trying to touch me up.'

His companions laughed, and I turned to find Craig still dawdling down the aisle. People were walking around him, throwing off angry looks as if being held at a green light. Still, his fingers dashed about his phone screen. I wondered if I could just make that phone disappear. Five minutes of regular conversation, that was all I craved.

'You look very tropical tonight.' I tugged at the hem of William's Hawaiian themed shirt. Its pineapple motif had been coupled with boardshorts and a pair of flip-flops. Havaianas. 'Very relaxed. I don't think I've ever seen you without long pants on.'

'Yeah, well.' His head dipped though he kept his eyes on me. 'I don't think I've ever seen you without your dress on.'

I tried so hard not to laugh, but the shocked faces of friends and the innocent grin on his face were too much. 'You're not supposed to say that.'

'It's not a lie.' He pressed a hand to his chest. 'I have not said an untruth.'

I tapped at his arm. 'Don't look at me like that.'

'Like what?' he pipped.

'Like *that*!'

A deep laugh sprang up. 'Why? Am I putting you off?'

With a hand on the small of my back, Craig reminded me he was still here. I reached around to him, slightly distracted and little self-conscious that it might have been me who'd left him behind in my rush to get to these seats. As it was, introductions were stilted. As usual, William was loose and happy, while Craig wore a look of distraction that told me he'd rather be someplace else. Next, I hobbled along the aisle to say hello to each of William's friends, all as fine and funny as their ringleader, while Craig skipped that part in favour of a comfortable chair. When I asked him if he'd like to get drinks, he simply replied that he would like a beer, and returned to his phone.

'He's a peach, Em.' William slipped a fifty over the counter as he placed an order. 'A peach that's fallen to the ground and is riddled with worms.'

'Oh, come on. He's busy with work.' I looked around. Yep, Craig was buried in his phone again.

'Luckily, I'm a doctor. I know how to treat worms.'

The bartender shot him a look, laughed under his breath, and popped a few more bottles of Samuel Smith.

'He's under a lot of stress right now. He's having trouble settling in at work, at least I think that's what it is. Tonight is the first time we've gone out in weeks. I just wish he'd shut that phone off.'

'You think that's what it is?'

I shrugged. 'It's hard to get a word out of him.'

'Could always throw his phone over the side of the building,' he said. 'That'll get the words going.'

'Sure.' I followed him back to our seats. 'That would work well.'

Throwing Craig's phone off the side of the building was looking more and more like a good idea the further the movie progressed. No amount of popcorn or alcohol, special effects or sex scenes helped draw his attention away from the tiny screen in front of him. Five minutes of solitude would pass, and the tiny distracting light would resume, and he'd be emailing, making notes, again.

I was an agitated mess by the time the closing credits rolled. The left side of me was completely disinterested and had only generic comments to describe the film. And the handful of boys to my right were already busy discussing plot points and action sequences. I desperately wanted to join in the lively chatter, stay back for a few drinks and maybe a meal, but Craig was yawning and ready to head home. I said a reluctant goodbye before joining the crowds in the stairwell.

Craig wanted to forgo a train ride home in favour of a taxi. His reasoning? Perhaps we could stop by a bar on the way through and grab a drink or two. Not bad considering only moments earlier he'd wanted to get to bed. As he stood by the kerb and tried to flag down a passing car, I felt a hand around my forearm drag me away. Far enough to be out of ear shot.

'Are you getting the train?' William asked.

'I think he wants to get a taxi.' I turned my body towards Craig.

'Right, okay.'

'I'll see you Monday?' I asked. 'We're not working tomorrow, are we?'

'No, you're good. I'll see you Monday.' William stepped away, before coming back just as quickly. 'I desperately need to ask you this before we part tonight. I admit it's mostly my own morbid curiosity but, also, because what the fuck, Emmy?'

I tilted my head just a slight. 'Sorry?'

'Do you love this guy? Like, really? You wake up and you think this is the best it's gonna be?'

I nodded, my mouth drying up like a summer shower. 'Yes.'

'Really? You're honestly telling me you're happy ... with that?'

'I'm happy.' I could feel my hackles start to rise. What matter was it to William if I was happy or not?

He blew his cheeks out and gave his head a tiny disapproving shake. 'Okay. Sure. Whatever. If you're telling me yes, then it's a yes.'

'What?' I guffawed. 'Why the questions?'

'Like I said, morbid curiosity.' With an indifferent shrug that seemed to say 'take it or leave it', he turned and walked away, back to his group of friends, and I turned to find Craig, glued to his phone again. Completely oblivious to the world around him. I snatched his phone and zipped it in away in my pocket.

* * *

My family had taken to sending me boxes of things from home. With two missed deliveries only a week apart, I decided it might be easier to get Mum to send any of her magical care packages to work. My new one, in its tattered brown box, had been whispering at me from its home beside the photocopier all afternoon to open it. It wasn't until we were all standing around with a cheeky end of week drink that I had my chance to open it.

'What's in the box, Ems?' William wriggled up beside me. 'Can we open it?'

'It's just something from home.' I sliced at it with a pair of scissors. 'Mum sends one once a fortnight, I suppose.'

'Really?' Pam cooed. 'Gosh that's sweet. The most I can get out of my mother is a shitty Facebook post complaining that I don't have kids yet. Or some pseudo political junk that's been researched by a three-year-old with a spinning top.'

'Oh, I get them, too.' I unfolded the lid of the box. 'For now, I'll stick to food babies.'

Everybody reached in and grabbed at things before I had a chance. Two packets each of both mine and Craig's favourite biscuits, a bag of ground coffee from my favourite café, an envelope of photos from Frankie, an old stuffed toy that had been dug up from somewhere and was missing an eye, and a magnet of the giant koala in Dadswells Bridge – a souvenir from my eagle-eyed parents.

'What is that?' Brian grabbed at the magnet. 'Is it really that big? It's kind of frightening.'

'It's huge, and great. Like the giant lobster, giant sheep, giant pineapple, giant strawberry, and anything else we can supersize and call a tourist attraction.' I unfolded a little letter from Frankie but, when I read the first line, stuffed it back in the envelope before it made me cry.

William flicked through the photos and pointed to one of Josh, Heather, and me at Josh's tenth birthday. 'Is this you? And Heather?'

'Who's Heather?' Pam asked.

'My housemate.' I filled the empty air as quickly as I could, not wanting to be drawn into a conversation about who knew who and how. 'It was a barbecue for Josh's birthday.'

'Speaking of barbecues,' William started. 'If you're all free tomorrow, I'm having a get together at home, just because.'

'Sounds great, count me in,' Brian said.

'That bloody wife of yours won't be there, will she?' Trevor asked.

What?

For a split second, I thought I might've been hearing things.

141

There were a lot of words that rhymed with wife … strife … knife … life. That was, until I saw the look on William's face, as white as a sheet and breaking out in a fine sweat. His eyes said everything his face couldn't in a room full of our colleagues. He handed my photos back and shot Trevor a look. I packed everything up and pretended I hadn't just found out I'd been played for a fool.

My heart scrambled to work when my brain couldn't, kicking about in my chest like a child with a soccer ball. It was sporadic and annoying and, worst, of all, I couldn't work out exactly what it was about his being married that bothered me. We were only friends, after all. Chatter around me had muted itself somewhere under the sound of blood rushing through my ears and, when I couldn't think of anything else to do, I drained the last of my drink and called it a night.

I raced ahead at the sound of footsteps shuffling up behind me.

'Emmy, wait!' He pulled me to a stop. I jerked my arm away from him.

'What do you want, Red?'

'Oh.' His eyes widened. 'So, I'm *Red* now?'

'Well, we're just colleagues, right? People who work together, not friends, because friends don't lie to each other.'

'I never lied to you, I just didn't tell you.'

'Oh, because lying by omission makes it better.' I shifted my parcel from my right arm to my left and looked over his shoulder to find everyone standing outside the clinic, waiting for my meltdown. 'I've been here almost three months now – June, July, August, and you couldn't tell me once?'

'It's a bit more complicated than that.'

'I'm not sure how telling the truth is complicated.'

'We're separated. We have been for months.' He sighed. 'I would really like you to come tomorrow so that we can sit down and talk about this.'

'In front of everyone? Some fun that would be.' I said. '"Oh, Emmy, just so you know, I've had a wife at home while we've been gallivanting around town, whiling away the hours without a care in the world." I suppose you were with her while we were in Edinburgh, too, were you?'

'Don't do that.' He shook his head. 'And no, I was single when we met.'

'Don't do what?' I asked. 'Do you have a problem with the truth?'

'Why not?' he asked. 'You obviously do.'

'What?'

'You have lied to me twice since you've been here, and I can tell because your left eye twitches when you do.' A long finger bobbed about around my eyelid. I swatted him away.

'Bullshit.' The nerve he had to turn this back on me. I wasn't the one with a secret wife now, was I?

'Not bullshit.' He held a finger up. 'Are you happy?' A second finger sprung up in support. 'Do you love him?'

Struggling to not let him see the tears in my eyes, I turned on my heel and walked away. The entire trip home, I repeated in my head: I am happy. I am very happy. He is just trying to throw me off kilter.

But, why?

* * *

When I arrived home to an empty apartment, I considered my options: television, dinner, wine, and a whole lot of dwelling on stuff I couldn't change, or I could go to the gym and channel my frustration into something a bit healthier. So, I hit the treadmill. Twenty minutes on that, and I felt game enough to waddle into the next Pilates session. I tied my hair back in a bun and hoped for the best.

There was a blue foam mat with my name written all over it in the far corner. Somewhere quiet I could zone out and work through my problems. I pressed the soles of my feet together and sat quietly as I waited for class to begin. I closed my eyes and listened to the room around me as, slowly, it filled with other students.

Listening to everyone was like sitting in a melting pot. The jangle of keys being dumped was coupled with girlfriends gushing excitedly about their weekend plans, while simultaneously reminding everyone that they were the only thing keeping their workplace afloat. Mothers bemoaned the second lot of headlice this year, wives complained about rubbish bins, and a few random guys were keen to get to the golfing green this weekend. One of them would just be happy if his boyfriend got the weekend off. It was a good way to take the focus off my own problems.

I took a deep breath and tried to zone out one shrill, insistent voice.

'Did I tell you what has happened this week?' It was her – the raven-haired woman I'd met previously. Oh boy.

The Whinger. Every class had one. That one person who sits in the corner and boo-hoos everything. I'd only seen her at a few classes before. More owing to the fact I'd skipped some in the last month in favour of doomed movie nights and random sit-ins at home. But, there she was, bold as brass, and ready to tell everyone about her awful husband. Again. Whoever he was, I felt sorry for him. The poor guy couldn't catch a break. When her companion remained silent, she kept going.

'Tells me he needs to work late. Likely story, right? And I say to him that if he had as much interest in saving our marriage as he did his job, we wouldn't be in the hole we're in now.'

A few sympathetic noises urged her on.

'And then I asked him, straight to his face, "What are you going to do about our marriage?". Do you know what he said?'

Opening my eyes felt like inviting trouble in, so I kept them closed and moved into another stretch. A guiding hand on my stomach and back helped steady me.

'He said, "You can move out. That's what you can do." And I said, "This is not about me".'

'Jesus, I wish she wouldn't,' said a familiar voice in my ear. 'Do me a favour, and don't engage?'

I sniggered. 'I'll do my best.'

'It's good to see you back.'

'Thanks.' I opened my eyes, stretching out of one pose and moving into the next.

'I'm Caroline.' She held out a hand and we shook.

'Emmy.'

'Mind if I join you?' She gestured to the mat next to me.

'Please.'

Like a pair of synchronised swimmers, we shifted into a new stretch. Our teacher walked through the room, mat rolled up under his arm. He inspected and fixed, pushed people into shape, and took his spot at the front of the room.

'I mean, it's not like he's even that attractive, really,' the whinger continued. 'Cock.'

Caroline and I shared a look, one of disgust mostly. Who did that to their husband? In public? He wasn't even here to defend himself. This was exactly like high school bullying. She probably got home, smiled, and offered to do his bidding for him. The rest of the room looked horrified. Obviously, the neon green Buddha statue in the corner wasn't wearing off on her. I was grateful when the class finally started. At least she shut up for forty minutes.

'Her poor husband probably looks like Henry Cavill.' Caroline rolled her mat up. 'She's probably right about the cock thing, just not in the way she's thinking.'

'I did consider whether this resistance band would double as an elastic band,' I said, laughing. 'Give her a good old snap in the eye.'

'Eh, it'll just give her something else to complain about.'

Out in the foyer, The Whinger still held court with her gaggle of friends. It struck me that this woman, who was so stupidly beautiful, could be so unhappy with her lot in life. I don't mean everyday beautiful, I mean she was billboard-make-up-selling beautiful. More fool me, she caught me looking somewhere in her immediate direction and waltzed over, bag slung over her shoulder.

'Hello.' She smiled. 'You're new here.'

'A little, yeah.' I caught sight of Caroline at the counter.

'A few of us are about to head out for drinks. Would you like to join us?' she asked. 'There's this great little spot around the corner.'

'No.' I gave my head a quick shake. 'I'm fine, thank you.'

'Shame.' She grinned. 'See you next time, then?'

'Sure.' I nodded and shrugged. 'Maybe, yeah.'

'If you're so unhappy, why don't you just leave him?' Caroline called after her. The Whinger stopped by the doorway, shoulders taut, but she didn't turn around. 'I mean, you spend all class pissing and moaning about this guy. You've only got one life, right?'

Without another word, The Whinger lifted her haughty chin and walked away.

'I think you just became my new best friend.' I laughed as Caroline and I swapped numbers. 'That was brilliant.'

Caroline waved her hand in the air, brushing away the compliment. 'We were all thinking it, someone just needed to say it. Don't be fooled by her drinks invitation, either. It's a black hole you'll never be able to get out of. I made that mistake once. Worst six months of my life.'

'Duly noted.' With promises that we'd both be at next week's class for moral support, we said our goodbyes and went in the opposite direction.

Chapter 17

Heather shuffled into the kitchen and switched on the light above the stove. Thankfully, she didn't scream when she found me sitting at the dining table, inhaling leftover apple crumble with half a pot of double-thick cream. The clock on the wall reminded us of the ungodly hour, and the gym schedule on the fridge pointed an accusatory finger at me.

'Jesus,' she said in a loud whisper.

'Not quite, but close enough.' I shoved the spoon in my mouth and held the bowl up. 'Want some?'

'Yes, actually, I do.'

Watching her try and get a chair out from under the table silently was like watching a mime artist who just wasn't quite sure of their craft. She tucked a foot under her and leant forward, spoon at the ready.

'What's wrong?' she asked.

'Today, about three minutes after I was invited to a party, I found out that William is actually, in fact, married.'

'Shit. Okay. Wait, how long has he been married?'

I shook my head. 'No idea. He was single when we met, or so he says.'

'What an arsehole. And how did that make you feel?' she asked, sounding more and more like her psychologist mother every day.

I sighed and tipped my head back. 'You know, I don't know. There's no reason for me to be jealous or angry, or any of it. He's not my boyfriend, or my exclusive friend. He's had a life while I've been gone, just like I have had a life. A life, by the way, which is turning to shit with each passing day. But, he's had one all the same. I can't expect that he sat around playing Tiddlywinks waiting for me to come back.'

'Of course not. And, like you said, you have Craig.' She reached for the tub of cream. 'But I sense that's not all.'

'Do you know of any cheap rentals floating around?'

Great blobs of cream dropped to the table as the spoon stopped mid-air. 'What? Em, have we done something wrong?'

I shook my head. 'No, of course not. Don't be silly.'

'Then, why? Is it Craig? Does he not like being here?'

I met her eyes. 'I meant for me. On my own.'

Her whole being seemed to deflate. 'Really?'

As I scraped the last of the cream from the tub, I let it all out. Once the verbal diarrhea began, I had a hard time stopping. We talked about William and the disappearing letters and shouty street fight, the quiet moments at work and how I'd caught him watching me on more occasions than I had fingers to count or wanted to admit. We tried piecing together a timeline but tumbled over each other so often we gave up.

Then there was Craig, with his work-life balance that was so far out of whack he wasn't sleeping properly and grinding his teeth, the Craig who'd gone from sweetest friend in the world to someone whose grumpy demeanour and demands for attention made him barely tolerable, let alone recognisable.

'I'm going to play devil's advocate, because I'm allowed to.' Heather pushed her empty bowl away. 'Is one angry because the other exists?'

I shook my head. 'I don't think it's that.'

'Can you promise me there's been nothing happen on your

148

weekend outings? I feel like an ass calling them dates. Please say you're just friends.'

'No, nothing's happened.' I rubbed at my nose. 'We are just friends.'

'But how do you feel about him? William, I mean.'

'I don't know.' I rubbed at my mouth. 'I don't know if I'm confused about him or because of him.'

'Here's the thing. When we first moved here, Josh and I fought *a lot*,' Heather whispered. 'It's hard. You're each out there trying to make new friends, all while trying to get your jobs rolling properly and adjusting to a new city. You think it's going to be easy because it's London. We speak the same language; how hard can it be? But it is, and he's still finding his footing, while you've hit the ground running. Not quite the same as us, we were both starting from scratch, but do you understand what I'm saying?'

Footsteps creaked above us. Josh was on the move and heading for the bathroom.

'He's still so heavy-footed,' I whispered.

'Oh, Em, he's his own herd of elephants.' She rolled her eyes.

'How was your weekend away?' I desperately wanted to change subject, if only to avoid anyone who was awake hearing it.

Heather grinned like the cat that got the cream. 'Lots of nasty holiday sex.'

'Oh my God,' I groaned, laughing too loudly for this time of morning. 'I don't want to know about Josh in that context.'

'Well, I do.' She drew her knees up around her chest. 'Now, are you serious about moving out? Because I'm going to be the mum here and say that I'll need to talk to Josh. Not for anything bad, I just want to keep him in the loop.'

'That's fine,' I said. 'It's perfectly understandable.'

'Can I give you my honest opinion, or will that just confuse your head more?'

'If you can't be honest with me, who can?'

'I think you're so far up a river in Egypt that you're about to be crowned Cleopatra. And I think that means you need to clean your house.'

'What?'

'Denial, Emmy.' She stood up and collected our plates. 'Which means you need to decide what, or who, it is that you actually want. Go to William's party, or don't.'

Leaning down, she gave me a peck on the cheek and my shoulders a gentle squeeze. 'Sort things out with Craig, or don't, but that will give you your answer.'

Chapter 18

Are you awake?
Let's grab breakfast.
I need to talk with you.
Please?

I squinted into the bright screen. The sun wasn't quite fighting its way into the sky yet, but William was already awake and ready to start the day. Craig rolled over, the mattress rolling like a ship at sea as he tugged the sheets away and buried himself like a cocooned moth. I had hoped my presence in bed might inspire a rather more positive reaction than that, but alas. I tapped out a quick response and got dressed.

A shade after 5 a.m., my day had started.

William sat in the corner by the window of the café, fingers threaded through shorter hair. A notepad and pen rested next to whatever he was reading, and a waiter topped up his coffee. I waited for the bus to pass and scuttled across the pedestrian crossing, narrowly missing the gift of a personal traction set courtesy of a Volkswagen Golf.

'Morning.' I dropped my bag by the side of the table and sat down.

'Hey.' William lifted his eyes to mine. 'Just reading up on heart disease.'

'And breakfast is a practice session, right?'

He chuckled and raised his mug. 'Emmy, I am about to treat you to the best fry-up this side of the Thames.'

I smiled gently, watching him as he went about behaving like last night hadn't happened. Move along, nothing to see here.

He held two fingers in the air. 'And an extra coffee, please. White and none.'

For all of William's theories about the best fry-up ever, it was just us and the old European guy behind the counter. He looked happy enough with his lot in life, grinning at William like they'd known each other for years. He tinkled his fingers at me like everyone's favourite uncle at a wedding before disappearing behind the strip door curtain. The décor was like any number of takeaway shops in the area, suspiciously grubby floors and a sheen of oil in the air.

'Two what?' I asked.

'Full breakfast. It's amazing, won't need to eat all day.' He flashed the screen of his iPad at me. 'Heart disease can be tasty.'

'I think that would have to be one of the worst ways to go, wouldn't it?' I asked.

'Certainly not the best way.' He sighed and began rattling off facts and figures, applying it to a patient he'd seen during the week.

I huffed a little laugh. 'Do you want me to start? I feel like you're stalling.'

'Yeah.' He stretched out across the table like a freshly woken cat. 'I'm stalling.'

'I thought about you a lot last night.' I placed my hands over his, trying not think about perfectly well they fit with mine.

'You did?' he asked, his face a perfectly balanced mix between wariness and confusion.

'I did.'

152

'And what were you thinking?' he asked.

'That we were never waiting for some point or event or whatever with each other. We were just really, really good friends. I do wish you'd told me sooner, but you're also too important to me for me to be angry about any of it.'

His bottom lip quivered. 'Emmy, it is so fucked up.'

'Do you want to tell me about it?' I snatched up the sauce as two overfull plates appeared at the table. 'We've got plenty of time before work.'

Post-Edinburgh, William's life had been a mess. The camping in Yorkshire, the offer of a room to rent, and a drunken night that ended in a shotgun marriage and supposed miscarriage. Throughout it all, all his descriptions and explanations, he remained calm. Only occasionally his voice gave him away, a tiny tremble as he danced over parts that felt too hard and elaborated on others.

'I just felt like a complete and utter moron, Em, you know? I'm supposed to be the smart one, but I failed to see what was right in front of me. Or wasn't, in this case.' He dabbed at his breakfast with toast. 'Like, there I was at this conference, surrounded by colleagues and mentors, and her doctor just says, "Son, I don't know what you're talking about". Okay, fair call you can't say anything about your patient, but he pulled me aside later and said she'd been in the week before for a smear test and had most definitely, "not ever been with child" like she said she was'

'And you didn't kick her out then?' I asked. God, this woman sounded horrible. How could a person lie so blatantly about something as important as this? 'Because that's lock-changing stuff for me.'

'You'd think, wouldn't you?' he said.

'What'd you do?'

'Naturally, I was furious. I'd started buying things for this child, you know. I was excited, even if it was a bit of a strange

153

situation. When I confronted her about it, she broke down and said she'd been to a different doctor and how dare I doubt her. She can be very convincing, so I felt like a right shit.'

'Oh, come on.' I sank back in my chair. 'That old chestnut?'

He shrugged. 'I should have just kicked her out and taken the blow. I tried, but somehow managed to be relocated to a spare bedroom while she, quote, "looked for a new place to live".'

'Is this only recent?'

'The last few months, yeah. I mean, the wedding was late 2012. I found out about the miscarriage that wasn't about six months ago.' He stopped. 'It sounds ridiculous, doesn't it? I mean, I'm a doctor. I should know this stuff inside out, right? I know how babies are made, I know about pregnancy and miscarriage, and this whole lot happens under my nose and I am completely bloody clueless.'

'Yeah, I don't know. I mean, there's not a lot to see. It's not like we break out in Baby On Board stickers, so it wouldn't be hard to fake, would it? I could tell you now that I'm pregnant and you wouldn't know.'

'Are you?'

'Please,' I scoffed. 'I'd need a boyfriend who wanted to touch me for that to happen.'

William made a noise.

'So, what happens now?' I asked.

'I kind of look at her like a bit of a parasite. She finds a host, latches on, sucks it dry, and leaves a husk in her wake. We currently occupy separate floors of my house and keep out of each other's way. Monday mornings we go to couples' therapy. I have no idea why, it makes absolutely no sense, but it's at her insistence. I agreed to try that before calling in the lawyers.'

'Is it working?' I asked.

'Nah.' He scoffed. 'The idea is laughable.'

My anger was replaced by great blobs of pity. I picked at his story as we ate. Not because I didn't believe him, but because I hoped to unravel threads, to work out exactly why he was being so generous. For the most part, he didn't want to elaborate. In the end it was simple: what began as a drunken night ended with a young guy scrambling to do what he thought was the right thing and getting himself caught along the way. It was a scenario as old as the hills.

'I've already told her to make herself scarce tonight. She's going out with her friends, so please don't feel worried about coming along. It's just us from work and a handful of friends.'

I tossed my napkin aside. Breakfast had well and truly defeated me; only a sloppy pile of beans and a few mangled tomatoes were left to show for my effort. I sunk back in my chair and rubbed at my tummy.

'This is my food baby.' A laugh burbled up. 'I will call it Black Pudding.'

William laughed. 'At least I'm actually responsible for that one.'

We fell about laughing like a couple of naughty school kids, which was a lovely way to end what should have been a solemn discussion. When we finally calmed down, we grabbed coffee to go and made our way to work.

'I'm so glad you laughed at that.'

William grabbed at my belly. 'I fucked up, Em, but I haven't lost my sense of humour.'

* * *

With a quick wiggle, my shoes flew off in different directions. Probably the second best feeling ever, coming in closely behind unhooking a bra at the end of a long day. I flopped down on the couch and revelled in the silence. Well, except for the occasional car horn and barking dog outside. After a full morning at the clinic, during which William avoided any or all further questioning, I was home alone. I let that sink in for a blissful moment and felt my thoughts unravel.

The shower, and first dibs at the hot water, was mine. I washed, rinsed, conditioned, loofah-ed, plucked and preened, and stepped out of the bathroom feeling like I'd been at a day spa for a week. After a few reruns of Hollyoaks and a glass of wine, I made a start on dinner.

The idea of going out tonight had grown on me over the course of the day. Our office hadn't had a group outing since I'd first arrived, and there'd been mutterings we'd been overdue for one. Above all that, it would be the first time I would see the house I'd sent so much mail to in the past. First, though, I wanted to have dinner with my friends.

Heather arrived with a bunch of flowers and box of chocolate for me. After the week I'd had, she figured I needed cheering up. When I stopped blubbering, Josh walked through the front door and offered me a hug and a kiss and a few words of his own brand of wisdom. Craig walked in just as I was dishing up dinner.

'Hey, good timing.' He grinned. 'Can I do anything to help?'

I moved just as he leant in for a kiss, and managed a brushed cheek. 'Oh,' I said, surprised. 'You can pour drinks? Please? Thank you.'

'Sure.' He did a double-take. 'You okay, Em?'

I nodded, biting down on my lip. Hard.

'You sure?'

'Dinner is almost ready,' I said.

I wanted to take his good mood on face value and run with it. He loosened his tie, dropped his jacket over the back of his chair and looked like he was relaxing into the night.

'Alright.' Heather shuffled around in her pyjamas. 'Tell me about your days.'

'You first.' I handed her a plate.

'Closed two big sales today and had an open house near Regent's Park this afternoon. Yay. Got a week off soon. Double yay.' She wriggled about in her seat, cross-legged like usual. Josh kissed her on the temple and mumbled his praise.

With the last meal served, I took my place at the table. 'I'm thrilled things have picked up for you, that's got to be a relief.'

'You and me both.' She smiled at Craig as he handed her a glass. 'Josh, your day?'

'I spent today playing with fancy watches and trying to write copy for them. Went for lunch in Soho. Made a date with another client for during the week. I'd say it was a good day.'

'Craig?' I asked.

'Uh, lunch on Southbank, meetings in the morning, paperwork all afternoon. Might've fallen asleep at my desk. Lunch was good.'

'Em?' Heather looked at me.

'I was invited to a get together tonight. I thought I might pop in for a while.' I glanced at Craig. 'Do you want to come with me?'

'Emmy.' It felt like his mood declined with each slow shake of the head. 'I've been at work all day.'

'It's just that it's been so long since we've spent time together,' I said quietly. 'I just thought…'

'You thought…' His voice drifted off. 'Jesus, Emmy. You want to spend time together? You're the one who swans about on the weekend with everyone but me. Yes, I work late during the week, but I try and get home for dinner on the weekend, only to wonder where the bloody hell you are. You tumble in on the stroke of midnight with an unsteady swagger and rosy face. You sleep on the couch half the time because you've decided … God knows what you've decided, really. Now, out of the blue, you want me to come and hang out with these new friends?'

'I don't *swan*,' I baulked, unsure of where this latest outburst had come from. And I certainly didn't come home at midnight, I knew that for certain. Any of my text messages could easily back that one up. Only moments ago he looked like he was embracing sweetness and light.

'Then what do you call it, Emmy? Because I'm not the only one who's noticed it.'

I did a quick check around the table. Faces as confused as mine stared back at me. 'I don't understand. Am I not allowed to have friends?'

'She is right.' Josh pointed his fork. 'She *can* have friends.'

'And isn't part of being a couple spending time with each other's friends?' I continued. 'Co-mingling and creating new groups?'

'Then let's go out. Just you and me, we'll go out for dessert.'

'That's not exactly what I'd call socialising.' I looked at him blankly until the realisation popped somewhere in the back of my mind like a slime filled balloon. 'Wait. Are you asking me to choose between you and my friends?'

He sniffed and got up from the table, leaving his meal half-finished. 'We can't just do this on your terms.'

'Well, are you and your friends going to sit around all night in your suits and congratulate each other about who owes who money, debits and credits and hidden cash burrows, and fuck knows whatever buzzword you're all on this week?' Craig's nastier side had a habit of breaking mine out too, and I was quite sure I didn't like it. In fact, I hated it. This was not a place I wanted to be.

'What's a cash burrow?' Heather wrinkled her nose.

'Just like you'll all sit around and talk about how wonderful you are because you saved someone from the dreaded flu, unjammed the photocopier without getting covered in toner, or answered your phone within three rings, which is really hard for Emmy to do with all the socialising she does between patients.'

My mouth popped open. Heather's followed, and Josh looked like he'd been slapped.

'Oh, don't look so shocked.' He poured more wine into his glass. I watched as it glugged and sloshed like an angry waterfall. 'What did you expect me to say?'

'Well, I certainly didn't expect you to insinuate that I'm nothing more than a dumb receptionist.' I stood and threw my napkin down on the table.

He sighed heavily, a deepset frown replaced by something more crestfallen. 'No, Emmy, no, that's not what I meant. I shouldn't have said that.'

'Really? Because it sure sounded like that's what you meant.' I walked down the hall. 'But, hey, maybe if I'm so stupid you should probably go and find yourself a smarter girlfriend.'

Unable to leave an argument well alone, Craig followed me down the hall. Mostly, he'd just quibble and mutter until the fight ignited all over again. The only other time he'd followed me was arguing over whether we should or shouldn't take a subject together in third year. Right across school campus and into the carpark. It was ridiculous then, and it was ridiculous now. He slammed our bedroom door closed with so much force that the small wardrobe rattled in sympathy. I tore a dress from a hanger and started changing.

'What the hell is going on with you, Emmy? Ever since we've got here, you've done nothing but disregard me.'

'What's going on with me?' I stabbed at my own chest with a raging finger. 'I'm going out and making a life with all my dumb friends which, by the way, I only do once a week. As for disregarding you, you clearly need a dictionary. The rest of my time is spent sitting about and waiting for you to get home. I wait for you to want to talk to me. I wait for you to look up from your phone long enough to hold a conversation.'

'Once a week? You're out at least four times a week.'

'I go to the gym,' I shrieked. 'With other women, so I don't turn into a bloody overstretched dumpling. I'm always home by eight, which is before you, and keep turning down the offer of drinks with people who have the potential to be great friends. And anyway, what's going on with you, huh? Where are you spending *your* time?'

He shifted from foot to foot, the defiant pose. 'You know I didn't mean it like that.'

'Then how exactly did you mean it?'

He stood, a little dumbfounded, shoulders up about his ears. 'I don't know, but it wasn't like *that*.'

'Right.' I tugged on my zip. 'Here's the thing. I'm going out tonight because my friend has invited me and I want to spend time with him. Yes, him. Now, you can either come with me and expand your circle, or you can stay home. I was only asking out of politeness anyway, because you looked like you were finally in a good mood and I thought it might be a fun thing to go together. Party, drinks, cake, sex. Apparently, I read that wrong. Again.'

In the silence that followed, I had the opportunity to study him. His clothes were sharper, and he'd moved away from his early Noughties Tom Cruise inspired haircut, opting for something more along the lines of early Dr House. Overnight, he'd turned into a stranger. Did he see me that way, also?

'What are you saying?' he asked.

'I'm saying I'm done.'

'Emmy,' he complained. 'We can't just be done. Don't be stupid.'

'Why not? You've just called me stupid *and* given me an ultimatum.'

'Maybe that's because I'm done with playing second fiddle to some people you've known five minutes.'

'Looks like we're both done then.' I forced a wild-eyed grin, buttoning my cardigan and pulling my hair free of my coat. 'Don't you think?'

Chapter 19

Thousands of random thoughts flew through my head as I stomped my way down the street. Each new idea that popped up was shot down like a clay target, shattering to a thousand pieces in time for next one to be flung into the sky. All the while, I was sure I covered it over with a glossy sheen of stunned mullet who didn't just pull the pin on Hand Grenade Craig.

The worst part was that William was getting caught up in these thoughts. Our breakfast was beginning to raise more questions than it answered, so I had those swimming about, tapping at the side of my head like goldfish in a bowl. *Tap, tap, tap.*

Digging around in my bag for a ringing phone made me feel all a bit too Mary Poppins for my liking. Past old receipts, a purse, swipe cars for work, a notebook that was too pretty to taint with pen ink (like, duh), and forty-seven million tourist ticket stubs, I eventually found my phone. The caller ID? The photo I'd taken of William at Tower Bridge. After this morning, it looked different.

'Hello.' I looked left, right, and jabbed the button on the pedestrian crossing.

'Hey,' he said. There was so much noise behind him that it sounded like he was shuffling through a mosh pit at a concert.

'Just checking to see if you're coming tonight? It's okay if you aren't. I mean, I'd really like you there, but I was just … curious.'

There was something about his call that made me feel like a live-action emotional pinball. While it was nice to know that I was wanted somewhere, I was just waiting for a paddle to give way and to drop through the bottom of insanity.

'Have you thought about what that entails?' I asked.

'I have.'

'When you get here, we'll…' I trailed off, echoing the start of many of our emails. It was a nervous moment to see if William would pick up on that.

'… drink cheap cocktails on my front fence where I'm waiting for you?'

I smiled. 'I'll see you in a few minutes.'

'That's the spirit,' he said. 'Literally.'

In a street lined with almost identical redbrick homes, William's stood out in a way only his could. Coloured twinkle lights shone from the window of the front room, and a small collection of red-headed garden gnomes looked after a small patch of dirt and a naked Barbie under the same window. As for the man himself, he was perched on the fence with a drink in each hand.

My arrival felt like the end of a mental marathon, years of planning and execution, and over in a heartbeat. I was looking forward to getting inside and drowning out my thoughts with loud music and even louder peers.

'I even got you a fancy tropical umbrella.' He raised a glass to me. 'Long Island Iced Tea?'

'You know how to make them?' I asked.

He grimaced. 'Not really. I just throw things together and hope for the best. That is not a guide for life, by the way.'

I sat beside him, though I turned to get a better look at the house. Music was thumping softly in the background, and the occasional screech of laughter could be heard over the top of it.

'So, this is it, huh?'

He shifted beside me. 'Finally. This is me.'

I threw him a sideways glance. 'Should we go in, or should we savour the moment a bit longer?'

The last of his drink gurgled up through his straw. 'Well, my drink is done, so I'm going inside. You can sit out here with all your friends if you like.'

I offered a gentle smile. If only he knew how close to the truth that was.

A small mushroom shaped light sat behind the front door and offered a welcoming glow through the side window to anyone sneaking in late at night. It was cute, and almost exactly what I'd expect of William. He paused and looked at me.

'You ready?'

'Yes.'

He pulled a face, and pushed the front door in.

We battled past coats that prevented the door opening completely, and a shopping centre's worth of shoes were scattered about like disregarded toys. William mumbled an apology and pushed them all into the cupboard under the stairs with one fell kick.

I followed him through the burrow of the house, eyes searching, drinking everything in to my parched memory. Every single crack, peel, picture frame, and smell was catalogued for future reference, some moments serving to reignite the memory of old conversation. Bannisters shone like a good French polish, and a shoe brush that had been discarded somewhere in the summer months rested against the wall like an exhausted worker.

'What's wrong?' William asked quietly.

'Nothing,' I said. 'It's just so…'

'Weird?' he asked.

'… big.'

'Well,' his chest puffed out, 'I don't like to brag, but—'

'—I meant the house.' I knocked his arm with my glass. 'But, yeah, a little surreal as well.'

Stepping out into the combined kitchen-dining-entertainment area was like stepping into an *Architectural Weekly* spread. The area was full of popping colours against crisp neutrals and designer furniture befitting a doctor on a decent wage. A bright blue kettle sat atop a gloss white benchtop, though all other appliances were scarce, hidden behind doors. William caught me, again, checking everything out.

Behind me, the rumbling displeasure of colleagues who'd waited so long for me to arrive. Their variations on the word 'finally', held more weight than any of them would know, and only added to the slightly floaty feeling I was experiencing, torn completely between opposing sides of my life right now. It was nice to hear that I was wanted, at least.

'How's that drink going? Do you want another?' William held his hand out, ready to take my glass.

'Same again, thanks.'

Despite my attempts to get comfortable in the corner with Pam, Brian, Trevor, and Bob, I was drawn into the outside world of manicured hedges and deck lighting. William's idea of a handful of friends extended to about thirty of his nearest and dearest and any children that sprung from that. Dinner had long been consumed, paper plates littering tables and empty beer bottles on their sides like inattentive toy soldiers.

I met university friends and mentors, neighbours, and the odd locally based cousin. If I got lost in the crowd, all I had to do was look for the hint of red in the crowd, which was more helpful than I thought. A nice warm tingle sat at the back of my brain and held me like only a grandmother could. It spread to a blanket-like warmth that protected me from the cold of the night and made choices a little harder to make. William and I tag-teamed on the drinks like a well-trained regiment. He'd leave me with school buddies to chat about his legendary pranks, only to return with a new mixer. Or, I'd disappear to the bathroom and magically find myself swinging past the kitchen on the way back.

My night began to feel like a carousel of colour and music, and it was exactly what I needed to counter how I'd been feeling earlier.

'Alright you two, photo. Squeeze in.' Someone I'd never met before appeared before us with their camera at the ready.

'Like you squeeze a lemon?' William shuffled closer to me. 'I can do that.'

I slipped my arms around his middle, ready for the perfect photo.

'Oh!' I gasped.

'What?'

'Heathrow.' I offered a nostalgic grin and threw in a few batted eyelashes for effect. He mimicked me, much to the delight of onlookers, who were now lined up with their own cameras.

William clicked his fingers at the photographer. 'Suze, I need these photos. Can you send them to me? Text, or email, or whatever. You know.' When his hand came to rest, his fingers spread across my backside like Patrick Star on a pub crawl through Bikini Bottom.

'My arse.'

'Is particularly nice,' he muttered through a smile. 'I can't believe I didn't think of that … Heathrow.'

'You were such a nice young boy then.' I grabbed at his hand and moved it up to my hip.

'I really wasn't.' He folded in on himself laughing. 'The only reason I didn't take you back to the hotel was because I didn't want to share you with the two other guys I was staying with.'

My jaw dropped. 'You are such a grub.'

'Actually…' His hand slipped away completely when the photographer left. 'I think that would be "gentlemanly".'

'Oh!' His words had triggered a memory. 'I have something for you.'

William made a show of looking around my sides, over my shoulders. 'You do?'

'I do.' I stepped away. 'Follow me.'

We buzzed through the house, bouncing from person to person and engaging in small talk until we found ourselves back near the front door. I picked through the pile of bags until I found mine buried somewhere near the back.

'I saw something in a shop recently that reminded me of you.' I held a small parcel between us, its grey wrapping paper shimmering in the low light. 'So, I thought I'd get it. Maybe open it on your own?'

'Oh,' he said softly, turning the gift over in his hands. 'That sounds intriguing.'

'It's only something small.' I hugged myself.

'Right this way.' He tipped his chin in the direction of the staircase.

My limbs were tired with drink, so I trudged slowly up the stairs behind him. Each heavy footstep clunked and creaked along clumsily behind me. Perhaps it was time to turn down the next glass that was thrust my way, however well-meaning it might be.

We bypassed the first floor altogether and moved on to the second. A light flickered to life and illuminated the small landing area and a bedroom door. I popped my head in for a look, expecting to find a grubby boyish mess.

What I got was rich wooden furniture, a bed that looked cotton ball soft, an on trend light fitting, and a bedside table littered with medical literature.

'Light reading,' he joked, holding up the latest medical journal, and bookmarked textbooks.

Oh, and two old coffee cups and a chocolate wrapper. It couldn't have been all perfect.

'It's lovely.' I let myself in to the en-suite. The fresh scent of shampoo lingered among the strewn toothpaste tube, disregarded toothbrush, and wet towel that hung off the counter.

'Really?'

'Considering you could fit my room in here twice, yeah.' I pointed. 'You going to open your present?'

William's eyes lit up in remembrance. A few muttered words were joined by the crinkle of paper. Continuing my tradition of kitschy gifts, I'd found a tattered copy of *William – An Englishman* in a second-hand shop. With a title like that, I could think of no one better to give it to, and tonight seemed like the perfect moment. Judging by the look of smug satisfaction on his face, I was right.

'It's me.' He grinned. 'Thank you.'

'No, no.' I forced the tattered, clothbound cover open. 'You've missed the best part.'

Inside the cover, a reprint of our Heathrow photo. A little larger and a bit more out of focus than the last, I'd had it printed recently on an afternoon in town. It might have been cheap, but it was cheerful, and a beautiful reminder of what started all of this. If someone were to ask what our favourite holiday souvenirs were, instead of our worst, this would be it.

'Oh, Em. I lost mine.' He flipped the photo over, just to be sure there wasn't something on the back. When he noticed the inscription in the front pages, he smiled broadly. '"Dear William – my favourite Englishman."'

'You're pretty much one of about four Englishmen that I know, so my options were limited.'

'Of course, of course,' he said, mouth in a downturned smile. He wriggled a come-hither finger.

'What?'

'Just come here.'

Before I'd had a moment to catch my breath on the landing, he'd cradled my face in his hands and was kissing me. And, for all my protestations and assertions of a boyfriend, I kissed him back. His mouth tasted like badly mixed cocktails. I'm sure his tasting notes would read something like: chocolate birthday cake with a hint of cherries, cream tea, and seduction. A gentle thumb drawn across my jaw threw me back to earth with an electric zap.

I clutched a handful of his T-shirt and pushed him back. 'Don't do that, please; please don't do that.'

But it was too late. Just as my lipstick had tinted his lips, I couldn't rub him off mine if wanted to. It added a whole new layer of confusion to the night, to my already scrambled egg life.

'What? Why not?' he asked.

'I can't do this.' I kept my eyes focused on the grey carpet between us, which blurred with angry tears. 'Don't confuse me.'

'I'm not trying to confuse you. This is what I want. Us.'

'How can you possibly know what you want?' I looked up at him, hoping he couldn't see right through me. 'You've barely separated, I've got someone at home, and all you've done is lie, so why? Why do this to me? Is it not bad enough…?'

'Is what not bad enough?' he asked. 'What are you scared of?'

'What am I scared of?' I asked. 'What if this job doesn't work out? What if I have to leave you behind like last time? I can't go through that again.'

'You've already decided you're not staying, then?'

I looked away. 'That's not what I said at all.'

William forced himself into my line of sight. 'That's a bit premature, isn't it?'

I shrugged. 'You're putting words in my mouth.'

'Shrug? What's a shrug, Emmy? You don't get to come back here like this and be wonderful you all over again and just leave,' he begged. 'Stay. Stay, and we'll, I don't know, get a home in the country. There'll be a couple of animals that nobody will take responsibility for, even though we were sure the kids promised they'd look after them. We can have a big family car full of mud and toys that I'll get angry about whenever I stand on them. We'll have weekend excursions to scary London because we're worried raising kids out in the country on *Famous Five* books won't prepare them for the big bad world. It'll be you and me and all those stupid, angry, annoying, tedious, beautiful things that we should have done years ago.' His chest heaved. 'Since you've been back, it's all I can bloody think of. I want it so badly I can smell the ink on the property paperwork.'

All I could do was watch him through blurred vision. How was it okay to just throw any of this out there? Tonight, tonight, my brain flitted about like a trapped bird.

'You don't get to do this to me.' I shook my head. 'You don't.'

'Do what, Emmy?' he said. 'Tell the truth?'

'You mean you want to tell the truth right now? Right this second? As opposed to all the other opportunities you didn't take?'

'That's hardly fair. You said yourself this morning we were barely anything.'

'Even if we weren't, you jumped straight from me to her, all the while you lied to me about it. Sorry, *omitted the truth.* Now, the minute she's gone, you want to get straight back on my horse again? No. Not on my watch. I'm worth more than that.'

William shook his head angrily. Lips pursed, his cheeks were marked with two dimples each, and I hated that I knew that look so well. It was just that it wasn't usually aimed at me, but at lab results that he didn't like.

'I don't want to argue with you, you're one of my best friends.' I rubbed tears away and tried to calm my breathing. 'So, what I'm going to do is go home.'

My brain was skittish at best, and crumpled like old wrapping paper at worst. All I could think was that I needed out. I had to go. Right now. William was hot on my heels, quietly protesting my leaving. How he thought it was okay to beg me to stay was beyond me. Even if I wanted to, I had to sort out what was happening at home. I wasn't going to leave Craig up in the air, and I wasn't going to cheat on anyone. As much as he had become a thorn in my side, he at least deserved that.

'Emmy, I'm sorry. I overstepped. Please,' he said in a loud

whisper while I dug about in the darkened hall for my handbag again.

'I can't stay.' I wiped a stray tear away. 'You know I can't.'

While I grappled with pulling the front door open, William tried to push it shut.

'Emmy, please. I just want you to talk to me.'

'What else is there to say?' I asked.

He shrugged. 'I don't know, I don't know, just … we should talk.'

I glowered at him and gave the door one last tug. This time, he didn't stop me. It was just my luck that, while I was snotty and teary, someone would be walking in my direction. I kept my head down and hoped for the best, but I'd barely made it onto the footpath before it became clear that she was heading right towards where I was leaving from.

'Well, hello. Fancy meeting you here, Pilates partner!'

I lifted my gaze only briefly. It was The Whinger from the gym. Her dark hair was perfectly styled, her black velvet dress a little rumpled, and her make-up unfairly perfect. I disliked even more that she got to witness me looking like a baked Desiree potato.

'W – what are you doing here?' I said. 'You two know each other?'

She gave a little self-satisfied snort. 'Of course I know him. I'm his wife.'

She looked at me, I looked at her, we both looked at William, and he swore under his breath like a sailor on shore leave.

'Angela, this is Emmy. Emmy is my … work colleague. Wait, how exactly do you two know each other?'

'*Emmy,*' she emphasized, 'is in my Pilates class. What a delightfully small world we live in.'

Her face did not move, but there was something predatory in the glint in her eye, causing a thousand thoughts to run through my mind. Did she know I had kissed her – *estranged* – husband?

170

Was my lipstick smudged across my face? Was it all over William's lips? I couldn't tell properly in the dark.

Oh God.

'What are you doing here?' William's voice punctured my thoughts, drawing me back into the conversation.

Angela had sidled up closer, resting a hand on William's elbow. 'Sweetheart, I *do* live here too, you know.' The laugh that rang out was more of a cackle than the wind chimes she'd tried for.

'You said you wouldn't come back until after midnight.'

'But I missed you!'

I fumbled with the remaining buttons on my coat. There was no way in hell I was staying for this. One way or another, it was going to be painful.

'I think that's my cue to leave.'

'Emmy, no wait, we need to talk.' William's attempt to extricate himself from Angela's grip was fruitless. She only held on tighter.

I sighed. 'There's really nothing to talk about. I'll see you Monday.'

'Goodbye, Emily! It was lovely to meet you again.'

With a pitiful wave, I took my leave. What had happened to tonight? First Craig, now William. Then … Angela. Tears threatened in the corners of my eyes.

Where had everything gone horribly wrong?

Chapter 20

By Sunday evening, it became apparent that Craig and I were avoiding each other. He spent the entire day at home and, if I walked into a room, he backed out quicker than a cat heading for the vet's. When he volunteered to buy us all pizza and a few bottles of wine for dinner, I refused. I'd have rather the time alone, soon finding myself scoffing hot chips in a local park while ogling a football team and batting away Chihuahua-sized seagulls.

I knew that ignoring our problems wasn't the best long-term solution ever, but the space it gave me to think was nice.

There was too much going on in my mind. The angel and the devil had retreated from my shoulders and were fencing somewhere around the tight spot in the back of my neck. *Allez!*

That night, he slept on the couch.

Heading into work on Monday morning didn't help anything. I was faced with more questions than answers. Where had I disappeared to on Saturday? Was everything okay? There was suggestion I was just too drunk and got an Uber home before it got ugly. To save face, I smiled and played along with that option. Explaining anything else was opening myself up to all kinds of scrutiny I wasn't ready for.

Nor was the issue of one missing Dr William Scott, and a cryptic voicemail left on my work phone.

'Emmy, it's me, William. Uh, I won't be in Monday or Tuesday. Brian already knows, just thought I'd give you the heads up. At this stage, Wednesday is a yes. So is the rest of the week, including Saturday, though maybe just don't schedule anything new for the weekdays. Please don't call me. I'll call you Tuesday morning if anything changes. Yeah … bye.'

I hung up the phone and looked at Pam. She was always good for gossip, but this time offered nothing more than a polite shrug and averted eyes.

'I haven't heard anything,' she said. 'Sorry.'

No one would give me any answers. All I got from Brian was that it was William's business. If he wished to share it with me, he would. In fact, everyone was eerily quiet. It made me feel like I was an outsider. The village leper.

That didn't help my mind one iota. I was awash with panicked theories. What if I'd sent him running straight back to his wife? What if they were busy right now, having insane make-up sex, the kind that makes your toes curl and skin sticky with sweat? William's toothbrush back in the communal bathroom and a box of torn condom foils strewn across the floor. It was enough to make me break out in a rash, but I was too scared to ask.

Instead, like the mature adult that I clearly am, I ate my feelings.

'There's no caramel popcorn left, Ems,' Josh announced from his perch on couch sometime between dinner and *Doc Martin* reruns. 'You ate it all.'

Sighing, I pushed aside a bag of salt and vinegar crisps and dug deeper. Two stray chocolate biscuits, a packet of stale cream crackers, and one rogue muesli bar. In the absence of Nutella, a jar of peanut butter wasn't such a bad option. I grabbed the first clean spoon I saw and settled onto the couch.

A cushion swung out and tapped me on the head. 'You alright?'

'I am a rainbow of fruit flavour.' I sucked my cheeks in and hoped to dislodge the tacky mess stuck to the roof of my mouth. It was bliss. I pulled the coffee table across the carpet and dropped my feet on top. 'I'm okay.'

'Sure.' Heather flopped beside Josh and spread herself out. 'That's why you're eating like a pregnant woman.'

Craig chose that moment to walk through the front door. Without making eye contact with anyone, he dropped his bag by the door and slipped off his shoes. Shoulders slumped forward and tie hanging limply from his pocket, he kept his head down and kept walking. Worry lined his face. For the first time in days, the bedroom door closed with a quiet click. He didn't reappear until the dishwasher was whizzing about with the dinner dishes.

While I was happy enough to not see him, because it meant I didn't have to deal with him, I hated the grubby atmosphere that made itself comfortable around the house. It wasn't just the two of us that it affected. Heather and Josh, and every conversation in between, had to tread lightly and be run through filters.

'Emmy, have you got a moment?' Craig appeared by the doorway, picking at his cuticles. 'In private?'

Josh was making grabby hands for the peanut butter before my feet had touched the floor. The last thing I saw was my spoon dangling from his mouth like a broken cigarette. He mouthed a 'good luck' as I followed Craig down the hall.

The closer we got to the (our?) bedroom, the heavier my feet fell, and my heart disappeared somewhere ahead of me in a nervous canter. I was quite sure it had nothing to do with the copious amounts of peanut butter I'd just hoovered, and everything to do with my own idiocy. I squeezed past Craig, rounded the bed and made myself busy folding the latest load of washing.

'Emmy, I've, ah…'

I lifted my eyes to meet his. He paced back and forth along the tiny path beside the bed. Doing his best little teapot impersonation, he placed a hand on his hip and threaded his fingers through his hair.

'Yes?'

'I'm going home.'

Shit. I knew things were bad, but was putting an entire continent between us going to solve anything?

I placed a T-shirt on his side of the bed. 'You're what?'

'This – us, me, living here. It's failed. I know it's only been a few months, but we haven't made headway at all.' He stopped on the spot and took a deep breath in. 'I've pulled the pin.'

'Oh.' Even with all the arguments and sniping comments, this all felt a little unfair for him. 'I'm sorry.'

'So, what I wanted to do was to have a chat, see where we were.'

'Where we were?' I asked. 'I'm more interested in why you've suddenly decided to go home without at least telling me what's gone so wrong at work.'

'I have been struggling with the workload,' he finally admitted. 'It's too much for one person, but the powers that be don't believe so. Today, I lost a million-dollar client. I was told I could leave or be fired.'

'Oh, Craig.' My shoulders fell. 'I'm so sorry.'

'I've been an ass, Em.' His shoulders relaxed, and bottom lip trembled. 'I know that I have been rude and awful and snappy and just not a nice person to be with.'

He blurred in my vision. 'Yeah, you have.'

'This was supposed to be our big start in life, you know? High flying and stepping up and out, and I've screwed it all up.'

'It wasn't all you,' I said, trying hard to share the brunt of the blame. 'We're both at fault. I just wish you'd told me sooner.'

'I guess what I want to know is if there's any chance you'll come home with me? We can get a place in the city and start over. I'm going to launch my own company. I'll work nine to five only, have a proper work-life balance, be home in time for dinner and have weekends at home. Hell, I'll probably work from home for at least the first twelve months.'

As tempting as it sounded, it was hard to accept that things could just be fixed just by moving cities again. Something had set in recently that had nothing to do with location and, now, we'd drifted too far from who we were when it all began.

'Maybe we can run it together?' He wiped at his eyes and gave a sad sniff when I didn't respond. 'I am so incredibly sorry that I called you dumb. I don't think you're dumb at all. If anything, I think you're one of the smartest, most compassionate people I know. And, you know, if marriage and kids is something you're keen on, then I'd like you to be the one I explore that with.'

I shook my head, sad at the last grappling words of a relationship. With Saturday night still zipping about my head I knew, if nothing else, I couldn't leave. I didn't want to leave. It was too much to give up again, and that scared me more than comforted me.

'I don't want you to want those things just because I do,' I said. 'That will only lead to more problems later. Resentment. I want you to want them because you're genuinely interested.'

'Emmy.' Heather tapped quietly on the door. 'You have a visitor.'

Strangely, Craig chuckled. 'Perfect timing, right?'

'Excuse me.' I slipped past him and followed Heather down the hall.

'Who is it?' I asked.

'Go and look.'

I opened the door to find William on the landing, peering out at the giant leadlight window that decorated a large part of the stairwell. On sunny afternoons, it made you feel as if you were walking through a kaleidoscope, and it was one of my favourite things about this building. My cardigan hung limp from his hand, his thumb rubbing gently over an embroidered flower. I loved that I knew how silky smooth that felt without having to do it myself.

'Hey.' I closed the door only slightly and moved towards him. 'Your hair – it's gone.'

'It has?' He looked confused, and grabbed for clumps of curls that were no longer there. In their place, a shorter trim. 'Shit. It must've fallen off while I was asleep.'

'At least you've still got the sideburns.' I smiled, wondering why it was so easy to do this, to talk with him. 'It's the small things, right?'

'Yeah.' His eyes darted about nervously and he scratched the back of his neck.

'Are you okay?' I asked. 'I've been worried about you.'

With lips pursed, his eyes darted about as he gave a quick nod. 'Worried about me? I've been more worried about you. Are you okay?'

'It's been an interesting few days,' I said slowly. 'Very … informative.'

'I am so sorry. For all of it. You shouldn't have been caught up in any of that.' He offered me my cardigan. 'I found this in the clean-up.'

'Thank you.' I shook it gently. 'Handy little thing.'

'I just wanted to drop it over before it got swallowed up or claimed by someone else.'

'Oh, right, okay.' While I wondered why he hadn't just waited to bring it to work, I also realised I didn't care. I was just happy to see him.

'Anyway…' He took a tentative step backwards. 'I have to go. Goodnight, Em.'

Without even the slightest backwards glance, William disappeared down the stairwell. The building door closed gently, and he was gone. In his all too brief appearance, we'd completely skipped over the elephant that joined me as I tore down the stairs and out into the street after him. What kind of friendship did we have if we couldn't at least talk about that? I was in the throes of losing one friendship tonight. I didn't want to lose another.

'William!' I popped out into the street like a vaudeville performer, bare feet and all.

Hands in pockets, he turned slowly and stepped back from the kerb. 'What's up?'

'Please.' I caught up to him. 'Please listen to me and hear me out.'

'Okay.' He smirked, and a dimple tugged at his left cheek as he waited for me to continue.

'It's just that, I feel terrible about Saturday night and about running off on you like that. I realise, since you've been away, that I haven't heard from you at all. You've probably decided to give things another go with Angela, and—'

'Another go with Angela?' He scrunched his face up. 'Where do you come up with this?'

'Don't interrupt me, please,' I said. 'I just want you to know that I'll stay out of your way and be the best support that I can be. Because you are my friend and I love you … as a friend.'

'See, the thing is—'

Above our heads, a window opened. I mean, it was exactly what I needed in the middle of declaring myself in front of William, even if it was just in the context of friendship. Josh leant out the window. I waved my hands at him, hoping to drive him away. It didn't work.

'Hey! I know you!' he shouted. 'You're Punchy McPunchFace. The first aider from Edinburgh you ran off with, right Emmy?'

William laughed and turned away. I, on the other hand, was mortified. After the discussion I was still having with Craig, this revelation was not exactly what I needed. It wasn't just the nail in the coffin, it was the decorative flowers and soggy-sandwich wake all overlaid by a thrift shop rendition of 'My Heart Will Go On' with the button stuck on repeat. A little bit not good.

I pointed to William with both hands. 'You can ask him, he's right here.'

A light flickered on across the street.

'Well, are you?' Josh continued. 'Are you that guy?'

William's smirk spread to a warm smile. 'I am. How have you been? Staying out of trouble?'

Josh hooted a laugh and slapped his hand down on the window sill. 'I knew it, I knew it. I told you, didn't I, Heather? I told you.' Heather's head popped out with an offering of silent apologies as she dragged Josh away from the window.

It closed with a loud protest, Josh still nattering away about how he totally knew and wasn't he clever. It was a wonder he managed sex at all, with that brilliant display of timing. But, in a moment, we were alone again.

I clapped my hands together. 'I guess what I'm trying to say—'

'Emmy.' William threw his head back and glanced at me through half-closed eyes.

'—is that—'

'She moved out.'

'What?' I asked. My train of thought screamed to a halt.

Back up, back up.

'We're not getting back together. There was never a chance of that.'

'Oh.'

Oh.

'She moved out on Sunday. I've spent the last few days sorting out our belongings and making sure she doesn't fleece me completely.'

'Can I change that to an I'm not sorry?' I blurted. 'No, actually, even that sounds horrible.'

He offered me a resigned smile. 'I haven't been in touch because I needed to do this on my own. I feel like I screwed everything up on Saturday, and the rest of it has proven not as easy as I thought, so … yeah.' He stepped forward and kissed my cheek. It was chaste enough to be innocent and lingering enough to say everything.

'I'll see you at work in the morning. I'll bring the coffee.'

I tried to shake my head, my nose brushing against his stubbly cheek. 'You didn't screw anything up.'

'Good,' he whispered. 'See you on the sunny side.'

With one more kiss, I watched as he turned and walked away, slipping from my fingers with a cheeky wink and a smile. I felt better knowing that the William I knew was still buried under there somewhere. I turned towards the house.

From the street, I could see Craig had taken up Josh's prime position in the window. With my nerves already on a knife's edge, I gave myself a tiny moment of silent composure. I couldn't pretend that my friendship with William had nothing to do with this when he was the reason I didn't want to leave. Hand poised on the handle, I rested against the door before, finally, walking in.

Everyone had cleared the room, leaving just Craig and me to sort out whatever was left of us.

'I guess that's my answer,' he said quietly.

'I can't go with you,' I said. 'I don't want to.'

'Just tell me one thing,' he said.

'Of course.'

'Did you follow him here?'

I shook my head, *no*. It was a half-truth, if anything. More and more I was realising that my dreams of coming to London were still entwined in my teenage fantasies. Did I intentionally follow William to London? No.

Unconsciously? Maybe, yes.

'Have you … slept with him?'

'God, no!' I baulked. 'Do you really think so little of me?'

'What I just saw doesn't exactly lead me to believe your answer.' He nodded his head in the direction of the window. 'Looked chummy enough to me.'

'Believe what you want.'

'I'm just saying.'

I threw my head back and counted back from ten. That knife's edge was looking sharper by the second. 'You know what, Craig? Just leave.'

His jaw dropped as if this hadn't been brewing for weeks, like he was completely blindsided.

'I have had enough,' I said. 'We moved here to start something new, like you said. But since we got here, you've become mean, boorish, and absolutely not the person I remember falling in love with. Thank you for telling me things were hard at work, I appreciate it, but it's no excuse to take your mood out on me. And, no, I haven't slept with anyone else. I wouldn't do that, you know I wouldn't. All I've done is go and make new friends and, as it turns out, find old ones. On Saturday, you gave me an ultimatum. You wanted me to pick between you, or my friends. Well, with the person you've become, I pick my friends. You can leave now. Don't wait until the weekend, find yourself a hotel tonight.'

Less than an hour later, everything was over. That sweet, sweet kiss by the fire in Sydney, the laughter that dotted study sessions, the lazy mornings in bed, and the sheer thrill of booking our flights here. It had dissipated like the morning fog. His bags were packed and rested by the front door, waiting for a black cab to arrive. I'd stripped the sheets from our – my – bed. It was all I could think to do to keep my mind busy in a small apartment that amounted to not a lot more than a tinderbox right now.

When a car horn sounded in the street, and the door closed quietly behind him, and behind the last eighteen months of my life, I wasn't there to say goodbye. I'd hidden myself in the shower, hoping no one could hear me cry over the sound of rushing water.

Chapter 21

There was a crack in the ceiling in the right-hand corner above the bed. How had I never noticed that before? Also, there was a heap of extra room in the bed, a very comfortable bed now that I wasn't sharing it with an octopus of arms and legs. I lolled about like a snow angel, all the while trying to tell myself that this was for the best. Upstairs, Josh's Clown Song alarm went off. Heather laughed, as she did every morning. A muted conversation was followed by footsteps down the stairs, a whistling kettle, and Heather creeping into my room with a cup of tea.

'Good morning, you,' she whispered. 'How are you feeling today?'

I felt like crap. Finalising the inevitable with Craig did not make me feel any better. In fact, I was riddled with guilt. I imagined anyone you asked would say, rightly so, that I was a horrible person.

My phone showed no signs of life, not unless you count an updated relationship status on social media, an attention seeking post, and a thousand photos of Craig's 'much more comfortable' hotel room. After reading the first few comments, and feeling my stomach sink all over again, I shut my phone down and lay there trying to work out where to begin the day.

'It's going to get better.' Heather climbed into bed with me. 'You're not naked, are you? That would be super awkward, though I'm sure my boyfriend wouldn't complain.'

I laughed, then crumbled into a snotty crying heap on her shoulder. Even a pillow over my head wasn't a lot of help. All it did was encase me in warm morning breath. Yuck.

'Oh, come on.' Heather rubbed my arm sympathetically and rolled out of bed. A gust of cold air followed in her absence. 'Neither of you were happy anyway, and nobody needs that. Let's get you up and ready for work.'

'Is this all on me?' I peered out from under the extra pillow.

'No, not all of it.' She shook her head gently. I listened to the clunk of my coffee cup on the side table and a whispered greeting from Josh. 'How much did he tell you about what was going on at work?'

I shook my head. 'Only last night. He admitted he'd screwed up, that it wasn't working.'

'Right.' She puffed quietly. 'From what Josh knows, he wouldn't take responsibility for his faults and, in the end, he lost a big client. He was asked to go. And, if he wasn't so busy heaping shit on everyone, and opened up instead of closing everyone off, maybe there wouldn't have been any room for anyone else.'

It was reassuring to know it wasn't entirely my fault, but it didn't exactly help me feel any better. Whatever had happened, Craig had been awful for most of our time here. I never wanted to be that woman waiting at home every night in the hope that her boyfriend or partner might throw a scrap of attention her way. I was going to go where I felt valued, and I did. I climbed out of bed, hobbling about like Grandpa Joe, got dressed, and took the slow walk to work. It was, without a doubt, a two-croissant type of morning.

While my life felt like a weather vane in a cyclone, you wouldn't have known anything was wrong in William's. At least not by looking at him. He arrived on that morning as if nothing were

183

wrong, challenging the idea that he'd been gone at all. He had a smile for everyone, and they all had one for him. There were quiet enquiries in even quieter corners but, if you missed any of that, you wouldn't have suspected anything. As for any patients who asked, he simply told them he'd been ill and didn't want to spread his germs.

'Thank you for looking after the last few days for me, ladies.' William passed behind the reception desk and tossed mail in the OUT tray. 'I do appreciate it.'

'It was mostly Emmy, you know.' Pam spun in her chair to look at him, dressed in his usual suit and coat. 'Are you okay?'

'Everything's great.' He grinned at her. 'Thank you.'

'You know, if you want to talk about anything?' she started. I kept my head down, focused on the spreadsheets in front of me, not wanting to engage. 'I'm a good listener.'

'I assure you, it's perfectly good and long overdue. Thank you.'

He maintained his position all week, though he ducked out for an hour or two at a time in the middle of the day. The only excuse he offered was that he had appointments. It was not technically a lie, and we all knew where he was going anyway, but it was the bare minimum of information he could get away with.

There were moments caught in the staff room, or shared looks that said more than words could in a sea of strangers. Quick emails began to resemble a private code in the off chance someone decided to go through my computer. It wasn't until Friday afternoon, in an almost empty clinic, that I caught him alone. I knocked on his door and waited.

'Come in,' he said quietly, distracted by an envelope full of results.

As I crossed the room, he switched the lamp on above his desk, his hair glowing brightly beneath its warmth. It was an odd sensation sitting in the same spot his patients did, looking at him as they did. I'd done it before, but so much had changed since

184

the first time that it felt different. A blood pressure monitor, prescription pads, and weird body part models were all crammed along the outer edges of his desk. The piles of thank you cards continued to grow around him.

I rested my elbow on the edge of his desk and dropped my chin into the palm of my hand. 'You okay?'

'Hmmm?' He barely glanced up.

'Are you okay?'

'Yeah, I'm good.' He nodded. 'Just trying to interpret the hieroglyphs in these results.'

I pressed my lips together. 'I wasn't talking about that.'

'I know what you're talking about,' he said. 'And, yes, I'm okay. Glad it's all over, to be honest.'

'Can I ask you a question?' I folded my arms and crossed my legs.

'You know the answer to that.'

'Where is your wife now?'

'Firstly, not my wife. Secondly, I have no idea.' His pen tinkled as it dropped from his ear. 'Why?'

'Yeah, so, she goes to my gym.'

'So I heard.' A frustrated huff blew his fringe about. 'This isn't making any sense. I'm going home. I'll call the lab Monday.'

William shut off his computer and snatched up his bag from the floor, while I filled him in about everything I'd seen and heard during my Pilates sessions. I wasn't incredibly comfortable going back there, but I'd signed a stinking contract, so I had to keep going unless I wanted to get stung with a massive fee to leave.

'So, what?' he said, fighting the key in the door lock. 'You want my permission to go to the gym? If you ask me, you don't need a gym. You're fit as it is.'

'I'm not.'

'You are.'

'Anyway, I just wanted to pick your brain,' I said. 'Do you think I should go?'

'Surely you've got some friends there you can mingle with? What's the worst she could do?'

* * *

Caroline flopped about on her workout mat, her body shuddering with laughter. Secretly, I hoped it was the small handful of drinks we'd scuttled at the local before sliding in the door of the gym with moments to spare. Experience told me, however, that is was me she was laughing at. Her rosy glow was not just from Mother Mojito, but from Eccentric Emmy and her Shitstorm Life, which had been explained very quickly and through much laughter as we split a plate of ribs.

'I love you,' she squeaked, pulling herself up into an impossible stretch to copy, before realising nobody wanted a remixed cocktail. She collapsed onto her knees. 'So, what now?'

'Look, if I can get through tonight without being knifed, I'll be perfectly happy,' I said in a loud whisper. The man in front of us swung his head about and glowered at me like an old leathery turtle. I flashed him a grin as he looked away in horror.

'I'm sure you'll be fine. It's not like you're dating him, right?' Caroline's ankle disappeared somewhere up around her ear. 'Plus, I'm always here.'

'She has to know, surely? I mean, she caught us on the steps of his house, and there was no way we could have looked innocent.' I blanched as something pinched in my back. I twisted back the other way and let out a slow, deep breath.

In the end, I didn't need to worry. As we settled into the first moments of meditation, Angela's whine was nowhere to be heard. I felt the anxious flutter float away from somewhere under my ribs. As for her posse, they behaved like I didn't exist at all. I was left to enjoy the painful stretching of my muscles in peace.

There was a beautifully soft calm that came with languid movements and tempered breathing. For most of the class, I kept

186

my eyes closed and cycled through the streets of my thoughts. For weeks, it had felt like there was fast moving traffic, blaring horns and tiny fender-benders, shouting drivers, and stop signs. But tonight, there was nothing but my tempered breaths and a friend by my side. If this was what I had to do to get some calm, clearly I needed to do it more often.

What was the saying – no pain, no gain?

Chapter 22

For the first time in what felt like forever, I took myself on a breakfast date. No William, no Heather, just me, one almost destroyed store copy magazine, and a healthy appetite. My favourite café, the one with the cute blue-eyed barista, helped me out with a pot of coffee and a huge plate of breakfast. French toast, grilled banana, decorative flowers that nobody ever eats, and a heavenly dollop of cream. If I didn't have to work, it would have been the perfect morning. I could've toddled right back off to bed to sleep it off, watched a bit of telly and relaxed.

Except I couldn't do that. I had to get on in there and process new patients, engage with older ones, who sometimes enjoyed nothing more than telling me chapter seventy of their lift story. Oh, and help open the door, it seemed. With his bag slung over his shoulder and a stack of papers wedged under his arm, William swore at the key as he wriggled it about in the lock.

'Hey you.' I grabbed at the pile of papers. Almost immediately, he stood a little taller.

'This bloody lock,' he grumbled. 'I'm sure there's some graphite inside somewhere.'

'It's in my desk. I'll sort it.'

He stopped still and looked at me, his pinched faced slipping with relief. He hoisted his bag strap higher up his shoulder. 'Thank you. How are you? Are you okay?'

'Good.' I smiled. 'Great.'

'Really?' He looked at me suspiciously. 'How was your night?'

'Excellent. I went out for drinks with a friend, then to the gym.' I followed William inside the door, watching on as he disarmed the alarm. 'I understand alcohol and exercise are generally mutually exclusive, but at least Angela wasn't there.'

'Funnily enough, I heard about your gym habits quite a bit last week.'

'You did?' I laughed nervously. 'Why didn't you mention something sooner?'

William rolled his eyes. 'I told you, you don't need to go to the gym anyway.'

'Because optimal health, good for the body and soul.'

'I can think of a few other things that will help with cardiac health.' He stepped backwards into the staff room. 'You're fit enough.'

'Aren't you supposed to be a doctor?' I narrowed my eyes at him. 'You should be telling me to exercise.'

'Do as I say, not as I do.' He dismissed with a cheeky laugh and a wave of the hand. 'You're chirpy this morning?'

'Like I said, Pilates. Good for the body *and* the soul.'

'Yeah, yeah, you've mentioned that a few times.' His voice was drowned out by the clanging of coffee cups and churn of the kettle.

Good thing for that cheer, too. After the door lock, and the graphite exploding everywhere when I tried to loosen the lock a little, I was a little bit over it all. Then, as if I needed it, Frankie began calling. That in itself was not a bad thing. I loved talking to her, and I knew I was well overdue for a call, even though I'd been laying low all week. The problem was that she didn't just call once, she called about ten times in the hour before we closed, and all I could do was watch as my phone lit up like a space rocket every few minutes.

As I returned from filing patient records, my phone began ringing again. I picked it up with a heavy sigh.

'Sorry, I've just finished work for the day,' I opened.

'Oh, so you still know how to answer your phone, do you?'

'What?' My eyebrows tripped over each other in confusion.

'I have been trying to get a hold of you all week. No one has heard a damn thing from you, and we've been getting worried.'

'You what? Why are you worried? I'm kind of on the other side of the world being busy and working and stuff.' I grabbed at the waste paper basket. 'As it is, I'm currently emptying the bin.'

'Exactly. You're on the other side of the bloody world and you just disappear. It makes it incredibly hard on other people. Think of someone besides yourself for once.'

'Where is this coming from?' My bottom lip wobbled like jelly. 'I've been busy.'

'And I've been busy worrying about you,' Frankie snapped. 'God, you can be so selfish when you want.'

'I'm sorry,' I squeaked, flabbergasted at this different tone of Frankie's. 'It's just, it's been busy, and things are happening, and I just … I've needed some me time this week.'

'You needed "me time"? We need to know that you're okay. Mum's tried ringing you, too, in case you didn't know.'

I placed a hand across my eyes and sobbed openly. After everything that had happened this week, I did not need this. I burbled something about not being a child, which only set her off on one of her big sister lectures about how I was absolutely behaving like one, and that they consider my safety in a big city a priority. Because I obviously couldn't look after myself.

William peered out of his office, careful not to disturb. As if it would give me a hint of privacy, he shut his office door.

'And what's this garbage about Craig coming back to Sydney?'

'We broke up.' I snivelled. 'I don't know where he is.'

'I'll tell you exactly where he is, somewhere between Dubai

and Sydney, probably chugging down an in-flight beer and trying to decide what crummy movie to watch. His mum called our mum like the bloody bush telegraph that they are, and it's been crisis meetings at ten paces. They're heading out this morning to console themselves over coffee and cake at that dodgy café down the street. I'm surprised the UN hasn't been summoned yet.'

'It wasn't all me.' I blew my nose.

Frankie huffed and, somewhere in the background, a door closed. 'Look, I know. It's never just one person. Just tell me he's lying about you sleeping with some guy you work with.'

'What?' I shrieked.

'You heard me.'

'I have not done anything like that.'

'Alright,' she said quietly. 'I believe you.'

'Quite frankly, I don't care if you don't. I haven't done anything wrong. I have friends. I love my friends. I love my life here, and I will not sit about waiting for someone to get home at some point before the sun rises.'

Frankie was silent. A rare occasion, as anyone would agree.

'Well, I'll just go then,' she said quietly.

'No, don't.' I leant back on my desk. 'Just, talk to me about life. Not him. What's done is done. I will fill you in on all the gory details when I'm home next. We'll make a day of it. Let's talk about something happier.'

My mother had started her own impromptu menopause support group. They met once a week to swill wine and whine; about men, about kids, about life, and their aging bodies. Ezra had disappeared into relationship bliss with his girlfriend. He was thriving as a stepfather and had stopped getting himself into trouble with his friends.

'I should call him, shouldn't I?' I asked.

'Yes, Emmy, you should,' Frankie said. 'He would be thrilled. He asked about you the other night at dinner.'

Dad had taken up boating with one of the neighbours. They'd

sunk a small amount of cash into a boat, bought themselves some fishing gear, and disappeared each Saturday morning for what they referred to as 'Hunter Gatherer Time'. Oh, and Frankie's baby was baking away nicely.

'Good,' I said. 'I'm really glad.'

'Me, too,' she said. 'Anyway. Thank you for finally answering. I can tell our parents you aren't dead.'

'If I were, I'd let you know.'

'Yeah, kind of doesn't work like that,' she chuckled.

'Anyway…' I spun around in time to catch William leaving his office, bag slung over his shoulder and ready to go. 'I've gotta go. I need to lock up.'

'Promise me you'll do better.'

'I promise I will do better.' My head lolled about like a dash-board doggie. 'You sound like Mum.'

'I'm practising!' she said, with way too much enthusiasm for that to even be considered a joke.

Eventually, I hung up, but not without a dozen more promises. I did have a few things to post her, I just hadn't had the chance to post anything on the back of my recent six-day working weeks. I tossed my phone aside and looked up at William, who held out a brochure for an open-top bus tour. I stood and took it from him.

'Doing anything this afternoon?' he asked.

'Why?'

'I thought we might pick up a bit of a bus tour. I know we've done one already, but this one comes with audio in sixteen languages.'

Right now, I could have listed a thousand reasons why that was probably not the best idea ever. A slideshow of images popped into my head. Craig, the picnics that became nit-picking, the arguments, and the breakup. They were followed down the water-slide by William, his wife, and *that* kiss.

'Really? After the week we've both had?' I asked.

'Uh, yeah,' he said. 'Isn't it what we always do on Saturday afternoons?'

I groaned. 'Are you sure? I don't think that's a good idea.'

'Why not?' His eyebrows crowded together as if I'd spoken a second language.

'Because we spend too much time together.'

'Oh, fuck off,' he said disbelievingly. 'We do this once a week for a few hours at the most.'

'And maybe that's what was wrong,' I said. 'Maybe this is my fault.'

'Maybe *what* is your fault?'

'Craig flew home this morning.' I swallowed down the knot in my throat. 'We broke up.'

'If he can't handle that, then screw him, he deserves to leave.'

I glowered at him. This time, despite the fact he'd just thrown my hurt in my face, I refused to get emotional.

'What?' he asked. 'There are no lies in that statement.'

'And, what, you're just gonna slip in and take his place?'

'Why is that such an awful idea to you?' he asked. 'We both know it would work.'

'Not right now, it won't,' I said. 'Do you want a list?'

'Sure.' His hands clapped against his legs. 'Why not add it to my shit list.'

'It's not a shit list, William. Think about it. Craig has flown home today, still a little raw, sausage on barbecue style. You are still married. Your wife, no offence, is not someone I want to be on the wrong side of. So, until that's over for you, and I've worked through my own mess, then that door is shut – as it rightfully should be. Right now, I don't need another boyfriend. I just need a friend.'

'Then fucking hell, Emmy,' he shouted through laughter, hands tossed above his head, 'let me be a friend at least. I mean, isn't that what I've always been? Or is that out the window now, too?'

I shook my head. 'No, of course not.'

'Then what's the problem? Let's go.'

'Fine!' I shouted, hands slapping against my sides. 'Fine. I'll go on your stupid bus tour.'

'Okay. Get your things, I'll lock up.'

'I've got my things.' I patted my sides down.

William looked around for the handbag I usually carted everywhere, his brow furrowing when he came up empty. 'Where?'

'In my dress.' I bounced on the spot.

'In your dress?' he asked.

I thrust my hip out at him. 'It has pockets.'

Chapter 23

Friends. It seemed like such a tame word to use after everything that had happened between us, but it's exactly what we did. And do you know what changed? Nothing.

In the weeks that followed, we still went on our Saturday afternoon post-work excursions. We went to art galleries and took in special exhibitions of touring artists. We sat in Potters Field Park and had picnic lunches made up at short notice of homemade sandwiches, cakes, and a thermos of coffee. We caught a matinee on the West End. The afternoon William argued for his bus tour, I dozed off, nestled up at the very front of the top deck of the bus in afternoon sun that was warm enough to be comfortable, but not hot. William woke me up somewhere by Buckingham Palace and pushed me off the bus.

I visited him on Sundays when I got bored of housework and listening to Heather and Josh argue about wedding plans. It was either spend time laughing with William or listen to whether fuchsia was out, and navy blue was in, and whether kids were invited or not. I turned up one afternoon to find his shoes spread about by the front door and covered in damp green grass, and the front door wide open. I found him on the sofa in the front room, sound asleep.

With one arm covering his eyes, and a hand stuffed between his legs, his shoulders rose gently with each breath. He looked so crumpled and comfortable, and the idea of curling up with him all too inviting. It would have been all too easy to do. We could have wriggled about and made room, but I left before I had a chance to act on that thought. I locked the door behind me and returned home.

Heather was pacing about the kitchen, muttering under her breath, and typing out some rapid-fire text messages. A polite disagreement with Josh about wedding venues became a niggle and, before you could say 'Do Not Throw Confetti', he'd taken a walk to calm down and clear his head before they dropped bombs on each other.

'You okay?' My keys jangled as I dropped them on the table. 'You look stressed.'

She clutched at her forehead and paced again. 'I am *so* stressed; this bloody wedding. We can't agree on a damn thing, and we haven't even had the engagement party yet.'

'I just…' I thought twice about telling her where I'd been or trying to offer the advice of the recently consciously uncoupled. 'Do you want to get coffee?' I asked. 'Let's get out of here, away from the magazines and colour swatches, clear your head for a while. Come on.'

Reluctantly, and only after the promise of cake, she grabbed a light coat and her keys and followed me out the door.

Cake turned into a shopping expedition when Heather decided she *had* to have a coat she saw in a glittering Regent Street window. It was still early enough in the afternoon that we could find a few shops open and, when she was done buying her coat, shirts, and shoes for a business meeting during the week, I forced her onto a cheap and cheerful Thames cruise.

In the boat's lower level café, Heather slid a tenner across the counter and scraped up her change. I collected the wobbly, over-heated takeaway cups and followed her back to the top deck.

After weeks of saying I would, I was excited to finally be on a cruise, even if it was just a short jaunt to Greenwich and back. That was enough. A sunny Sunday was all the excuse I needed. Thinking ourselves near enough to locals now, we dodged a few tourists and wayward kids, and wrangled the last of the empty seats in the back row. Heather spread her shopping out beside her in the hope that no one would try and join us.

'So.' I held Heather's cup while she shook two sugar packets into her coffee. 'What seems to be the problem?'

She sighed heavily, her body trying to fold in on itself. 'I want Sydney, somewhere on the bay. He wants one of those Agatha Christie, everyone-gets-murdered-in-the-end, manor houses outside of London.'

I pushed my bottom lip out and considered the options. While both venues sounded appealing, one would have more people travelling than the other. Still, it wasn't my wedding, so it wasn't my choice. 'There's a lot of variables, isn't there?' I asked. 'Aunties, uncles, cousins, kids, parents, grandparents, all coming over here. Whereas, having a wedding in Sydney would mean what?'

'About thirty or forty friends travelling to Sydney, some with their kids.'

'You could do both.' I sipped on my coffee. 'If you felt like it. Have the ceremony at home and a party here. I would love to help organise a party here.'

'That's because you're a social butterfly.' She smiled. 'But I do like that idea. It's not so bad, is it?'

I wasn't sure about the social butterfly thing. I could count my friends on one hand recently. William, Heather, Josh, and Caroline, who was quickly becoming my post-Pilates food and drink buddy.

'Personally—' I held a hand to my chest '—I think the ceremony is important for family. As for friends, they like the booze, right?'

'That they do.' Heather sighed, still undecided.

Beneath us, the motor putt-putted to life as one final last

197

passenger ran the length of the berth, hoping for the best. A crackling overhead announcement warned us of safety procedures and floatation vests, 'in the very unlikely event that we needed them'. And then we were moving.

Heather crossed one leg over the other and joined the masses by whipping out her phone and snapping a few photos of landmarks along the way. We got our shit together in time to snap a selfie as we sailed under Tower Bridge. The trip, and the silence, gave me just enough time to wonder what this boat's commentary would be like if William were in charge. I gave my head a shake, hoping he'd drop out of my thoughts like a rock in a shoe.

'Enough about weddings! How are you?' Heather dug through her handbag for lip gloss.

How was I? I thought about it for a moment and, while I could've picked up all the niggling negative things that had happened, I hoped they were just hiccups on the way to a better life. My job was amazing. I loved spending my days laughing at Pam's latest antics, and I got to spend weekends with my best friends in an amazing city. William refused to double-up on restaurants, so we were always trying somewhere new for dinner. We laughed ourselves senseless at his tour guide commentary, and I was ticking off my London List like it were some magic quest that would give me access to another world at the end. Maybe I'd power up with one of Mario's magic mushrooms. What could be bad about that?

'I love my life.' And it was true. Without the negativity bubble that was Craig hovering over one shoulder, and William's disappearing act slash wife saga on the other, I could say it with confidence.

'So, what's your boyfriend got planned for your birthday?'

I hung my head back and groaned. 'Firstly, not my boyfriend.'

'Lies, lies,' Heather muttered, sucking from her straw. 'Wait, have you slept with him yet? Why have we not talked about this?'

I scrunched my face. 'Because there is actually nothing to talk about. And, no, I haven't slept with him. I don't want to.'

She tossed her head back and laughed. 'You are so full of shit.'

I huffed, especially at the niggling idea that she might be right. 'I have no idea what William, who is not my boyfriend, has planned.'

'Right, well, Josh and I are taking you out for dinner on the Friday night.' She tossed her can in the bin, and I secretly wished she'd offered the rest to me. 'No questions.'

'Okay, sure,' I said, looking at Heather suspiciously. 'And?'

'Bring William.'

Clearing my seat, I pointed a finger at her, as if that would stop her allusions. 'It's not a date.'

'Yeah, whatever.'

'It's not,' I called to her back as she walked away and gave me a dismissive, over the shoulder wave. 'Heather, it's really not.'

199

Chapter 24

Birthdays are funny things. The older you get, the less excited you're supposed to be about them, busy being an adult and all that. But I'd been looking forward to mine. It wasn't a particularly special day, just another Friday in October, but it felt like an important marker. Normally people mark things off in six- or twelve-month increments, but it was my first in London, and that felt important. William and I had almost run the gauntlet of things to do on the weekend, so when I mentioned my birthday to him, I was both surprised and cautious to hear he'd already planned something.

'What do you mean you've planned something?' I asked, taking another spoon of ice-cream from his bowl.

'It's your birthday, of course I have.' He dipped his chin and tipped his head to the side. 'And stop pinching my ice-cream.'

'Will there at least be cake?' I sank back into the couch and kicked my legs out across his lap.

'What do you think?' he said.

'Can I have a tip?'

'Always floss.'

'What?'

'You said you wanted a tip.'

And that was exactly how he answered any further questions. It was that, or I was met with a hand clapped over my mouth, and text messages were replied to with a simple change of topic. 'Can I have a hint?' earned me a 'You are a very nice cook', or 'That dress looks lovely today'. The only thing I knew for certain was that we were going out for dinner on the Friday night – the night of my birthday.

William raced down the stairs at the station, knees bent like coat hangers as we stepped into a carriage halfway along the platform. Heather had organised the entire day's activities through a string of group social media messages that would make any Wimbledon official's eyes water. This included a comically big and sneezy bunch of flowers delivered to the clinic early this afternoon, which arrived precisely ten minutes after the local bakery delivered a gooey almond flour and orange syrup cake courtesy of the clinic.

Everything had been planned down to the last minute, including the formal dress and super-secret venue. All we had to do was meet at the station by seven o'clock. At five past the hour, we'd resigned ourselves to the idea that William had either screwed up and was making his own way there, or that he wasn't coming at all.

But, there he was, flustered and pink and wearing the look of a shamed child. Apologetic greetings were exchanged for hand-shakes and air kisses as we walked the length of the carriage. A quick search offered up no chairs, but a small speck of real estate on a stanchion. It was maximum comfort for my big day.

'I'm so sorry I'm late,' he said.

'It's five minutes, I don't think it's too much, is it?'

'I don't know,' he said quietly. 'I feel like Heather is very keen on punctuality.'

His perceptiveness made me grin. Not bad for someone he'd barely spent time with.

'You would be right with that.'

'How's your day been? Have you had a good birthday?'

'So far.'

He toyed self-consciously with his suit, with its tightly cinched waist and crisp lines. He patted his tie down, checked it was stuffed into his jacket properly, then checked the buttons on his jacket to make sure they were done up.

'You look fine,' I said quietly.

'Yeah?'

'Of course,' I said. 'Very dashing.'

'In a White Sergeant kind of way?' he asked. 'Or just your regular mannequin in a window kind of way? Because I know how much you like those shopfront dummies.'

With Heather preoccupied with Josh and his Captain America bow-tie, I leant into William and whispered, 'You are still *very* White Sergeant.'

'Still can't dance though,' he lamented with a cheeky smile that curled up in one corner and dimpled his cheek.

'Now, I know first-hand that that's a lie.' I slipped my hand around his waist as the carriage swayed and turned my heels into tiny, unrelenting pogo sticks. All I hoped was that I didn't snap an ankle as the train careened around the next bend.

'We'll have to do it again, then?' he suggested.

'I'd like that.'

'Would you?' He tugged at a strand of hair that had come loose from my bun. As he kept fiddling, his elbow came to rest by my shoulder. That such a seemingly innocent act could feel so intimate wasn't confusing. In fact, I welcomed his touch.

'Yes.'

'Really?'

'Of course.' I scratched at a piece of fluff on his coat. I'd only replayed our night Edinburgh in my head so many times I thought I was a broken record. You know, the one that sometimes skipped and missed the best parts of the song. 'I already can't wait.'

'It makes me happy to hear you say that.'

'It does?'

'Absolutely. I think it's a great plan.'

We peeled apart reluctantly at Baker Street, swapping hands on backs and arms under coats for a rowdy passenger on the Circle Line, who entertained us with her picnic spread across several seats. I would have stayed a few more stops for the sheer entertainment of it all, except I was hungry, and she kept dropping sliced tomato and cocktail onions on the floor.

Finally, we arrived at Tower 42, which stood out from the streetscape like an Emerald City reject. Heather looped her arm with mine and dragged me through the revolving door, all the while I was busy peering up at the immensity of twinkling glass and concrete above us.

'Have you been here before?' William leant into my side as the elevator doors parted at restaurant level.

My hand instinctively searched for his, tugging it from his pocket and weaving my fingers between his – an automatic balsam in the loud din of an unfamiliar environment. 'No.'

'No, me either.' He chanced a quick glance down between us.

Tables were draped with starch white cloth, perfectly folded napkins, glinting cutlery, and fluttering tealights. As the sun dipped further behind the skyline, the open space, with its quiet chatter, took on a soft romantic feel. It was somewhere I could see myself curling up for hours with friends, regardless of the price tag. We'd sip quality wine, dine of delicacies, and discuss world politics like we were clever. And we did.

Over a degustation menu and bottles of dusty wine that left crimson rings across the tablecloth, chairs got progressively closer, and the briefest grazing of skin became comfortable touches and held hands. This was beginning to feel a lot like falling off the edge of a boat and drifting into relationship sea. I wasn't sure that this was what I wanted just yet, no matter how good it felt.

'You know, I'm desperate to know.' Joshua rubbed his hands over his thighs and rocked a little. It wasn't highly noticeable, but it was a nervous tick. 'What did you think, William, when Emmy walked into the clinic that morning? You're all there, ready to work for the day, and in she walks. What's the first thing that goes through your mind? Were you excited? Happy? Terrified?'

Heather looked at Joshua like he'd just proposed six children and a litter of kittens. I shifted uncomfortably, wondering exactly where this line of questioning was going to lead. Sure, I'd pondered that question myself briefly, though I suspected our initial reactions to each other had put those thoughts to rest.

I swigged at the fruity red wine and prayed that we'd all drunk enough that the question would land softly, maybe flail about like Mel Gibson when he leapt from the building in the first *Lethal Weapon* film.

'My first thought?' William chewed absently as he refilled our glasses. The last remaining drops splashed into his glass. 'I mean, it was just after lunch, wasn't it?' He looked to me for approval. Like either of us could forget. 'I panicked. Absolutely shit my pants. I mean, wouldn't you? After all this time, and you think someone is no longer anything more than this sad, happy, beautiful memory—'

'Sad happy beautiful?' Heather looked confused, like someone had just asked if she really did want the chocolate-laced dessert.

'That's exactly what it is.' William looked at me again. 'It's like those moments we had that made me really happy, but I didn't get to have them anymore, so also sad. Also, she's completely beautiful, so: sad, happy, beautiful. And utterly terrifying.'

Joshua laughed, throwing himself back into his chair. 'You scared him, Emmy.'

'She did!' William laughed nervously. 'It was a very ... confronting moment.'

'I'm terrifying?' I asked, a smidge of hurt in my voice. 'You could have tried being me in a room full of people I didn't know, and someone who pretended not to.'

I hadn't meant that to slip out like that. Well, not entirely, but

I suppose it was bound to at some point. I mean, why were we only worried about how William felt? The table went quiet, his face fell, and the others shuffled uncomfortably.

'No, no, it's nothing like *that*. Confrontation is not always a bad thing.' William squeezed my hand gently between both of his, as if he hadn't just announced to my best friends that I'd upended his life like a canoe full of teenagers. 'So what I mean is that it forced me to deal with a lot of things that I'd long ignored in the hope they'd just work themselves out. Of course, that doesn't generally happen. So, it forced me to act.'

'Look at you, Em, force for change.' Joshua's convex face winked at me from behind a balloon glass that sloshed with alcohol. I imagined that's what fish saw from inside a bowl when we peered at them.

'Hah.' So, I *was* a homewrecker. Was I? If you looked carefully, you might have seen me physically harrumph, then pull myself together. Little things had been niggling at me lately about this entire situation, and how it looked from the outside. If someone at the eye of the storm thought that, then it was probably best I draw back a bit. Nobody wanted to be known as the homewrecker.

I tuned out of conversation for a bit.

'And she's good to work with?' Josh looked at me. 'Sorry, Ems, I'm just really curious.'

'It's fine.' I waved his concerns away. Like it could get any worse.

'She's wonderful, naturally,' William said, as if the question were rhetorical. 'I get to work with the best person I know every single day. I love it.'

'Thank you,' I said quietly.

Heather beamed at us. 'So, my question.'

'Sure.' William shifted in his seat as another round of empty plates disappeared.

'What's on the agenda for tomorrow?' She held an empty wine bottle above our head. Was she surrendering for the night, or planning on being carried home? Our waiter sashayed back across to us … and we were getting another bottle.

'I can't tell you that,' William chuckled. 'But, it's good. At least I think it is. I just hope Emmy agrees with me'

'Why can't you tell me?' Heather pouted.

'Because it won't be a surprise then, will it?' He stuffed a breadstick in his mouth and gave her a sly smile.

'I like that this is all happening while I'm here, by the way.' I waved at the table. 'Just … over here being a leper.'

William placed a gentle hand on my thigh. 'You'll love it. Promise.'

'Promise?'

'Absolutely.' He looked horrified at my questioning. 'It's been a long time coming.'

Chapter 25

William blew through the door the next morning like a gust of wind down a tube tunnel. At the sound of him, I rolled over to face my bedroom door. He apologised to the pot plant by the sofa for scaring it, muttered not so quietly about the wall behind the door, making sure he hadn't put the handle through it, and said a quick hello to Josh. His footsteps got heavier, until his shadow tickled the gap underneath my bedroom door.

He pushed it open slowly. A shock of his beautiful hair was the first thing I saw through barely open eyes. His smiling face followed and, when he found me in my scarcely conscious state, he slipped into the room quietly and closed the door behind him. I pulled the duvet tighter around my ear and closed my eyes again.

'Good morning, sleepy head.' He tiptoed across to the bed. 'Happy Day After Your Birthday.'

'Morning,' I grumbled.

'You don't sound so great.'

'I drank too much last night,' I said. 'We might've kicked on with a bottle or two once you went home.'

'No,' he gasped. 'You did not. And you didn't invite me?'

'No, we really did.' I closed my eyes and let my body sag back into its familiar rut. 'Sorry for the lack of invite.'

Though it had been an incredible night, and we spent way too much time chatting out in the cold when everyone had gone inside, I insisted William go home. He had tried for an invite, but I wasn't ready to jump into the unknown yet, not after the night's discussions. Besides, was there even a time limit on ending things with one boyfriend and taking up with another? I didn't want to just hop, skip, and jump into another set of issues. And then...

'Can I get into bed with you?'

'I'm not wearing any pants,' I slurred into the pillow.

'Okay. Alright.' He looked about the room for the briefest of moments, until a thought flashed across his face. He reached for the button of his jeans. 'If I take my trousers off, we'll be matching.'

'What?'

'Don't look though, I need to protect my modesty.'

'You? Modest?'

'If I'm not careful,' he said over the sound of a zip coming apart, 'I'll pull my underwear down, too, and no one wants my penis flopping about like a discarded pool noodle.'

'What? Not a sea cucumber? But a full pool noodle.'

'Uh-huh.'

One eye popped open, and I caught sight of him carefully pulling the last leg of his jeans off. They landed on the floor with a soft puff.

'And God knows I've seen so much penis in my time that I don't need to engage in any navel gazing.'

'You what?' I laughed. 'What the hell are you talking about?'

'I'm a doctor, Emmy, I see quite a few. Daily. It's almost a sport.'

'Do you think there's a plural for penis?' I mused.

'I believe the Latin term is penii. Like cactus becomes cacti.'

'Makes sense,' I chuckled. 'They can both be a little ... prickly.'

Even with all my back and forth rhetoric about how I didn't want this to be a thing yet, I didn't stop him getting in my bed;

I just couldn't be bothered. After a small gust of cold air, I felt myself sink further into the middle of the bed as William slipped under the covers, all the while eliciting a high-pitched giggle at my attempted joke. The bed wobbled about as he got comfortable and pulled the duvet up around his shoulders. His bare knee brushed against mine, sending an electric charge up the back of my legs and into my stomach. It was too early in the morning to feel like this. I took a deep breath in and enjoyed simply existing. A quiet Saturday morning in bed with William. The rest of the world rustled about outside the door but, for now, it was just us, and I was free to enjoy that, wasn't I?

'Open your eyes,' he whispered.

'Why?'

'Because I have something for you.'

'Not your pool noodle?'

'Pfft. No,' he mocked. 'Look, I mean, if you want that, too, I'm sure I can look the other way. Would be terribly awkward and uncomfortable for me, but I'm willing to take one for the team.'

I pushed my face into the pillow and laughed loudly. 'You're incredible.'

'Let's not get too excited,' he chortled. 'I've still got my pants on.'

When I opened my eyes, he presented me with an oversized cupcake. Complete with greasy wrapper, it was piled high with pink buttercream icing and an edible image of a rainbow.

'This isn't one of those edibles you get down near Camden Market, is it?' I asked, sitting up next to him and crossing my legs. I had to admit, he did look naturally comfortable in my bed, and it kicked my heart up a notch. Already, this early in the morning?

'How the fuck do you know about them?' William laughed disbelievingly. 'Of all people.'

'I know about them. I get around.' I licked the strawberry flavoured icing from my fingers and offered the cake back to him. 'You want some? This is really good.'

'No, what's really good is that shirt.'

'This?' I looked down at the white business shirt I'd been wearing. I'd picked it up twelve months earlier in the clearance bin of a men's store. For five dollars, it was way too big, but had been the most comfortable sleeping gear I'd ever owned. 'Are you serious?'

'It's, you know, it's a bit of a turn on.'

'This?' I tugged at the hem again.

'You should wear it today.'

'I can't do that, I've slept in it all night. It's crumpled, and it probably smells.' I scrambled off the bed, did the sniff test, and looked for a pair of jeans to throw on. 'I've got something that fits a bit better. Close your eyes while I change, will you? I'd ask you to leave, but I'm assuming you've seen plenty of backs in your time.'

'Guess where we're going?' he asked, his gaze following me about the room as I tidied up and tried to make it look as though my life these past few weeks hadn't been an utter mess.

'Camden Market?' I cleared away a damp towel and old pyjamas, tossing them into a makeshift washing basket in the corner. 'Don't say home decorating. You don't have enough friendship tokens for that.'

The last time I'd volunteered to help him decorate, on one of our Saturday adventures, he'd started a charge of kids across the tops of beds in IKEA and got us kicked out.

'No.' William took my hand and pulled me back onto the bed, close to him. There it was, that unmistakable burst in my chest and tingle in my toes. 'You'll need an overnight bag. Think of it as our weekend excursion, just on a grander scale.'

'Really?' I reached out and laced my fingers through his hair. If he was surprised by my sudden urge to touch him, he didn't let on.

'We've both not had a great time of it lately, so I figure we could do with some cheering up. Also, I'm quite sure I have some birthdays to make up for, so here we are.'

210

'Just one night?' I slipped away, already missing the feeling of my hand in his, or the brush of curls between my fingers. I stuffed some clean clothes into a backpack, grabbed some essential toiletries, and turned to face him. He was so unfairly beautiful, even as he clumsily pulled his pants back on.

'Just the one.' He peered up from his hunched over position.

'No hints?' I tried.

'*Non.*'

'None at all?'

He grinned, entirely pleased with himself. 'Are you ready? You've got five minutes.'

'We can't just go,' I baulked. 'Can we?'

'Actually, we can. This is 2014, not the middle ages. Anywhere from London to Istanbul is a four-hour plane trip away. We have the whole European continent at our doorstep. But, if you don't get your shit together, you won't find out.'

I narrowed my eyes at him, bag sling over my shoulder. 'You sound like *National Geographic.*'

'Isn't it wonderful?' He clapped his hands. 'Let's go.'

'It's Edinburgh, isn't it?' I asked. 'A pokey hostel, cheap beer. Oh, God yes.'

'Maybe.' William pulled my bedroom door shut behind us. 'Maybe not.'

* * *

William powered on ahead through St Pancras station. His backpack clanged around behind him, while I dawdled up the rear. I was sure I'd never been here before (how?) and wanted to stop and admire the iron beam and red brick architecture. It had been a mad rush from King's Cross, through underground walkways, avoiding suitcases and bypassing queues of tourists clambering to work out the Oyster machines. I felt a strange sense of pride, knowing I'd almost be considered a local now.

'Come on, quick.' He yanked on my hand and pulled me back into the here and now, the overwhelming, snaking queue of people shuffling their way through turnstiles. 'We can Fortnum & Mason to our heart's content when we get back.'

'We can what?'

'We're going to be late.' With a hand pressed against my back, he ushered me further along toward customs. 'We can stop and look at all this when we get home. I promise. I'll buy you anything you want.'

William steadfastly refused to use the ticketing machine until I swore to turn away and not peek over his shoulder. I was sure I looked like some weedy little bodyguard, ready to be snapped like a twig as I stood about listening to him mumble booking numbers and tapping the touch screen. The only thing I was privy to was the mechanical whir as the tickets spat forth from the machine. Oh, and the overhead screens, which gave me the options of Paris, Lyon, Brussels, or Belgium. I was completely okay with any of them. Except for one slight problem: I did not have my passport.

'Okay.' He stuffed the tickets face down in his passport. 'Let's go.'

While some people revolt at the idea of elaborate surprises, I was not so secretly loving the shit out of it. Nobody had ever gone to *this* much effort for my birthday, post the oversized toddler birthday parties. As we progressed in the queue, William refused to budge on the destination, right up to and including the moment he spoke to the customs officials in perfectly enunciated French. When he slid my passport across the counter I did a double-take.

'How did you get that?' I shrieked.

'Last night at dinner.' He looked as if it had been the easiest play in the world. He shifted feet and leant against the counter with his hip out. 'Also, since when do you have a British passport?'

'Since when do *you* have my passport?' I looked at him horrified. Not only was he master of the mystical art of medicine, he was apparently also a champion sleight of hand.

'Heather gave it to me last night while you were on one of your seventy-eight toilet trips.'

And since when did Heather even know where the hell I kept that?

'I don't wee that much,' I baulked. The customs officer barely raised a brow at our discussion, though William managed to oblige with answers between taunting me.

'You do, and you were bound to go at some point. Get a bit of vino in you, and you become the Trevi Fountain.' He grinned as we were handed our passports back. 'So, whose fault is the passport? How long have you had that?'

'Since birth.' We shuffled through baggage check and into the waiting area. I watched as William checked the overhead monitors and took hold of his hand as he drew me towards a quiet corner.

'You never told me that.'

A tiny laugh burst forth. 'You never asked.'

'If I had known that at Heathrow, I might've asked you to stay.'

I laughed loudly. 'You would not have!'

William shook his head, eyes blazing bright blue. 'You don't know that.'

* * *

On the train, he was three steps ahead of me, seeking out seats and tossing backpacks in the luggage rack by the door of the carriage. I squeezed past the nesters taking off jumpers and settling in like it was a long-haul flight.

'Window seat for *mademoiselle*.'

'You're too kind.' I slipped past him and into my seat.

Until now, this had all felt like something that could have been pulled from under me – that this had all been a huge practical joke. Customs might turn us away, or William might tell me it was all just an elaborate ruse to get me to McDonalds for breakfast. But, as the train hummed to life beneath us and pulled out of the terminal, it began to feel a little more real. My tummy fizzed like I'd swallowed a handful of pop rocks and litre of cola. It was a sweet moment of excitement, and a feeling to savour.

The overhead screens lit up and, as they did, gave away our mystery destination. Safety instructions flashed up in dual languages, French and English, along with an expected arrival time.

We were going to *Paris!*

I turned in my seat so quickly I thought I might have my own Linda Blair moment. William laughed to himself, completely proud of his efforts.

'Paris?' I asked. 'Really?'

'*Oui.*' He nodded. 'We are going to Paris.'

I squeaked.

'Unless that's a problem for you.' He cast a sideways glance my way.

I shook my head wildly, mouth Sahara dry. 'No, no, no, not a problem at all.'

'If it is, we can always get off the train, and I can take you for a fancy lunch at your local Costa or Greggs,' he teased. 'I'm easy. We may even be able to find a few of yesterday's sandwiches left at St Pancras.'

'No!' I clutched his hand excitedly as he stood up. 'Paris is perfect.'

'You sure about that?' He narrowed his eyes. 'I'm not entirely convinced. I should get our bags.'

I yanked him back down into his seat. 'It's incredibly thoughtful.'

'It is?'

'Yes. A thousand times, yes.'

I settled back into the seat beside him, flipped the armrest up, down, and up again. The complimentary magazine stuffed into

214

the seat pocket proved to be the most interesting thing I could find to read, what with its restaurant and shopping recommendations. Galeries Lafayette? Sign me up! That, and the drinks menu. In the end, it was more entertaining to get William to read the French articles aloud, and then translate them. I didn't even have a book stashed somewhere in my bag. But it didn't matter, there was too much happening outside the windows that was otherwise claiming my attention.

Unknown backyards, graffitied walls, and industrial complexes zipped past in a haze of concrete walls and red bricks. When the city became the country, and grey was replaced with green, wind farms and tiny brick cottages became more prominent, which ended abruptly with darkness.

'We should go to Dover for a weekend.'

I turned to my right, surprised to be hearing anything at all. For an hour, he'd had his eyes closed, and arms folded across his chest. After the dozenth time that I'd laughed at his French, he'd decided he'd had enough of reading the magazine to me and announced his plans to sleep. 'The cliffs are fantastic, and there's a great boat cruise you can do around the harbour.'

'Have you been?' I watched him in the relative darkness of the cabin, eyelashes spread across cheeks, and hair everywhere, and the finest hint of five o'clock shadow. A ridge set between his eyebrows, as if trying to sleep required maximum concentration. I loved his crumpled white T-shirt; it only served to highlight how colourful he was.

'I took my sister for her birthday a few years ago. Mum and Dad came across on the ferry, and we spent a weekend down on the coast.'

'That sounds like a beautiful weekend.'

'It was lovely to spend time together, just the four of us.'

'No wife?'

'She was "working",' he said, finger quotation marks in full effect.

215

As darkness became light, and green grass melded into the cityscape, I settled in and watched the French countryside zoom past our windows. When we pulled to a slow stop at the Gare du Nord. I peered out the windows at the arched ironwork, bulbous lights and graffiti covered walls by the train's entrance. So much to see in such a short space, and I wasn't even in the city yet. Uncertain excitement was blooming like a flower in the morning sun.

I leaned into William's side. 'Where are we going first?'

'Where do you want to go first?' he asked, shifting just enough to look me in the eyes.

'I don't know.' There were a thousand places I missed last time, and just as many that I wanted to revisit. The boulangeries, the riverside cafés, and the Eiffel Tour was a must.

William checked his watch. 'Good thing I do.'

'What have you planned?'

'A few things,' he said.

'But you're not going to tell me, right?' I asked, a slow smile spreading.

'You're a fast learner.' William stood, and stretched up to touch the roof of the carriage. I peered over the top of the seats, waiting for the crowd to disperse. 'Ready spaghetti?'

I was ready – for anything.

Chapter 26

Paris is synonymous with romance, more than any other city in the world. Look it up in the dictionary, and there'll be a wobbly little pencil drawings of the Eiffel Tower and kissing couples, rich foods, and bubbling champagne.

My memory of it is full of glittering lights and golden historic bridges, classic tourist moments, antique buildings and funny photos outside La Louvre. However, while this was all true, it was also suddenly terrifying to someone who barely spoke a lick of French beyond *merci* and *s'il vous plaît*.

Even if I had been here before, a quick dash through the City of Lights on a tour bus at nineteen felt like it didn't really count for much anymore. We got as far as a coffee shop inside the terminus, when feelings of inadequacy began to taunt me. I listened to William order coffee and ask for directions as if it were second nature. God, I loved his brain. It was so full of ridiculous titbits, factoids and, sometimes kind of important, ability to save a life kind of information.

'Alright.' He handed over a warm paper cup. 'What's on the agenda today?'

I popped the lid and let the rich aroma of coffee hug me gently. 'Sorry?'

'What do you want to do? It's your birthday weekend, so you tell me where we're going.'

'You mean you haven't planned anything?' I narrowed my eyes at him. 'Why not?'

'Oh, I have, but we'll fit your things around that,' he said.

Sure, I'd had a few hours to think about it, along with all the other leftover thoughts from last night, but was I supposed to be able to condense what I wanted into 280 characters or less?

'Uh, food, I guess? I'm quite hungry. The Eiffel Tower? I don't especially want to climb it. I mean, we can, because yay, but I'd really just like to sit in the park underneath for a while and just be?'

'And?' He gestured for me to continue.

'Can we just wander the streets and make it up as we go along?'

He gave a sharp nod. 'Sounds like a design for life. I like it.'

'Alright,' I said. 'Did you bring Steve?'

'Steve?'

'Your shark.'

'Oh!' His eyes widened. 'No. I have something better this time.'

'You do?'

He waggled his hand at me. 'My hand.'

I looked at it waiting there in hope and peered up at him.

'Come on.' He twinkled his fingers. 'I've lost you in a foreign city once before. I don't want it to happen again.'

Without thought, my fingers slipped perfectly between his, as if they'd been searching out each other all along. I looked at our hands clasped together for a moment. Over the weekends we'd spent in the city, and random other outings, he'd taken my hand before, but not like this. Last night, this morning and, now, this. It was different, a step in another direction. I adored how one small act seemed to have a finality to it that wasn't there earlier.

'So, we're going to get the Metro into the city and go from there.'

'The tower?' I let him pull me through the station towards another set of turnstiles.

'We'll get there, I promise.' He handed me a tiny card stub. 'Did you use the trains here last time?'

I shook my head.

'Really easy. Little ticket in, through the gates, onto train.' He grinned. 'Want to follow me down the rabbit hole?'

'Too late for that,' I teased, squeezing my way through to the platform in time for a rickety train to come hurtling towards us.

I was a little grateful that the carriage was so full. After sitting for the last few hours it was a good chance to stretch my legs. With a white-knuckle grip on a stanchion, I watched as another world whizzed by in a cacophony of noise and brake dust. The tiny nuances that made Paris feel like a world away, from signage to etiquette, were spectacular and altogether beautiful. For William, though, it seemed like a run of the mill afternoon; something he'd seen a thousand times before. Social media kept him entertained until we arrived at our station.

We climbed the stairs to street level, and the sight before me made the hairs on my arm stand up. It was hard to decide what to gawp at first – the Pont de Bir-Hakeim, with its dark arches and multiple levels, or the Eiffel Tower. As always, the tower stood proud and stoic, overlooking all corners of the city. I came to a slow stop as I peered up at the iron giant, a pedestrian bumping me out of the way with an annoyed grumble. I reached out absentmindedly for William. He slipped his hand into mine in what was beginning to feel like a purely perfect thing.

'So, I think what we should do is check into the hotel first. Then the afternoon is yours.'

'Where's the hotel?' I asked.

A lanky finger made like E.T. phoning home. 'Right here.'

The Pullman, with its sleek tiled floors and red accents was about as far away as possible from what I was expecting for the night. I stood admiring the opulence while William checked in and collected room keys. I think I asked more than once as we took the elevator up if we were in the right hotel. He assured me we were.

'Totally selfish reasons.' He tipped his head towards me sarcastically as we stepped out of the lift. 'I've always wanted to try this place. You were just a good excuse.'

'You're so full of…'

Our door opened with a quiet swish to a room that looked like something out of a dream. I had thought maybe a couple of lumpy beds with flimsy pillows, a kettle with instant coffee, and a bathroom full of roaches that partied until midnight. I did not imagine a room with a prime real-estate view of the Eiffel Tower, a downstairs bar to make every cocktail dream come true, crisp white linen, Nespresso machines, complimentary robes, and … one king-size bed with linen whiter than white.

'This is … wow.' I pointed. 'But just one bed?'

'To be fair, it's a king, so you won't even have to touch me,' William said. I flinched, wishing I hadn't just asked the question. 'You know, if you don't want to.'

I looked at him. The air in the room changed, shifted from expensive hotel to awkward encounter. Words flash through my mind like a bloody Bob Dylan video clip; marriage, separation, divorce, homewrecker. No, there would be no penis involved in tonight's activities. Also, it raised more questions for me than it answers. What about last night, the insinuation that I was the one who came in like the proverbial wrecking ball. And what about those blasted letters? I shuddered to think of what this all looked like from the outside.

'I mean, unless you *do* want to.' He grappled for the coffee machine behind him. 'Like I said earlier, I'm happy to take one for the team.'

I crossed the room and pushed myself up against the window. A door lock gave way with a quiet click and I stepped out onto the balcony. The tower was so close and so bit it was almost as if I could reach out and touch it. I peered down at the tiny bodies making their way around the park and wondered exactly whether any of them held any answers for me.

While William answered a knock at the door, I pulled my hair from its limp ponytail and gathered it up again. A porter stood just inside the entrance, picnic hamper and blanket, champagne and drinking glasses, and an embarrassed smile, probably glad he hadn't interrupted something seminal.

'What's this?' I asked, hair tie between my teeth and arms up around my head.

He held up the wicker basket. 'Just a little something extra I organised. You've always said croissants by the tower was your favourite memory of your last trip, so figured you might be interested in lunch under Gustav's finest. If you're still hungry, that is?'

'Starving.'

We dumped our bags, along with anything we didn't immediately need, and began our afternoon of exploring in the Champ de Mars. With grass greener than a frog's rear end and trees perfectly bronzed for autumn, the only problem we had was in deciding where we were going to park ourselves. As it turned out, finding a spot with a clear view of the Eiffel Tower that wasn't otherwise obstructed by tourists was a challenge.

'Here?' William pointed to the ground.

I dropped the blanket by my feet. 'Perfect.'

Spread out with our lunch around us like a prized loot, I struggled to choose what to eat first, and I loved it – what a terrible, awful, horrible decision I had to make. Did I want the flaky croissants, salty butter, and jam? Or did I feel like any of the array of miniature cakes that seemed to keep appearing from the bottom of the basket like Mary Poppins had done a break and enter at a bakery?

William was content to kick back, resting on his side with an elbow bent and his head resting in the palm of his hand.

'What do you think?' he asked.

'I think you're incredible.' I looked around. 'Though, this does set the bar quite high for future birthdays.'

His eyes met mine, softly proud. 'I meant the food. What do you want first?'

'I don't know.' I pulled a face. 'I'm not sure what to eat first.'

'I'll make it really easy. This has all come from my favourite café, which is not far from here. Whatever you like, we can get more of for breakfast in the morning.' He plucked a sticky paper from around a cake and bit down before passing it to me. 'Try this one.'

I bit down on the soft chocolate mousse centre, and hoped like hell there was another in the bag, because it was perfection. Also, because it would be the perfect antidote to the hard question that was swirling in my mind.

'You look like you want to say something.' William sat up. 'Do you?'

'Me?'

'Yeah, you kinda have that frowny thing going on again. You're thinking, but you're still working out the words.'

'Last night at dinner, you kind of insinuated that I was a bit of a homewrecker.'

'No, no, no, Emmy. God. I would never think that.'

'I get that, really, I do.' I put my cake down. 'But, is that how everyone else sees me? Because, if so, then maybe you and I aren't a good idea at the moment. I know this sounds completely ungrateful because this is just amazing, and you've obviously gone to a lot of trouble, but I don't ... should we wait until your divorce goes through? We should, shouldn't we?'

God, I'd hurt him. His face was crestfallen. I may as well have asked him to shave his head and set fire to the remains. 'I don't think we should wait.'

'No?'

'Emmy, I want to tell you something.'

'I'm all ears.' I licked my lips and reached for the bottle of

222

champagne nestled between us, because at least that was going to help temper whatever was coming.

'That first day you arrived, I honestly felt like I was a colour wheel of emotions.'

I offered him a far too full glass of bubbles. 'Tropical Cyclone Emmy.'

'The night before had not been great. I'd asked her to move out, again. So the day already started with this black cloud following me around. Then the grey ambiguity of everyone we worked with who had zero clue, and I wasn't about to tell them either.'

'I haven't told them. They don't need to know.'

'Pam was this little pink-faced loon looking at me to accept this gift she'd just brought to my attention.'

'Some gift, huh?'

'And there you were, and you were looking at me for this desperate level of approval. Like, "Please, don't tell me I dreamt all this", and I couldn't give it to you.'

I swallowed around a strangled throat. 'How could you have?'

'I wanted to though, that's the stupid thing. I desperately wanted to. It was ridiculous. Standing right in front of me is this incredible woman I had thought was long gone, who I dreamt of in the dark of night, who I hoped was okay, who I was scared I was never going to encounter again.'

I said nothing, instead choosing to down the last of my champagne before cuddling up on the rug next to William. He reached across and pulled me in under his arm.

'It was terrifying,' he laughed nervously. 'Suddenly, I had to confront all this shit I'd left on the backburner.'

'I don't want people to think I did that, though. That had to have been your decision.'

'I know that. And anyone who asks is getting the right story, at least from me.'

'Just because I was back?' I asked. 'You were just settling? Why

223

would you settle for *that*? You deserve better than that, anyone does.'

'Seeing that that photo of you and him that night at the pub.'

'You did look at it for quite a while.'

'It tore at something in me.' His eyes met mine. 'I wanted you back. Right there.'

'Oh, please,' I scoffed. 'I did have feelings for him. They just weren't as intense as … anyway.'

'As for me?'

I nodded, closing my eyes and lifting my face to the French sun.

And there it was, the admission that had been pinballing around my head since the moment I stepped through the clinic doors. No one was ever going to live up to him, to Edinburgh, and all those whimsical wonderful feelings it evoked in me. Hell, all I had to do was hear bagpipes on the television at home, and it was all over bar the haggis.

My words hung in the air above us, close enough to touch. But, instead of reaching out to grab them, we stayed quietly as we were, tucked up with each other under the shadow of the tower. After I fired off a few photos, and a handful of selfies, I closed my eyes and simply enjoyed whatever this was.

'Are you still awake?' William whispered into the top of my head.

I was. Barely. I opened my eyes slowly, still wanting to pinch myself at the sight before me. How did I get this lucky in the lotto of life? Saturday afternoon, light breeze, full of sweets, direct view of the Eiffel Tower, and the most wonderful person I knew as a pillow. I lifted my head and looked at him.

'Just.'

He tucked hair behind my ear. 'Want to go for a walk and wake up before we lose the rest of the day?'

'I would, yes.'

With no set plan, nor a destination, we dropped the picnic

basket back at the hotel and wandered the streets of Paris for the afternoon. We slipped into museums if something appealed, or just gazed in shopfronts and took in the atmosphere of full cafés with bustling crowds and ancient bookshops. It was a shame that we'd arrived so late in the day, because the hours ticked away even faster than normal.

'Did you want to climb the Eiffel?' I asked, realising we were heading back in that direction, back towards the hotel.

'I think they'd likely be sold out for today, I can try for tickets in the morning. We could go after breakfast,' he said, busily tapping at his phone as we strolled over another ornate bridge, statues covered in gold and richly coloured paint. 'We just don't have the time to stand in a queue for hours. Sorry.'

I grabbed his hand. 'It's okay.'

'I just want you to have a great weekend.'

'Great?' I knocked into him. 'It's already perfect. Whatever we do now, it's just a bonus.'

'You really believe that?'

'Yep.' I hooked my arm through his elbow. 'I love it.'

What I didn't love were the layers of conflict fighting for top place. My brain said a very big no. There were a thousand reasons not to get involved with William, no matter the sleeping arrangements or the extra care that had gone into this weekend. I might be leaving again in the next few months, unless my contract was extended. He was still married; I didn't need to get caught in the crossfire of divorce.

On the other hand, my heart was already dreaming of the country house, a clinic where he made his own hours and, the most important, the pocket full of children. I wanted that, desperately, and couldn't imagine wanting it with anyone else.

'You sure?'

'William, *you* are enough.' I grabbed at his hands. 'That we're here, just walking around even looking at all of this? I was kind of just hoping for a birthday cake, maybe a bottle of wine.'

'Speaking of wine.' He turned us around. 'We have twenty minutes until our dinner booking.'

'What's for dinner?' I asked.

It soon become apparent we were heading off on a very fancy dinner cruise, with river view seats, a cute little candle, and unlimited alcohol. We floated through the centre of Paris, which began to glitter as the night got darker and street lights came to life. Bridges took on a magical quality, for their shared history as well as beauty, and landmarks were lit up in a show of national pride. We ate and drank some of the most incredible foods: seafood and pasta, pork, and panna cotta with a rich berry sauce. I didn't dare question the cost, but I did help myself to as much wine as the waiter would allow.

When the boat returned to dock, we disembarked, completely buzzed and laughing hysterically at a joke that should have stopped being funny an hour earlier. I raced ahead of William, up the embankment and towards the street. As he reached me, he slipped and arm around my waist and pressed his lips against my temple. His spare hand came to rest against my cheek. Was there anything better than skin-on-skin contact? Whether it was hands, bodies, or lips, sometimes it told you more than the words you heard.

'Where do you want to go now?' he asked, mouth still up near my ear. 'You pick. You're in charge now.'

I tilted my head enough to kiss the palm of his hand. 'Follow me?'

'Anywhere.'

After a quick dash over the road, we scuttled through the doors of the hotel and past reception. I pulled up quickly, seeing the bar still open, and took a detour for a few late drinks. I wasn't sure William, with his follow-you-anywhere ethos was particularly excited by the prospect, but he stood patiently by the bar with me.

'I've always wanted a late-night drink in a hotel bar.' I wriggled clumsily onto the stool.

'One drink.' He laced his fingers through my hair and scratched at my scalp.

'Two.' I held up the equivalent fingers. 'And we get the second to go.'

We finally left the bar as soon as drink three was poured, right after I leant up from my stool and placed a kiss in the nook of William's soft, warm neck. It was a race to see who could toss their credit card at the counter quickest as we rushed to the elevators and jammed down on the Close Doors button.

As the doors closed, he kissed me. Far from being the slow romance I was expecting, it was fast and urgent, deep breaths, and a fistful of my hair in his curled up hand. He tasted of sugar syrup, the lolly water of his last drink, which hung limply at his side. When he tried to stop, I let him, before giving chase for one long, last kiss.

'Why the hell did we wait so long for that?' I asked breathlessly.

'Well…' His eyes searched mine. 'That's my thing I've always wanted to do.'

A loud ding announced our arrival at the fifth floor. We poured out into the hallway full of electric charge and nervous energy. Our door was second on the left.

'Emmy, before we go inside, I want to ask you something.' He boxed me in, his hand against the door, and the handle pressing into my back.

'No.' I took another sip, gurgling the last of my drink. 'Let me ask you something.'

'Sure.'

'What side of the bed do you want?' I arched a brow and waited for the slow spread of surprised recognition to register on his face. It was beautiful and illuminating all at once in the dimly lit hallway.

'I want the middle.'

I dragged my bottom lip through my teeth. 'So do I.'

With a mechanical click and a beep, I tumbled backwards

through the door, pulling William in behind me. Somewhere in the corner of my mind, hidden behind a kiss, I registered that our glasses had landed upright on the counter by the door. I reached for his shirt and pushed it up over his head. William fiddled with the buttons on my shirt, turning the unbuttoning into an advent calendar style event, revelling in each new piece of skin he caught sight of. As the edge of the mattress met the back of my knees, I stumbled backwards and dropped my jeans over the edge.

'You okay?' William asked, slipping off the rest of his own clothes.

I laughed at how ... simple that question seemed right now.

'What?' he chuckled, climbing onto the bed, above me.

'I'm great.' I mumbled against his mouth as he pressed his lips to mine again.

And, as for the whole 'no penis' idea I was toying with early today? Yep, no, there it is right there. Definitely broke that rule. And, by God, was it incredible.

Chapter 27

I stared blankly at the computer screen in front of me. My brain was still skipping giddily along the Seine, my mouth was still savouring the hot coffee and pastries of Sunday's breakfast, and my heart was still stuck in bed with William and his white-knuckled grip. What was he thinking, I wondered, as he criss-crossed the office, patients in and out, and collecting his files with little more than an office regulation smile.

'Are you okay?' Pam leant into my vision, twisted smile on her face. 'You've been doing that thing with your hair for ages now.'

I pulled my hand away from my head. 'My hair?'

'Wow, you are out of it today.' She chuckled. 'Good weekend, then?'

I wasn't sure either of us got a lot of sleep that night. We talked, fumbled, and spent an inordinate amount of time exploring each other's bodies. William strolled across the room naked and made coffee at two o'clock in the morning, just in time to watch some evangelical Christian television and, eventually, I fell asleep in a contented bliss somewhere near the first purple wisps of dawn.

A breakfast rich in butter and jam was provided by the bakery next door. We hopped on the Metro again, preferring this time to stroll through shopping centres that showcased brightly coloured stained-glass ceilings, drank champagne in the food court of another, and William bought a small handful of French novels to take home. As if he hadn't spent enough time showing off already, he wanted to add bilingual books to his shelves at home.

Heading home didn't exactly feel like punishment but, after stepping off the train at St Pancras, I did feel a little like someone had put a pin in my bubble. All those lazy cuddles, unconscious touches, and words we didn't need to say were now all coupled with the reality of going our separate ways and preparing for the week ahead.

Now, as I typed in new patient records and tried to keep my mind on the job, all I wanted was to go back there, back to bed, and back to him.

'It was.' I nodded. 'Lots of fun.'

'What'd you do?' she asked. 'I went to Westfield. Yay for payday, right?'

She wasn't wrong, I could have done with some new clothes, but I wasn't sure I wanted to tell anyone what I'd really been doing. In the excitement and flurry of trying to cram in as much as possible, and sleeping most of the trip home, we hadn't even talked about what this was. And until it was more than a flash-in-the-pan naked weekend, perhaps it was best to keep everything under wraps and separate. Our office was tight-knit. The last thing I wanted to do was jeopardise that. Before my big mouth let me down, I slipped away to the staff room for a few minutes.

'Look what the afternoon breeze blew in.' William didn't have to look to know it was me sneaking in to grab a coffee.

'How did you know?'

'Because I've listened to you shuffle about to the loo in the dark of night.'

I smiled coquettishly and leant into his side. 'And what does that sound like?'

'Like that stampede at the start of *The Lion King.*' He bit into his apple. 'That's after you've stubbed your toe on the doorway, cursed like a sailor, and turned on so many lights anyone would think Clark Griswold had moved in.' He leant in and kissed my cheek. 'But I wouldn't have it any other way.'

He walked away before I could say anything else.

Stolen moments like that became precious commodities. Gold chips in the sludge of a punchy work day, they provided that loved-up, sherbet buzz feeling that never got old. Our usual place of rendezvous was the staff room, because how romantic was it to whisper sweet nothings to each other around a benchtop littered with spilt sugar and baked on coffee granules.

Despite any assertions to Heather that I wanted to maintain some level of independence, nights and weekends were soon taken up by William. On nights I went to the gym, he'd be waiting on my couch when I got home. Other nights, I would go to him. I was turning into a regular old coupled-up woman, and it felt like something I'd waited my whole life for.

With my London List almost finished – I had one or two items left – weekend outings were replaced with sleep-ins and paint brushes. Saturday morning shifts were ditched in favour of staying in bed and enjoying copious amounts of sex, and restaurant hopping was left behind in favour of home-cooked meals. It was a sweetly domesticated existence that we slipped into naturally without meaning or planning to. We went on like this for weeks, completely uninterrupted and thinking this was the greatest life ever.

In our turn of domesticity, we'd been making headway repainting William's house. Well, it was mostly him, but I often got dragged into it when I visited. The only room I wasn't allowed to help with was the bedroom. That was his to fix, he said. It meant a few weeks where he'd stayed with me instead of the other way around.

'I'll bring a bag.' I reached up to press my lips to his. 'Seven?'

'Seven's good.' He kissed me again. 'I'll cook.'

'Really?' I used my back to push the door closed again, stealing another kiss. 'What are you making?'

'It's a surprise.'

Mostly, his version of cooking involved a delivery driver but, when I arrived just before seven o'clock, he was busy cooking. I dropped my overnight bag on the dining table and offered him a hug.

'This looks interesting.'

'I bought new pots.' He kissed my forehead. 'After getting on the scales and realising pizza wasn't the friend it promised.'

'Doctor, doctor, how very insightful of you.' I buried my face in the warmth of his neck and laughed. 'How was your day?'

'The parts that involved you were fun,' he said. 'Otherwise, all as usual.'

'Pam asked me what we were laughing at this afternoon,' I said, hoisting myself up onto the bench and helping myself to a glass of water. 'Apparently we looked very chummy.'

We certainly felt very chummy. Laughter continued to permeate the afternoon, single words leading to a red-faced William crouched beside my chair trying to hide his face from everyone. All it took was a single word reminder of something we'd said in Paris and, snowballing from a joke he'd told earlier, he lost control.

'Good thing she won't be seeing us in a few short hours.' William switched off the stove top and held his hand out to me. 'I have a surprise for you.'

'I think you've used that line before.'

'Ah, this is a proper surprise. No lies.'

'No overselling?' I teased.

'You cruel, cruel woman.' He laughed, low and guttural.

I slid from the bench and followed him. While he took the stairs two at a time, nattering excitedly about all the things he'd done around the house, I was happy to dawdle along behind him.

Last time I saw his bedroom, a frame surrounded the bed, but none of the other furniture had been assembled. Instead, it sat boxed up in the corner until he could get around to painting the room. Like P.T. Barnum on a good night, he gestured to the door with a flourish and pushed me in with a tap of his foot on my backside.

'Oh, wow.'

Dirty old white paint had been replaced with delicate greys and navy blues. Bedside tables complemented the bed frame perfectly, which had now been pushed up against the far window of the room. With the addition of a soft fabric wing-backed chair and a few cushions and throw rugs, the room looked like something out of a catalogue.

'This is magic.' I rubbed at his chest while taking everything in. Wall and light switches had been replaced with designs more fitting of a period home, and the ceiling light threw shadows across the roof in a way that felt cosy, like you'd never want to get out of bed.

'Thank you.' He collapsed into his new chair and crossed his legs over. 'At least it'll be a bit nicer for you to stay in now.'

I sat on the end of the bed. 'You know that I'm quite okay with staying over as long as you're involved.'

'Yeah, well, comfort is good, too, and this is proper comfortable now.'

'Did you paint everything?' I gazed about the room.

'Everything except the floorboards,' he said. 'And there's one more thing.'

'More?'

'Come on.'

William was out of the room and gone before I could so much as stand, his footsteps thudding on the stairs that led to the third floor. The previously abandoned room was now painted, had a lounge suite, cinema system, and project. Wall to wall shelves ran behind the lounge suite, which was a rich caramel colour.

233

I laughed. 'Get out.'

'Good?'

'Good? This is incredible. You've been doing all this between work and banishing me and divorcing someone else.'

'I don't really need to do much with the whole divorce thing. That's why I pay other people.' He squinted. 'But, yeah, I guess I have.'

'Are you not exhausted?'

'Have you seen how quickly I fall asleep lately?'

I threw myself down on the couch and waited for William to join me.

He crawled over the top of me. 'You did say that your bookshelf was already full and, well, I want you to think of this as a long-term thing. You and me, like we should have always been. I want you to feel at home here.'

'William.' I held his face away from mine.

'Yeah.'

'You are incredible.'

He lifted himself from the couch. 'I'm not so bad, am I? Come eat dinner, and I'll tell you about the rest of it.'

* * *

A student volunteer handed us visitors' stickers and schedules. Heather flipped the paper over in her hand, gave it a quick look of approval, and handed it to me. In my all too brief study of schools in the area, King's College London kept coming up as the place to go for all things nursing. As I wandered around the Waterloo campus, talking to staff and students, I got that jittery feeling that, even if I wasn't entirely sure what I should be looking for, my options were only limited to how much work I was prepared to put in.

'What do you think?' I walked beside her down Stamford Street.

'It's a bit fancy, Em.' She nudged me with her shoulder. 'I think you'll do great.'

'It'll be a huge change.' I craned my neck to peer up at one of the buildings.

'But you've got the scores, right? This is a cakewalk for you.'

'As long as there's no entrance exams,' I said. That wasn't a total joke. 'But there is. And it's full-time, so I would have to work somewhere else. Probably at nights and weekends.'

'And here's the crux of the issue.' She pointed a finger and walked backwards as we talked. 'A, you have a really lovely ... boyfriend?'

'I do.' I smiled inwardly.

'And you're enjoying lots of ... food right now.'

I laughed loudly. 'Food, yes.'

'But have you discussed future plans?'

'Actually, this is a question that deserves to be answered over a meal.' I looked up from the map. 'Have you got the time?'

'Do I have the time for seedy gossip and sex chat? Boy-o, yes I do,' she laughed. 'I can already tell this is going to be good.'

Heather might jokingly refer to herself as The Mum, but it did feel like that sometimes. She was number one for advice, even if she was a little thirsty for gossip, but at least I knew it would go nowhere once I told her. Except maybe for Josh, but he was one and the same anyway. We split an overpriced sandwich from a café near Waterloo Station, and splurged on hot chocolate with chocolate whipped cream, because that was the non-alcoholic drink of the gods. After that, we wandered about Southbank until we found a few free seats.

'Alright, Globetrotter, what's going on?'

'Globetrotter,' I scoffed. 'Please.'

'You are. Look at you, mad sex weekends in Paris—'

I giggle-snorted. 'It was pretty incredible.'

'Even madder sex weekends at home, thanks for letting us hear that last weekend.'

'Oh shit.' I pulled the neck of my shirt up over my head and hope it hid me. It didn't, and I laughed until I cried, probably out of sheer embarrassment.

'It's okay, it's fine.' She smiled knowingly. 'It's part and parcel of living with people. It's cool.'

'I am *so* sorry.'

'Are you though? Because you didn't say sorry at the end, you thanked him.' Heather folded in on herself and fell about laughing. 'It was so pure. Like, thank you kind sir for helping me out of a hole there.'

'Or in one, as it were.' I laughed all over again.

'Alright, spill. What's happened recently that's making you think twice about school?'

'Who says I'm thinking twice?' I asked. I loved that all these people around me thought they knew what I was thinking before I did.

'Because you flinched when I said, "future plans".'

I let out a deep breath and looked at her. 'William's asked me to move in with him.'

'Oh, Em.' Heather clutched at her chest. 'Yes, but no.'

'Yeah, but nah? How does that work?' Truthfully, I'd kind of hoped she was going to tell me I was being a bit precious and should jump at the opportunity. That it wasn't going to be the death nell that I thought it would be.

'Too soon, too soon.' She waved a hand about, careful not to splash hot chocolate on her. 'I mean, do you want to spend every second of the day with the guy, or what?'

'No, not really. I, you know, I have feelings for him, but I don't need him around all the time.'

'That's exactly what it will be if you live with him.' She pulled a face. 'And what's this "I have feelings" shit? You've only had your kids' names picked since the minute you met him.'

I really hadn't. I glanced down at the show bag bursting with school fliers, free drink bottles, and random landfill items. 'Maybe

I should go back to school and work nights. That way we won't be in each other's faces. That could work.'

'You want to say yes.'

'I kind of do, yeah.' I shrugged. 'Is that so bad?'

'No, no, please don't think that it's bad. That's not what I'm saying at all. What I'm saying is you need to be careful. Everything's a bit tender for him, you've said yourself that you don't want any more run-ins with his wife, so maybe keeping separate spaces until that's settled is a good idea.'

'What's the financial impact for you if I do?' I asked.

'Oh, please,' she scoffed. 'That's not an issue. Seriously, scratch that from your mind. We were surviving fine before you, and we'll be perfectly good after you. It's a non-issue. For us, it was just a bonus.'

'Okay, alright.' I bit into my sandwich and let the quiet filter through for a few moments. 'I'd still need to pay rent at William's, so I'd need a night job.'

'Emmy, you won't be boarding, you'll be banging.'

If I survived lunch without choking, I was going to go home thankful. 'Stop it.'

'It's true, Ems. He won't charge you board.'

'He should,' I said. 'Mortgages don't pay themselves.'

'No, he shouldn't. He's asked you to move in.' She held up a finger. 'And another thing. How long is this course? Have you thought about what you want to achieve in the next four years? I'm all for further education, you know I wouldn't try and talk you out of this, but ... marriage? Kids?'

'I hear you.'

'Is it too early to have those discussions with William?' She looked at me.

'He's a doctor, he's meant to be able to talk about the hard stuff.'

'Well, we all know about his bedside manner.'

'Oh, stop it, you.' I tossed the last of my roll at her. 'Enough.'

237

Chapter 28

Since living in London, I'd learned that your phone ringing in the middle of the night did not necessarily mean an emergency. It was more likely that your family hadn't thought to calculate the time difference. Or, like the call I got very early one Monday morning, my sister was in labour and wanted me to share in every gasp, cry, groan, or screamed curse from thousands of miles away.

Aaron Sumner popped into the world a little after 4 a.m. my time. Everyone dissolved into perfectly happy tears, before my phone was bombarded with photos I couldn't possibly look at until I ended the call. All that mattered was that he was healthy, my sister was okay, and that there were no issues. I'd promised I would visit as soon as I could and hung up knowing that the world was perfectly balanced.

William cuddled into my back as I scrolled through the handful of photos a dozen times.

'You okay?' he whispered.

I wiped away an ecstatic tear and snivelled. 'I am so thrilled right now.'

'Good.' He kissed my shoulder. 'He looks like you.'

'You think?' I peered again at the photo of a screaming, vernix covered little boy. 'How so?'

'He's screaming, probably about being woken up or being hungry. It's a look you've perfected.'

Laughing, I'd shifted in his arms to look at him. 'You're awful.'

'And yet, here you are.'

My phone and all social media became a hotbed of activity, bombarded with so many photos, I was sure I could piece them together to make a flip book movie. Almost every little burp, squeak, nappy change, and face pull was captured in digital glory for the world to see. Looking at those images on heavy rotation would have to do until I got a chance to fly home; which brought me to Brian's office.

More recently, Brian had mastered the art of two-fingered typing. He did that thing my mum does when she sits down at the computer: glasses on, squinted eyes, hunched over at the keyboard. It was a hoot to watch, because how did you end up a qualified GP without getting some serious typing practice in?

'I'm always losing the keys,' he mumbled. 'M, there you are.'

'Sneaky little sucker,' I laughed.

'Right.' He straightened up and gave me a look of grave concern. 'All of December?'

'Sort of?' I tried. 'Maybe the second week of December until the end of the first week in January?'

He took his glasses off and raised his brows. 'Funnily enough, Red wants to come back on the same date.'

'Really?' I looked about nervously, scratched the back of my head, and I was sure I was completely busted. To add authenticity, I leaned in to look at the computer and did my best surprised face. 'What are the odds?'

'Depends on who you ask.' Brian slipped his glasses back in place. 'Any exciting plans?'

'My sister just had a baby. I'd love to go home and see her, them, all of them. Some not as much as others.' I snorted. 'Plus, I'm happy to go without pay, so it will cost you exactly zero pennies to let me loose.'

'No pay?' His gaze settled on me. 'Don't be silly. I'll sort something out.'

I nodded, a little surprised and touched by his concern. 'I just need to cover the airfare.'

'You'll be entitled to something, Emmy. You got here on such short notice, which helped get us out of a huge hole, and Pam hasn't requested any time off, so it's only fair. I've just clicked the approve button.'

I stood so quickly my head spun.

'Oh, and Oz?' Brian passed some papers across the table. 'It's a week or two shy of six months, but I thought you might like to sign this before you leave.'

A brand-new shiny contract, permanent full-time, no six-month expiry. I snatched the bundle of paper up and flipped through it quickly. This ranked as one of the best things that had happened here so far. I'd done okay, I'd got through my probation without being flung out into space. I was staying.

I clapped excitedly. 'Thank you. Thank you. I'll send a postcard.'

I was out the door before Brian had a chance to change his mind. As for my own mind, I was floating somewhere up in the clouds, two weeks away from a month off work, and tapping away madly at my phone. There was no hope of a cheap airfare at this late stage but, without having to pay for anything else, I did not care in the least.

Select dates, cheapest fare, midday flight. I settled back into my desk and spat out my credit card number without thinking twice.

Done.

I was going home!

'Earth to Emmy,' Pam stretched out and tapped me with a ruler. 'Ding, ding!'

It appeared I had a queue. That almost never happened. Trevor was keen to offload his filing while requesting a follow-up on some results that were late, and the Royal Mail delivery girl looked like she had one thousand other places to be. She probably did. An overstuffed parcel landed on the counter with a heavy thud. My name had been scribbled in giant black marker, smiley faces all around it and flowers in the corner. Frankie had obviously overseen this delivery. If Mum had sent it, the handwriting would have been in a swirling regal font that suggested discipline by cane at early primary school.

The moment everyone had been sent on their way, the scissors were out, and I was tearing at that packing tape like a rabid five-year-old on a sugar high at a birthday party. There were more than a dozen packets of sweet biscuits, an offering of Savoury Shapes, Caramello Koalas, and it looked like she'd bought out the local supermarket of Cadbury Dairy Milk. But the real gold was hidden in an envelope that was slipped between the biscuits.

Digital photos were fun and instant, but I still loved the look and feel of printed photos, the kind made in a dark room with pungent chemicals. Just as I was earmarking a few to put in frames at home, I felt the grip of one hand on my waist and spotted another making like an octopus as it dug through my parcel. Two packets of biscuits and a block of chocolate were quickly confiscated.

'Thanks, sweetie.' William made a show of kissing me on the cheek.

'But they're mine,' I complained. 'Will, don't do that.'

'You love me, remember that.' He pointed his stolen stash at me as he retreated to his office. He turned his attention to his elderly patient. 'She loves me.'

Pam swung on her chair, completely scandalised and mouth popped open.

'Pam, you look like a sideshow clown,' I laughed.

'Really? Because I don't see anyone putting balls in my mouth.' She turned away. 'Shame, really.'

I shrunk down on my chair, behind my parcel and laughed. One of the most perfect things I'd ever see was watching Pam try and compose herself enough to answer her next call.

The second she was free, she turned her attention back to me, face twisted up in confusion. 'You know, someone's very handsy with you today.'

'You should try sleeping with him,' I mumbled, rifling through the parcel. 'It's like sleeping with a face hugger. I had a finger in my mouth the other morning.'

Oh shit.

I was sure I could hear Josh's Clown Song alarm in the background as her face dropped again. 'What did you just say?'

Double shit.

'I think I might have said that I'm sure sleeping with him would be like sleeping with a face hugger?'

'You did not say that at all.' Slowly, her face turned from one of shock to that of someone who was sure they'd just won the office gossip jackpot. 'Oh my God, Emmy, what is that even like?'

I gave her a sideways glance.

'Oh, come on,' she whispered. 'Please? It's only you, me, and a hundred contagious patients.'

'It's ... good?' I laughed, trying to hide my face. I was so, so embarrassed.

Armed with her newfound knowledge, Pam wasn't letting the subject go anytime soon. I was questioned up and down the afternoon. Was he a good lover? Great. Does he know what he's doing? Absolutely. How did we even happen? Long story, trust me. Every time William appeared, she roared with laughter, which only left him confused and checking to see if his fly was undone or hair was unusually unruly. Try as I might to change subjects, she wasn't letting go. Before my big mouth got me into even more trouble, I slipped away to the break room to tear open a fresh packet of biscuits.

Because the universe likes to sometimes back me up, and not always leave me outside in the cold, I returned to my desk to find Angela tapping bright red manicured nails on my desk. There was an immediate panic, as if me being happy was wrong, and I hoped it didn't wear on my face.

'Hello.' I smiled. 'Are you after William?'

'He's so hard to catch sometimes.' She smiled. 'You don't know where he was all weekend, do you, Emily?'

Again, with the name. Also, I felt a smug satisfaction in knowing we'd barely left my bed all weekend, but I was not about to say that out loud.

'Me? No. Your guess is as good as mine.' I pushed my parcel to the side of my desk and made like I had a pile of work to do.

'Is he in today?' she asked.

'I'll just call him.' I picked up the handset and dialled his extension.

'Hey you,' he answered. 'I'm with a patient.'

'Dr Scott, your … Angela is here to see you.'

'That all sounds very formal. I'm almost done here, I'll be out in a moment.'

Despite asking her to take a seat, she insisted on hanging around reception. She tried to drag Pam into a discussion about the weekend, but Pam had slipped from eager anticipation into complete shock trying to compute my news, while recognising that Angela was standing in front of me.

'You didn't go anywhere at all?' Angela directed her question at me again.

'No.' I shook my head. 'Just stayed home.'

'Well, sometimes that's best, isn't it?' Angela looked towards William's office as he appeared. 'Keeps you out of trouble.'

Even though I had done nothing wrong, guilt crawled up my spine and sat upon my shoulder. I was driving along a highway, and she was a police car hot on my tail. It was enough to make me want to run, far away and as fast as I could. To do just that, I grabbed an armful of filing and disappeared to the data room.

Try as he might, William couldn't get rid of her unless she got her private audience. For all her smiles and warm politeness, it wasn't my first glimpse of a woman who was prone to belligerence. With a low voice, she stood at the desk and demanded she

243

be allowed to air her newest grievances. William marched her straight out the front door. As she shifted through, in perfect slow-motion, she glared at me in a way that said she knew, and that her questions earlier were only the tip of the iceberg.

I turned to find Pam watching me. 'What?'

'Oh, Emmy,' she said.

Oh, Emmy, indeed.

Chapter 29

William scuffed across the floorboards in his socks, two glasses hanging between his fingers, and a bottle of wine under his arm. This was the type of couple we'd become. Sitting at home with a hot pizza and a bottle of wine had taken the place of getting dressed and heading out. I hadn't moved in, but it was almost a little comical that I took thrill in unlocking the door with my own set of keys, while William emptied the letterbox and brought rubbish bins in.

'I have to tell you something funny.' I held the two glasses up as he poured drinks.

'Go for it.'

'Pam knows.'

'I know.' He grinned. 'She's so proud of herself for finding out, too. She sent me an email this afternoon just before I left saying, "Hey boyfriend, your girlfriend has just left the building". I popped out of the office to look at her and she just about fell over laughing.'

I tucked my feet up under me and watched him get comfortable. 'What else did she say?'

William shook his head. 'Nothing, really, which is a surprise. She's all very cat that got the cream about it though.'

'You mean she hasn't gone and told everyone?' I twirled his hair through my fingers.

'No,' he said. 'At least not yet.'

'Miracle of miracles.'

It had never been a conscious decision to not tell anyone at work, it was just something that happened naturally, so we never bothered. It wasn't as if we could or would run about holding hands anyway, so if it wasn't interfering with our jobs. It just kind of slid into the background. We were happy, wasn't that enough?

'We could just tell them.' William looked at me. 'What do you think?'

I shrugged. 'Up to you. It's not going to change anything, is it?'

'I shouldn't think so.'

'Oh, and I did something else today.' I crossed my legs and just about propped myself up on my knees.

William offered me the box of pizza and changed the television channel again. Now, instead of rugby, we were listening to some of the most fantastic shit from the Eighties. It was the television equivalent of getting stuck in a 2 a.m. YouTube rabbit hole. Sequins met Michael Bolton mullets, and Michael Jackson was still king of the world.

'What did you do?'

'Firstly, I signed a permanent contract.'

'Hey, cheers!' He tapped his glass against mine. 'I had a meeting about that last week. "What do you think, William? The board thinks we should keep her on, how do you find her?"'

'She snores after too many carbohydrates and stomps about the house in the middle of the night, but otherwise, yes,' I laughed.

'I didn't quite say that.' He smiled. 'And what was second?'

'I booked my flight home.'

His face twitched a little, and I suspect he was trying not to look confused.

'What?' I asked. 'What's wrong?'

'You didn't think to ask me if I wanted to come?' Suddenly, he was more interested in staring at his pizza than at me.

'Did you want to come?' I asked.

'It's a bit late now.'

'Not exactly,' I said. 'I'm sorry, I just didn't think it would be something you would be interested in so soon.'

'What, after all our letters where we talked about it? You thought I wouldn't be interested?'

'So, book a ticket and come with me. I'm sure there are seats left. We could sit together,' I said. 'Why does this need to be an argument?'

'I'm not arguing, Emmy, I'm just saying that it would have been nice, as your boyfriend, for you to talk to me about what you were planning. That way, we might be able to do something together.'

'Did Brian approve your leave?' I asked.

'No.'

'So, you can't come anyway.'

'I'm just saying, it would have been nice to have been asked.'

I reached across and touched his forearm. 'I'm sorry. I didn't think.'

I wasn't saying that simply because that was what he wanted to hear. He was genuinely right. We were together, this was a real, living, breathing thing, and I should have told him first. I waited for him to take the empty pizza box out to the bin before I snuggled into him on the couch.

'I'm sorry.' I pressed a kiss into his shoulder. 'You sure you couldn't convince Brian?'

'I tried,' he said quietly. 'What are you doing while you're over there?'

'A whole lot of nothing.' I looked up at him. 'I'm getting off the plane and spending two weeks at my parents' house doing nothing. Maybe eating copious amounts of seafood over the Christmas period, but otherwise, I'm sleeping.'

'Next time, hey?' he said. 'We should probably sit down a few months out and plan anyway.'

'Yes, otherwise you'll be stuck at home with my family. I promise next time.'

'Speaking of family, what else did they send you?' he asked.

'The usual, biscuits, lollies, snacks, photos. You know about the biscuits, because you stole some.'

'But they're just so good.' He gave me a sideways glance. 'Emily.'

'Don't you start.' I gave him a playful tap.

'She's just being spiteful, you know that, right?'

'You know, after Angela arrived today, I kind of forgot about my parcel. I didn't even bring it home, so I'll have to remember to grab it tomorrow.'

* * *

There were two letters in the box. One from Frankie, in which she poured her heart out onto the page like I never thought possible. She was great at the phone chats, but I'd never seen her write anything down in her life. It was a whole different side to look at her as a completely doting, over the rainbow mother, even if she was struggling and completely overwhelmed at times. After work, I'd purchased some small photo frames. New photos of Aaron littered my bookshelf and one of the bedside tables.

The second envelope was an old letter from William. It was already open. I figured Frankie must have found it in the back of a drawer when she took my bedroom and decided to send it to me. That was lovely of her. I sat down on the bed and unfolded the thin paper.

13th June 2012

Dear Emmy,
    I've thought about you a lot lately. The truth is, I miss you.

248

I know that sounds ridiculous, I know. I've been playing those words over in my head the fortnight, and I can't shake it. I moved onto the next phase of training at a new job, and forgot to take your email address with me. Sorry, my fault.

I'm going to put my phone number at the bottom of this letter. Please call. I need help, advice, support. Something. I just want to hear your voice. Tell me I'm wrong, tell me I'm right. Either way, please call. I want to hear your voice.

Yours,

Will

I wasn't sure if I believed what I was holding onto. It looked like a letter, and it was in the same type of blue envelope William had always used. The date stamp said June 2012. There was no way Frankie could have possibly found it at home. A quick text to Frankie confirmed she had no idea. The only envelope she put in there was hers. No more, and no less. When William didn't answer his phone, I left for the gym. I could talk to him about it later. Surely there was an easy explanation. Maybe Frankie was mistaken.

I picked up my gym bag and walked out the door.

* * *

I kept an eye out as class filled up. The usual suspects rolled in, almost at the same time every week. I was glad for the sight of Caroline, who shuffled quickly over to our corner. Away from the prying eyes of the world, we spread out little pile of bits about us like a picnic.

'I didn't think you'd be here today,' she whispered.

I looked at her, confused. 'Why not?'

'Because we have company.'

My head spun about like a spinning top. Arriving like a float in a civic parade was Angela, her posse trailing behind her. Heads were held high, and smirks were set on each face like a membership card. I knew I caught her eye as I looked away. As quickly as I tried to turn away, I didn't need a chiropractor trying to set my neck back in place later on.

She was silent. It was the first time she'd turned up to class and not had an op-ed about William, or her hard knock life. She did her open-leg rocker with the rest of us, and only bothered to chance a look at me as we stretched out into a position subtly known as a birthing squat. I thought that was hilariously fitting and had a giggle.

'What's funny, Emily?' Angela's voice shot across the classroom. Somebody tried to quieten her, but good luck with that.

'Me? I'm not laughing at anything,' I said. 'Dust allergies.'

Now, it was Caroline's turn. She snorted and collapsed flat on her back. I shot her a 'please help me' look, and she quickly got to her feet again. Our instructor floated about the room in his sea of zen and happy feelings.

'Shame you're not allergic to other people's husbands, Emily.'

I straightened up, and secretly cursed the creak in my knee. Already? This was happening already? I wasn't even close to thirty. Angela was still posed perfectly, watching me from the corner of her eye.

'You mean the husband you tricked into marrying you? Or the one whose mail you hid?' The words tumbled out before I could take them back. A seed of doubt that had threaded its way into my mind as I'd sat looking at the letter that couldn't possibly be true.

Judging by the look on her face, I'd hit jackpot.

'Oh.' Her voice was filled with glee. 'You got my letter, did you?'

'Yeah, I got it.'

'What letter?' Caroline swapped sides.

'She used to write love letters to my husband.' Angela cackled. 'My Lovely William. Yeah, well, he was mine. I got rid of you once, Emily, I can do it again.'

Caroline stretched her arm over her head. 'If you're going to insult her, at least get her name right, you oversized twat.'

'Ladies, enough.' Our instructor looked between the three of us as if we'd committed the greatest sin of all, talking in class.

Angela collected herself only long enough to look at me properly. 'Would you like to continue this outside?'

'Fuck yes, I would.'

'Shit yeah, me, too.' Caroline was hot on my tail and then, because everyone loves a good fight, half the class followed us out into the reception area. Only the instructor and a handful of students were left behind, wondering what an earth had just happened to our tranquil pilates class.

I felt like an extra in some pokey mid-Nineties teen movie when two girls have a scrag fight and pull hair over some guy who turns out to not be so great anyway, when the ten-years-later highlight reel showed there was no pot of gold at the end of the rainbow. It was just six screaming kids and a family van with enough fingerprints on the windows to make it look like privacy glass.

'Alright, spit it out.' I tried to stuff my hands in my pockets, only to realise my pants didn't have pockets, so I folded my arms across my chest instead.

'Don't get defensive with me...' She paused. 'Emmy.'

'I'm not defensive. I just don't have pockets.'

'You need pockets.' A voice came from behind me.

I shook my head. 'I haven't got all night.'

'You stole my husband.'

'Nope.' I shook my head.

'You lied and manipulated and took him from me.' She shifted nervously.

'Funny you should mention lies and manipulation.' My mouth twitched into a smile. 'Didn't he marry you because you were supposedly pregnant?'

'Not supposedly. I was.'

251

'That's not what your doctor said though, is it?' I asked. 'And your own "husband" is a doctor, so he was going to figure it out in the end.'

And the posse was shook. Mouth after mouth dropped open, gaping little fish on the back end of a sea trawler.

'Then there's the little issue of the letters,' I said. 'I got your letter yesterday. Pretty bloody stupid to give me one in which your husband, writing to me before you married him, told me how much he missed me.' I shrugged. 'So, what, you hid letters to section him off from his friends? What kind of a wife does that?'

The silence was deafening. I could almost pinpoint the moment each of her friends began switching off from her. One by one, the light of love and friendship was snuffed out.

'So, he wasn't cheating on you. He couldn't, because you isolated him from everyone he cared about.'

'Did he send for you?' she asked.

'What?' I laughed. 'No. You were intercepting his communication, so that would have been a little hard anyway.'

'I wouldn't call it intercepting, sweetie. After all, he has all the letters.'

I stared at her blankly, determined not to flinch.

'He's had them all along. I don't know what he's been telling you, but he's had them.'

'How long is all along?' I asked. 'That's not incredibly time specific.'

'All along,' she said again, stepping out her words like a *Hooked on Phonics* cassette. 'The. Whole. Time.'

'Why would he do that?'

'Because he's William, and you don't know him like you think you do.'

With that, she turned and walked back into class, apologising profusely to our instructor for my interrupting the class.

'Well.' Caroline looked at me. 'That wasn't quite what we expected, was it?'

Chapter 30

William looked different this morning. He sent an early message, asking me to meet for breakfast. I declined, as politely as I could. If it was true he'd had those letters and had known about them for as long as Angela said, I was dealing with someone very different to the person I thought I knew.

There was always a huge chance that Angela was lying. She hadn't exactly proven herself to be a bastion of virtue at any stage of this process, so why start telling the truth now? Unless, of course, there was a benefit to her doing so. The whole situation was enough to give me a migraine, which I was sure I could feel as I walked to work.

'Did you get my message this morning?'

I looked up to find William walking through the door. He looked concerned, in a state of ignorant bliss.

'I did,' I said. 'I wasn't hungry.'

'You didn't reply?' He checked his phone again.

'Didn't I?' I responded vaguely. 'Sorry.'

'Are you okay?'

'I got an interesting letter last night.' I grinned at him. 'And then, wouldn't you know, ran into your wife at the gym.'

His jaw twitched. I didn't want to assume, but it felt like a decent indicator that he knew exactly what I was talking about. But, if he did, he didn't show it. He goofed about as usual all day, trying to get a rise out of me. All the while, I sat at my desk, having had minimal sleep, trying to work out how to best broach the subject with him.

'Hey, Emmy.' William approached from his office, newborn baby swaddled in his arms. 'Look at my new friend, George.'

I glanced up and gave George's mother a polite smile. 'Hi, George.'

'Have you got babies on your London List?' he asked, squatting beside me. 'Look at him.'

George was cute, a tiny button face and a mess of thick black hair. He reminded me a little of my nephew, which only drew out my frustration at having to wait to visit. Not long to go, I reminded myself.

'What do you think?' William looked at me hopefully. 'Ours might have brighter hair though.'

George's mother gave a thrilled laugh. 'You'll have the best time.'

'I think he's beautiful.' I looked at William. 'But you need to stop.'

It was probably the nicest thing I could think of at that moment, with the hum of office life in the background, and Pam making noises about how we should totally have all the babies. I threw her a look and ignored William as he sent George and his mother on their way.

'Let's talk after work, Emmy.' William walked away.

'Sure thing, Red,' I called after him.

When he turned back to look at me, his face was twisted up in anger.

* * *

Though the office was almost empty, it felt like the eyes of the world were on me as I walked down the short hallway towards William's office. Office doors were closed, and everyone was preoc-

254

cupied with tidying up from their afternoons, but it still felt like, somehow, everybody just knew. I knocked on the door and waited.

No words, just a wave of the hand to draw me in.

I closed the door quietly and crossed the room to sit in the patient's seat.

William looked exasperated. 'What is going on today, Emmy? I've been wracking my brain all day, and I cannot work out what the problem is. Yesterday was perfectly fine. I know we didn't spend last night together, but surely that's not it?'

'No.' I shook my head. 'That's not it at all.'

'Then what? What have I got wrong?' he asked.

I slid the envelope across the table. 'I found this in the box my family sent me earlier this week.'

'So? It's an old letter.'

'Yes, but I sent all your letters back to you.'

He glanced at me as he unfolded the solitary page. I was sure it was the colour draining from his face, and not the sun setting outside the window. He was whiter than rice, if that were possible.

'I never got that one,' I said. 'Do you want to tell me how your wife ended up with it instead?'

'She's not my wife.'

'I don't care about semantics right now, William.' I crossed my knees and fought the battle to keep my tone measured and profes-sional – one of us had to be. This was embarrassing enough without setting off an emotional fire sprinkler. 'I want to know what you know about this letter and how your wife came to leave it on my desk.'

He said nothing. His head shook in annoyance.

'Please don't lie to me again,' I said as calmly as possible. 'How long have you had them?'

'There was a lot of back and forth with lawyers, but I got them back the week after Paris.' He stuffed the paper back into the envelope and dropped it onto his desk. 'She was upping demands constantly and, as you know, I figured she was the only one who could have done this, so…'

'So?' I urged him on.

His shoulders lifted around his ears. 'I just threw a demand back that said she'd get nothing if I didn't get those letters. Gave her a counteroffer and sent her on her way. I had them two days later.'

'And you never thought to tell me?' I asked, affronted, my brain not quite knowing what part to process first. 'After all our conversations, all our *fights* and you just had them? This is not a difficult thing to discuss, William.'

'For Pete's sake, Em. You know it's not that simple.'

Not that simple? What the bloody hell was so wrong about fronting up on my doorstep with a box of tattered letters and a bottle of wine? It wasn't like we were talking classified war documents.

I took a deep breath and watched him, tried to read his face. I couldn't work it out. I couldn't read the lines or the tics and quirks. Even his eyes were empty. 'I think that's me done.'

'Done with what?'

'Us.' As I stood up, his face fell in equal measure. 'I can't keep excusing things, William. It feels like it's been one thing after another since I arrived. The way you treated me, hiding things. Whatever this is, it's over.'

'No, Em.' He scrambled as I made to leave the room. 'Can we just talk about this?'

I held a hand out but yanked it back as he tried to take hold of it. 'Stop. Just stop. There's nothing to talk about. I'm not going to yell or scream or get into an argument. I am tired, I am so tired, and I'm done. From now on, we're nothing more than colleagues, okay?'

His brow wrinkled. 'No, Emmy, that's not okay.'

'It's going to have to be.'

As I pulled the door open, feet disappeared through doorways,

256

not unlike that scene with the hallway in the Yellow Submarine movie. I took the walk of shame, stopping for no one. I slung my bag over my shoulder and took one last glance over my shoulder. William stood in his doorway, pleading silently for me to call him. I shook my head and left for the night. The sooner I could get out of there, the less chance there was of making a complete farce of it all.

Chapter 31

If I'd learned anything in my time here, it was that relationships don't just go quietly into the night. They bubble like a dropped bottle of cola and, while everyone will stand around and not touch it for fear of getting sprayed, eventually, the bottle will burst and there'll be a mess everywhere.

I thought I had done my best. That was as much as I could say. I was quiet, cordial, and applied myself to my job as best I could. William, too, though he was trying to chip away at me as if he were taking an ice pick to carbonite. And, while others may have tried fishing for information, I was tight-lipped. Professional, calm, courteous. That's what I was there for, after all.

It was only a week. That's what I told myself as William appeared in the front door each morning, despondent smile on his face. Five working days, and I could get on a plane and enjoy crowding my thoughts with family and friends instead.

Frankie was running up her text message bill like a gambler at a casino on pension day. Last minute plans and bookings were coming to fruition, supplemented by dozens of 'just checking' messages, and quickly making my trip look like a tourist expedition. Admittedly, that felt strange. I mean, I was going home, wasn't I? Was it supposed to involve climbing the Sydney Harbour

Bridge or dinners booked in expensive restaurants, or museum attractions I wouldn't normally bother with? Really, I would have been happy with a packet of biscuits and cuppa in front of the cricket. Okay, maybe not the cricket, but just the television in general.

Dad, in one of his rare turns of communication, offered up a list as long as his arm of local sweets and spreads he wanted me to bring home. Through mutterings of, 'I haven't had them in years' and, 'we used to ride down on our bikes and get them from the shops', I was entreated to stories of his childhood that I'd never heard before.

I managed to hunt down as much as I could, though I wasn't sure customs were going to love me when I landed and ticked that box that said yes, indeed, I did have a picnic spread of food in my luggage.

I debated for a few days, packing and unpacking a suitcase, when I gave in and just threw everything together in a jumbled mess. I was only going for a few weeks. I had clothes at home. The food would be fine if I declared it, surely. If not, a stint on one of those border security type shows was looking likely.

My ears pricked up at an unusually loud discussion by the front door. It was muffled, but the strains were enough to understand that it wasn't an altogether pleasant exchange. As far as I knew, it was only Josh and me at home. He'd prepped dinner while I did a load of washing and cursed that my favourite comfy undies were still stuck in a spin cycle as I packed. If I just kept my head down, I would be able to sail on through whatever was happening without being bothered, continue packing my things and be done.

'Emmy, you home?' Josh knocked on my bedroom door before he walked in.

'For the time being,' I teased. 'What about you? Are you home?'

'You lucky thing,' he said. 'We have to wait a whole week more for our flight.'

I pouted. 'I know, that sucks.'

'Why didn't we organise this a bit better?' He tapped his chin. 'Really. It would've been great fun: a whole row of the plane, a few shandies, some blankets. I'd be in the middle, of course.'

'Next time,' I said. 'Promise.'

'At least we get to party when we do get there.'

'I'm so excited.' I bounced. 'I am sorry I haven't done much to help though.'

That was something else I'd realised in my last week of over-abundant time. I'd been a shitty friend, leaving Heather and Josh to organise their engagement party. Not that they needed my help, of course, seasoned organisers that they were, but they had asked, so I should have been there to pick up the slack when needed.

He gave a tight shrug. 'You've had stuff going on. It's okay.'

Josh stood quietly for a moment, his mouth paused mid-word and finger in the air. He was on the cusp of something important but wasn't entirely sure what to do with that information. It was the same face he made the first time he tried to tell me I'd upset him. About what, I couldn't remember, but I did remember that face.

'What's up?' I asked. 'Are you okay?'

'Yeah … so you have a visitor.' He made to leave but doubled back. 'I feel like we say that to you quite a bit.'

'Not that much.' I tossed a pillow case in his direction. As it landed on the floor, something else settled in the room, something a bit heavier; more solemn.

William appeared in the doorway. He stepped over the pillow-case and into the room. In his arms was a small transparent plastic tub. It was stuffed full of envelopes and, at the very bottom, I recognised the eggshell blue tea set, and reference book William had once sent me. I looked at it, then at him.

'Hi.'

I fought with a small cardboard box, trying to nestle it in the corner of my suitcase. 'Hello.'

'Are you leaving soon?' he asked.

I looked at my bedside table, still decorated with Craig's alarm clock that had to go back to him. 'I've got a few hours yet.'

William shifted uncomfortably, from foot to foot, one hand scratching at the other. 'Emmy?'

'Yes?'

'Before you leave, can we talk?'

'If you'd like,' I said.

'I've brought our letters.' He placed the box gently on the bed that stood between us, as if they were a sacrificial offering or rare gift; gold, frankincense, and feather-light airmail paper.

Right now, my stripped-down bed felt like a chasm. He may have only been on the other side of it, still close enough to touch but, emotionally, it was a world away. After all our midnight discussions and under the cover laughter, this must have been what emptiness felt like. I peered into the box, quickly fingering the bundles of letters, boxes of gifts, all things I'd thought lost long ago. My eyes met his, and he looked away nervously.

'I didn't ... I mean, I meant to tell you. It's just so stupid in hindsight, I know.'

'Well, it's not that difficult, William.' I angled my body away from him, dumping another bundled T-shirt in my suitcase. 'These should have been a thing of celebration, shouldn't they? They're not tainted.'

'They have all been read.'

I looked at him disbelievingly. 'Really? That was what you were worried about?'

'No, Em, no, of course not.' His head lolled about.

'How did she get them?' I asked. 'Do you know?'

'She needed a room to rent, so moved in about six months before the letters stopped. Given that she worked odd hours, she would volunteer to run errands. I'm talking bills, groceries, the mail, so that's how she got the incoming and outgoing stuff.' He rubbed at his stubble thoughtfully. 'Really simple in hindsight.'

'And how did you get them back?'

'There was correspondence back and forth with her lawyers. You know, the usual divorce type stuff. It was all getting a bit messy, and one point stood out because I was sure I'd only ever told you that particular fact. I started piecing it all together, and it just made sense, like a missing piece of a jigsaw puzzle. So I played her at her own game. Told her lawyers I refused to move forward with anything unless she gave back all the letters she stole, or I'd have her up for stealing mail. The next thing I knew, there was a box on my doorstep and it was full of you. I mean, it was a bit more convoluted than that, but...'

I frowned, and pulled one of the old letters out of an envelope. 'Here's the problem I have with this, and it's not actually this box. It's all the shit that led up to this. This just happens to be the icing on the cake.'

'Honestly? I didn't know how to handle you being back.'

'You didn't know how to handle it?' I shrieked. 'I'm on the other side of the bloody world. My social circle consists of maybe ten people, even less at the time I discovered that you were still here and, suddenly, the one person I'm thrilled about had turned into a complete ass in the time since I'd last seen him.'

'Did you come here for me?'

I laughed loudly. 'Are you kidding? No. I had no idea where you were, you asshole.'

'At least you're honest.'

'Which is more than I can say for you.'

William took a deep, shuddering breath. 'Emmy, I never meant to lie to you. I just thought it would be better to get all of my stuff sorted, get it out of the way and done, and then I could come to you and say, "Here, look what I have".'

'But it's not just the lying, William.' My voice rose. 'It's the humiliation that came before it. That first week at work; I didn't know anybody, and yet, there you are telling me how to write on envelopes, ignoring me when it suited you, refusing to work with me even though you'd been told you had to.'

'Em, I'm sorry.'

'At the pub with that bloody drink, then out in the street where we argued for all and sundry to hear. It was humiliating, William. And from you, of all the people. *You*. I don't want to fight with you, I don't, but come on.'

'I know I've made mistakes,' he pleaded. 'I know that, Emmy.'

'And you're still so bloody nonchalant about it. It's no big deal, Emmy, I've said sorry, what do you want me to do?' I mocked.

'And what *do* you want me to say?' he shouted. 'I can't do any more than what I'm doing now!'

'Right now, I feel that maybe I shouldn't have been friends with you again, maybe I should have kept that distance.'

'Don't say that.'

'Why not?' I asked. 'I've lost a boyfriend and half my friends over this, because he went home and declared I'd been cheating on him. I've had your wife haul me up in front of an entire gym class and make me look like a homewrecker, so obviously I am. That's clearly how it looks to everyone. I mean, when does this end? When do I just get somebody who's going to treat me with a little bit of respect?'

'Now, Emmy.' He pointed to the floor. 'Me, me, I can.'

'But you can't, Will. You've proven that. Why am I supposed to buy into it now? What's the big difference?'

'So, what, what, that's just … that's just it?' he asked, looking around the room frantically. Was he looking for something to grip on to? Something to stop him floating away?

'I'm going home, William.'

'Are you coming back?'

'Honestly, I don't know.' I shrugged. 'After everything, not coming back is looking like a good option right now.'

His chin dimpled. 'I don't want you to go.'

'Why not?'

Right then, it felt like I was watching a small child crumble in front of me. There were hands that didn't know what to do with themselves, eyes that filled with tears, and a trembling lip. 'Because I love you and I don't want to have to watch you disappear on another plane again.'

My eyes, heart, throat, it all stung. 'Could you please leave?'

'Can I get some contact details for you? Would that be okay at least?'

'You already know how to contact me.' I nodded in the direction of the box.

Chapter 32

Frankie met me at the airport, a bunch of balloons in one hand, a WELCOME HOME FROM PRISON sign in the other, and my nephew all swaddled up against her chest. God knows how, though. Even inside the airport, the air held that sweltering warmth that only Sydney could provide in summer. It only got marginally better as the sliding doors opened because at least then the air was forced to move about. Ezra was there, too, ready with a hug and the offer to carry luggage.

'How'd she get you out here?' I squeezed my brother in a way I perhaps hadn't ever done. There was something there about absence and hearts and fondness, but I didn't want to ponder that too much in my state. I refused to let go until he did.

'I'm just here so you didn't have to catch the train down so early in the morning.' He lifted me off my feet. 'Also, because Mum said so. And because I missed your face. Welcome home.'

'How was the flight?' Frankie pinched at my arm as I gathered around her, stealing my first real-time peek at Aaron.

'Yeah, the usual,' I mumbled as Aaron was passed over to me. I wasn't ready to elaborate on any of it.

William had left quietly, collecting the box of letters and shuffling out of the apartment with his tail between his legs and a

265

dozen variations on his apology. Not that it helped me out of my own sore spot. If anything, all it did was leave me questioning myself. Maybe I was being too harsh, or maybe not strong enough. Or, maybe I just needed to accept his apology and get on with life. Through all my customs checks, airport terminals, and weepy in-flight movies, it wasn't as if I could get his face out of my mind. I just hoped that a few weeks away from it all might give me a bit of clarity.

'He is so, so pretty.' I threw an arm around Frankie's neck and kissed her cheek. 'How are you, Mum? Are you okay?'

'It's a shock.' She gave an embarrassed smile. 'But I do love him. He's pretty peachy.'

'He is.' I pushed his hair back from his forehead. 'He's so heavy. It's so deceptive, isn't it?'

'He likes food.'

'Well, he's mine now,' I teased. 'You can't have him back.'

He was even more beautiful in real life, a little button mushroom nose and mop of dark hair already. Added bonus: he was happily asleep. All I had to do was keep him that way until we got out to the carpark.

We glanced up to find Ezra battling his way out the doors and towards the car park. Taking our cue, we dawdled slowly behind him.

'Where are Mum and Dad?'

Frankie rolled her eyes. 'Currently on some Murray River Cruise. You know what Mum's like with the discount vouchers on the back of shopping receipts.'

I scrunched my face up. 'Sounds classy.'

'They'll be home tomorrow, or the day after.' Ezra turned to us. 'Enjoy the peace while it lasts.'

Arriving home and ditching everything in one of the bedrooms was one of the strangest feelings. There was the ease of being at home, that I could truly unwind and, even in the heat, just lump about, enjoy a cold drink and close my eyes for a few moments without any of the stresses that London had brought. I think it was because I was so physically removed from all of my issues, I could pretend like they didn't exist. For the first week or so, that worked incredibly well – after the two days of jetlag wore off, that was.

My parents returned from their cruise, delighting us with photo after photo of the murky Murray, and all their tiny town pitstops along the way. Dad unpacked all the food I'd brought him, commenting on label changes and reduced package weights, and I revelled in more stories as he cleared a place in the cupboard for them all.

Days rolled into each other. I stole Aaron away from Frankie so often she announced I could keep him, and that she was putting her 'going out' clothes on and disappearing with friends for a night, and I even chanced an overnight trip down the coast to see where Ezra had set up home with his girlfriend and her daughter.

Socially, I crammed in as much as I could and, when Heather and Josh arrived, it only ramped up more. Their engagement party was strung out over a few days' worth of events – just to make sure they covered off as many friends as they could while they were around. We had a small beach party at Bondi with friends, went to dinner at a winery outside the city, and climbed the Sydney Harbour Bridge.

It was something I'd done once before but was more than happy to indulge in again when someone else was footing the bill. Last time, standing at the summit and posing for photos held a feeling of achievement but, this time, something flinched inside me. There was a niggling annoyance that had been following me around all week. Until that moment I'd been unable to put my finger on it. But, as the flash fell across our smiling faces, I realised that all these things I'd been doing were exactly what William and I were looking forward to doing together. It was essentially our list of things we'd do when we travelled together. But he wasn't here, and the realisation was awful.

When our climbing suits and safety harnesses were returned, I split from the group. I didn't have anything special planned, I just wanted to clear my head and gather my thoughts. I promised I'd be at the party later that night and farewelled everyone.

At Circular Quay, ferries bobbed about in their terminals, and a preternaturally huge cruise ship seemed to lumber over the top of the harbour like an all-seeing, all-knowing deity. I took a quick walk along the dock, just to get closer to the enormity of it, before heading into the twenty-four-hour restaurant just by the water.

When you get to know people well enough, you can tell they're walking up behind you just by the fall of their feet, that distinct shuffle of the left foot and clobber of the right. Or, you can pick them out in a crowd because of how they tucked their right foot behind their left ankle as they leant against the bar.

Craig.

The Good Lord was apparently intent on cramming just the right level of Told You So into my trip as possible. Before I had a chance to hot foot it out the door and find a cheap eatery under the bridge, he spotted me in the bar's reflection and, altogether too quickly, spun to face me.

'Emmy?'

'Hey,' I said, although what I really wanted to do was run for the hills. 'How are you?'

He bobbed his head about a bit. The casual summer shorts and polo look had returned, his hair was shorter again, but he looked fresh, happier, well-rested. 'I'm really well, thank you.'

'Good. Great. I'm glad.'

Cue the awkward standing around while we both struggled with what came next. I looked around the restaurant like it had the most fascinating décor ever. I skipped over my options. Running would get back to my parents and make yet another bad story. It would also mean more flack for me and, even though I had every right to walk away, I kind of just stood there and waited for fate to decide.

'Do you have time for a coffee?' he asked.

'Me?' This was certainly a change of pace for the same person who told everyone I'd cheated on him. My suspicions were aroused at the flash of memory, momentarily hazed by surprise.

'Well, yeah. I'm not in any hurry to be anywhere. Unless you're here with someone?' He looked over my shoulder. 'I just thought, you know, catch up for old times' sake.'

And that was how I came to have coffee and afternoon tea with Craig in what was fast becoming a very strange trip indeed. We picked the furthest table in the quietest corner and hoped that this would all go smoothly. He smoothed his clothes down as he sat, tossed me a packet of sugar and a spoon for my cake.

'So, how are you?' he asked. 'Are you well?'

I nodded. 'I'm not too bad, thank you. You?'

'Good.' His own spoon landed on the table with a clang. 'Uh, so, I didn't start that company. Not just yet, anyway.'

'No?' I asked. 'What are you doing?'

'Back in the family fold.' He shrugged. 'But I'm piecing things together each night when I get home from work. Hustle, hustle.'

'I'm sure when you do get there, you'll be completely fine.' I distracted myself with cake in the mouth and watching a small child drop a perfectly domed, fresh ice-cream on the ground.

'Are you just home for Christmas?' he asked. 'When did you get here?'

This all felt way too familiar and distant all at once. He was polite, completely rational and calm. And, while I didn't expect anything else of him – he always was all of those things – it just seemed so at odds with how I expected our first post-breakup meeting to go.

'About a week ago.' My head bobbed a little. 'It's been really good to catch up with everyone.'

'And how's work?'

'Still a dumb receptionist,' I blurted.

'God, Emmy, I'm sorry. I never meant that. I was angry and

269

irrational, and not an entirely nice person to know around that time.'

So this was fast sliding into territory I wasn't sure I wanted to enter. I yanked on the handbrake and tried angling the conversation towards things I'd been doing with family since I got back. I was scared that, if the conversation kept on its current trajectory, we'd end up not so much discussing, but fighting over the English elephant in the room.

'I'm really glad you're having a good time here, Emmy.'

'You are?' I said from behind a napkin.

He nodded. 'Sure, I mean, I was upset when I came home, but I don't wish you any harm.'

And that was officially the red rag to a bull moment.

'But didn't you tell people I'd cheated on you?' I asked. 'That was pretty hurtful. I lost a lot of friends from that.'

'I didn't tell them that.' He shook his head gently. 'But it was very clear you weren't telling the truth about your relationship with him.'

My eyes widened, possibly to the size of the saucers on the table. 'Sorry, what?'

'Your friend from work? He wasn't strictly that, was he Em?'

'No, you're right,' I admitted. 'I'd known him a while longer.'

'You could have just told me.' He pushed the last of the cake towards me, but I'd lost my appetite. 'Friends are cool, but you deliberately didn't tell me that there was history. I think that's the part that hurt the most, because it said all it needed to about the friendship.'

Christ, he dropped that wrecking ball right through the lounge room window. My own words to William began ringing very loudly in my ears.

'I'm sorry.'

'I take it you're dating him?'

I shook my head. 'You know what? I can't do this with you. This is too strange.'

270

I left. Quickly. I slipped up a stairwell and onto the first train that took me in the right direction. I wanted home, only my question now was: where exactly was home? Was it here, in the warmth, protection, and ease of family? Or was it on the other side of the world, choosing to sit down and iron out a few problems to make sure William and I didn't completely combust before we'd even given ourselves a chance. The realisation that I had been just as awful to others as I thought he'd been to me was a little ... sickening.

* * *

'You look like you've seen a ghost.' Frankie's voice held a twinge of smugness which was only slightly covered up by the squalling baby in her arms.

'I think I did.' I dropped my bags on the kitchen stool and held my arms open to take Aaron. 'The ghost of Emmy's past came to visit.'

The ride home had been a bit of a foot-jiggling, hand-wringing angst-fest. I was sure a small family approached the seats across from me, only to turn around and hotfoot it up to the second level of the carriage. I didn't blame them, really. I scrolled through the numbers in my phone over and over, the digital screen rolling to a spinning wheel stop at W for William. I debated calling, not just the once. More like The Police would – a thousand times a day – except it was clear that nothing I was doing was magic.

'Huh?' She shook her arms about, glad to have them freed up for even a few moments.

'I just ran into Craig.'

She was silent, but the raised brows and O-shaped mouth said it all for her. 'Right, well, I suppose you might. He lives around here still, so, you know.'

'I was a bit of an asshole to him.' I followed her around the kitchen as she filled the kettle, switched it on, kicked the door

271

shut on the dishwasher, and searched the cupboards for coffee cups. 'Not today, of course. I mean, when he was in London.'

'I wouldn't go that far.' She held up a box of tea and a jar of coffee.

'I would,' I said. 'Tea, please.'

'And what makes you say that?'

I rewound that tape right back to Edinburgh and laid it all out. My brain hit download, and Frankie copped a torrent of whatever was happening in my head. I told her all about William, my friend from work, who wasn't strictly just a friend from work, but an important piece of my history. We went back and forth about Craig and the stress of his job, and everything that had come to pass before he came back to Sydney and, when I relayed William's life plans, she sighed like it was it was the most romantic proposal ever. Despite reminding her it wasn't a marriage proposal, she wasn't buying it. Paris and everything after was covered off quickly, because there was no way she needed to know all the gory details, though I suspected she not-so-silently lived for it. By the time I wrapped up my fight with William, we were resting on banana lounges outside with ice-creams and oversized hats.

'So, you see, I've been an awful person,' I said. 'But I don't know if I'm sure what to do.'

'I don't think you have,' she said. 'But you both did some stupid things, neither of you could possibly deny that.'

'Correct,' I sighed.

'Now, this isn't excusing anybody's behaviour, but do you think he did those things to hurt you? Honestly, sit and think about it for a second.'

'I'd like to think not.'

She swung her legs off the lounge and sat up to look at me. Or Aaron as it turned out. He was fast asleep, sprawled out on my front. 'Just being selfish, right?'

'Yeah.'

272

'Which isn't that different to you not wanting to share him with anyone else. What do you think would have happened with Craig if he knew about William's history?'

'I think Craig would have come home earlier.'

She shrugged. 'Probably.'

'We've both been ridiculous.'

'Now she gets it.'

'I should call him.' I squinted into the sun. 'Shouldn't I?'

'Yes, you should.' She stood up and took her son. 'Do it before the party tonight. Get it out of your system. You know, like deadlines. Do them, get them done, then chill out.'

Chapter 33

There were no two ways about it. William didn't want to be found. I didn't call him when Frankie suggested. Later that night, at the engagement party, and after one too many drinks, I stepped out of the darkened venue and into the carpark. I dialled once, then twice. When his phone went straight to voicemail, I resorted to an email and hoped that, in the sober light of morning, he would find it as Drinking Emmy did right now.

William?
Can you call me?
I'm bored.
Call me when you can?
xx E

I realised that having an epiphany in the middle of someone else's engagement party was probably not the best way to handle things, but they happened when they happened, and all I could do was roll with the tide. I watched on absently as speeches were made in the decadent Edwardian building overlooking Sydney Harbour. We were sat around tables with crisp white linen and ornate centrepieces, indulged in share plates of that didn't seem to stop, and danced to a DJ who span tunes on a platform normally reserved for a bridal table. It was, in essence, a wedding in place of the one they'd decided to have in London. With the cocktail dresses and men in suits, the only thing it was missing was the exchange of vows.

I still had no answer as I climbed out of a taxi and into bed in the early hours of the next morning. When I took to helping Mum with the Christmas baking the next day, my phone sat silently on the counter. Did I try again? Only if I wanted to look like a complete nutter, though I wondered if that wasn't too far from the truth given the last few months. Mum was on hand with a bit of quality side-eye, but thankfully didn't air her thoughts.

* * *

Christmas morning began with sweltering temperatures, wrapping paper strewn across the house, and the smell of lunch wafting through from the backyard where it was already set to cook. Even though I'd told everyone not to get me anything, they'd chipped in and, after arranging it with Heather, had got me a lovely little gift card for my favourite clothing shop in London. I was beyond thrilled, though I made them promise they all had to come and have lunch with me next year.

Family arrived, seemingly one or two at a time, and then all at once, extra tables and chairs spread out across a backyard that would normally feel quite large. It was nice to be back in the throng, among aunties and uncles, long unseen cousins, and the platters of seafood and nibbles, party hats and Christmas crackers. I was a thing of curiosity, questioned for miles about life in another country, but there was one question I deflected each time it was raised: 'So, who's the lucky fella?'

Good question. Or, maybe that should have been: Where's the lucky fella?

I tried to call again just after lunch, assuming it was enough of an allowance for the time difference, for William to crawl bleary-eyed out of his toasty warm bed and get started for the day. If he was already in Paris, which was his Christmas, maybe I'd been using the wrong phone number. No, I told myself, roaming would see him right. I dropped my phone in the pocket of my shorts and tried to forget about it.

And, then, right as I was in the backyard on bottle duties with my nephew and shooing away flies, the chatter seemed to drown out to a whisper. I thought maybe I had a rogue vomit somewhere down my back, because it had happened, but when Frankie wrestled Aaron away and spun me around like we were prepping for Pin the Tail on the Donkey, it wasn't vomit at all.

'Hello, Bored.' He smiled. 'I'm William.'

'No!' I laughed.

I'd never before felt such a mix of wonder, relief, and excitement all at once. Though, I wasn't sure how he felt as he stood there looking like he'd worn his own clothes through the washing machine and, possibly, hadn't slept in days.

'Please tell me you travel business class, because that flight was balls,' he joked, to the amusement of his audience.

My knee buckled as I stepped down from the back porch and onto the grassed area. If I made the short walk across to him without face-planting, I'd be quite happy with being thrown up on again at some stage later today. It seemed like a fair trade.

'It's good to see you.' I wrapped my arms around his neck and hugged him tighter than I ever had. 'I'm so glad you're here.'

'Well, that's a relief.' He drew back to look at me. 'Wasn't quite sure what I'd do if you said bugger off.'

'I'm quite okay with this.'

'Good, because I think I just lost a day, didn't I?'

'Sort of, but you have travelled forward in time,' I said.

'Makes sense. I am a doctor.'

I skipped introductions and instead opted to drag William

276

inside and lock him into my bedroom. Except, we didn't do a lot other than look at each other for the first few minutes. He dropped his coat and backpack on the bed, finished tearing his tie off and found the air-conditioner vent to stand under.

'It's like breathing in lukewarm water here. It's awful.'

'I'm really glad you're here,' I said. 'Because I have a lot of things I need to say to you.'

'Can I go first?' He pinched at his chest and fanned his shirt. 'That's better.'

'No.'

'No?'

'No.' I leant against my old desk that had been transplanted to my new room, complete with world map and teenage graffiti. 'I think it's actually me who owes you an apology. I've held you to this sometimes ridiculously high standard when, as it turned out, I was doing all the things I accused you of, to other people. So, not only am I a hypocrite, I'm a stupid one at that.'

'What do you mean?'

'I had coffee with Craig the other day.' I scratched at my forehead. 'And he said something that just made everything click.'

William looked at me warily, the mention of the ex-boyfriend. 'Oh?'

'He was asking how I was, how things were with you.'

'Really? He asked about me?'

'He did,' I chuckled. 'And all he said was, "I wish you'd told me about who he was sooner, so I didn't have to find out about him the way I did." All I could think of was that moment at work when I found out about you being married, and said something very similar to you.'

'I never did any of that out of a place of … malice.'

'I know.'

'Maybe some of the stuff at the start, I was genuinely being hurtful. I don't have an excuse for that. I just shouldn't have done it. But the whole Angela thing, and then the letters. It was over before you arrived, so no excuse to not tell you. I can't whip out some bullshit about trying to protect you, because that's all contradictory. I think I know why, and it was as simple as I just loved spending time with you, and I wanted to keep us in that little bubble.'

'It was a nice place to be.'

He smiled. 'It really was, wasn't it?'

I nodded.

'And the letters? Well, you were right – they're a thing of celebration, so I should have just said something. I think I was hoping to just pack everything away until after the divorce and then show you, thinking everything would be totally fine when it wasn't.'

'Well, I was the fool who said she wanted to wait for all that to be done, too, so maybe that's another one on me, too.'

'What I want to say, I suppose, is that I have seen people take their first breaths and I've seen them take their last. And the only, only thing that these two moments have in common is love. No matter who they were, they were surrounded by love. For me, that means you. You are my love. You, our letters, and everything they stood for – even when we thought they were just silly ramblings, which many of them probably were, but they always said more than that. You are who I want to surround myself with – as impossible a thing as we are. Statistically speaking, we should not be. I mean, how many times do you go around getting punched in the face? But here we are, which is why I need to hold onto you all that much tighter.'

'Oh, God, that is so getting you laid,' I said through laughter. And maybe a few tears.

His beautiful face wrinkled up into a tired but satisfied smile. 'Not if I don't pass out first, I am absolutely shattered from that flight.'

'Seriously, though.' I stepped forward and threading my fingers through his hair. 'I did my share of stupid things, too.'

278

'I realised very early on how ridiculously much I loved you and was petrified that you'd hit your six months and disappear again. So, I scrambled like an egg.'

'I love you too much to do that,' I said quietly. All I could think about was how he smelt like home. 'Start over?'

He leant in and kissed me. Soft and slow, I was suddenly wide awake in the face of a food coma, and feeling everything – the flutter of deep breaths against lips, the brush of his unshaven jaw, and the roar of hearts that beat to our own song. This is how Edinburgh was supposed to end last time, a long slow kiss under the fireworks before walking off into the dead of night. The moment it felt like he was moving away, I slipped my arms around his neck and pulled him closer.

'I really missed this part,' he mumbled.

I laughed against his mouth. 'Just this part?'

'Oh, there are other parts, just being socially appropriate.' He wobbled his head about playfully. 'You know.'

'You? Socially appropriate? I won't hear of it.'

'Hey, Em.'

I held the back of his neck and scratched my fingers through his hair. 'What?'

'One last thing.'

I regarded him with uncertainty. 'Yes?'

William leant back and rustled through the front pocket of his backpack, a tattered envelope plucked out of obscurity. He pulled out a piece of paper and turned it to face me. 'Your Death List has one thing left on it.'

'Hogmanay,' I mumbled. 'Really?'

'We have tickets,' he said. 'If you're keen, that is?'

279

Chapter 34

From our hidden vantage point at the top of the hill, we had the perfect view of Edinburgh. We'd started the night much the same way we had a few years before, with dancing, dinner, and a few drinks in the same tiny pub we first visited together. This time, we made sure we were out in the street and on our way well before the clock struck midnight.

William's trip to Sydney was a whirlwind to say the least. He fit in fantastically with family, who were both curious and excited about their new family. When I hadn't heard his laugh filter through the yard, I went looking for him, only to find him fast asleep on top of my bed.

Accounting for flights William had booked into Edinburgh, we had exactly four and a half days to cram in all of the things he wanted to see. It was impossible to get to everything, but Bondi Beach was easy enough, as was the boozy lunch and stroll around Darling Harbour. We took a ferry to Manly, which proved to be a thing of wonderment for William, even though it was just a normal part of life me. He likened my lack of enthusiasm for this to his own lack of enthusiasm for the Tube. Still, we were cramming things in right up until we boarded our flight home.

We slid from one celebration to another after landing in

Edinburgh as smidge after midday on December 30th. From the airport to the hotel, and directly onto the torchlight, where I absolutely did not tempt fate by getting involved in any of the arguments we saw break out.

Not minding the lack of sleep, we were still jazzed after days of touring, talking, and enjoying the company of each other's bodies. We crashed heavily our first night, sleeping until after midday, and enjoying a slow stroll through the city that culminated in us now, up on the hill with a tray of coffees and a bag of hot jam donuts beside us.

'So, Emmy, got any resolutions?'

'Hmm.' I popped a yeasty morsel in my mouth. 'I was thinking nursing school.'

'Sexy.' He looked at me approvingly. 'As in nursing your own child, or getting a nurse's outfit, because both are completely cool with me.'

I laughed. 'Nurse's outfit. You can close the baby door for a little while.'

'But, but, but…' He leant into my line of site, hair sprawled across my lap. 'You just look so good with a baby in your arms.'

'I'm not saying I don't want one. I'm just saying maybe let's just enjoy this for a little while, have fun.' I pushed William off of me. 'What about you? What are your plans?'

'I have a few thoughts on that.'

'Which are?'

'Well,' he began. 'I wouldn't mind my own practice. I've thought about moving out of London, getting a place in some tiny town somewhere.'

'I don't know if I want to leave London. I'm comfortable in your place, my place, wherever I split my time.'

'Does that mean you want to move in?'

I chuckled. 'You are straight on in there, aren't you? Setting up house, making babies.'

'Both of those are fun options.' He pointed at me. 'Especially the making part.'

'Oh, good Lord.'

'Alright, how about this.' He held his hands up when I went to say something. 'Let's just make like Paris and see what happens? Nothing concrete, minds open to what the world gives us.'

'I like that plan.'

William leant in and kissed me, just as the first firework exploded in the sky above us and, if that wasn't the most perfect way to end a night, then I had no idea what was. When it came down to it, in this moment, I would have relived the last six months of my life all over again, just to experience something this pure.

Acknowledgements

As it turns out, book two *is* actually harder than book one. Even if book two is actually book seven, but was originally book one about four years ago. I know, hectic, right?

The first version of this book was self-published in 2015, and it's been quite the adventure ever since. Getting the original version out of my head and trying to reimagine William and Emmy's story was difficult and took a little longer than anticipated. It was all very Doctor Strange navigating the mirror dimension. But, here we are. We're done. I think. It's time for the credits to roll.

Since I feel like I missed thanking a whole heap of people after *A Recipe for Disaster*, you're stuck listening to me prattle on today.

Kathy Palmer – the first stranger to tell me you loved my work, in a very long message, very early one morning. I still have that message printed out and tacked up on my notice board. Thank you so much for your endless support, and I hope you love this version as much as you loved the original.

Kat Betts – for answering all my stupid grammar questions and keeping me occupied in the midnight hours.

Hannah Smith – thank you for offering this over-excited idiot a contract. I'm not going to question why, I'm just going to roll with it.

Charlotte Mursell & the HQ Digital team – thank you for the patience, the covers, the support, and for letting me email in a panic at 2am. This past year has been spectacular to say the very least. I'm sure this is only the beginning. Looking forward to seeing you all soon.

Rebecca Raisin – you, my friend, are a rare find. Wading into the world of publishing is confusing enough for a newbie. Your advice and counsel have been priceless. I'm so glad I have you to bounce from. London awaits us.

Hannah Membrey – from that strangely fantastic weekend at UNSW, to today. Thank you so much for the laughs, the re-reads, the bouncing of ideas, and the edits. You were there in that pokey Sydney hotel last August when *A Recipe for Disaster* was born. And you've been there to make sure this book especially is way better than the original ever could have been. Words cannot express my gratitude. I only hope that we're pulling 3am finishes to finish your own book soon.

Cheryl Farinola – my sister from another mister. Though, you never know what our genealogy studies will turn up. I love you. You've got this.

Shane McInerney – you are the best person I've ever met.

Last but not least, to anyone who bought, reviewed, Tweeted, or contacted me about *A Recipe for Disaster*, thank you so much for trusting me with those funny little things we call words. I'm just glad my humour translated, and that you enjoyed the read. Random Tweets first thing in the morning make it all worthwhile.

See you next time,

B. xo

Dear Reader,

Thank you so much for taking the time to read this book – we hope you enjoyed it! If you did, we'd be so appreciative if you left a review.

Here at HQ Digital we are dedicated to publishing fiction that will keep you turning the pages into the early hours. We publish a variety of genres, from heartwarming romance, to thrilling crime and sweeping historical fiction.

To find out more about our books, enter competitions and discover exclusive content, please join our community of readers by following us at:

🐦 *@HQDigitalUK*

f *facebook.com/HQDigitalUK*

Are you a budding writer? We're also looking for authors to join the HQ Digital family! Please submit your manuscript to:

HQDigital@harpercollins.co.uk.

Hope to hear from you soon!

Turn the page for an exclusive extract from *A Recipe for Disaster*, another enchanting story from Belinda Missen...

Belinda Missen

A RECIPE FOR DISASTER

Life's not always a piece of cake

Chapter 1

Wedding cakes have always fascinated me. When I was a young girl, they'd be the centrepiece of any drawing I fashioned up in school. Big ones, small ones, plain white ones with that awful marzipan icing, or the ornate beauty of a royal fairy tale. I marvelled at television programmes that featured cakes; each one of them a work of art. Someone had spent hours toiling away in a kitchen, hair in a net, poring over finer details of lace, ganache, height, and taste.

Now that job was mine.

As a baker, it was almost a shame to see your work sliced and served in greasy paper bags at the end of a long night. I'd woken after countless events to find a squashed slice of chocolate mud in the bottom of my handbag. I hated to think of wedding cakes ending their life like that, but I also loved seeing them enjoyed.

The history of the wedding cake was simple, stretching back to the time of Arthur and Camelot. Wealth, prosperity, fertility, and good luck were all said to come from consuming said baked delight. For me? It was all about the art. Was the icing set? Did I get that flower just right? What about the topper? Is the cake even cooked? Never mind the brides they were designed for.

Today, my bride was Edith. Keeper of chickens and knitter of ugly sweaters, she lived exactly four houses away from me in our not always quiet country town of Inverleigh, ninety minutes south-west of Melbourne. It was home to exactly one pub, one general store – which served as bank, post office, chippy, and advice line – a restaurant that closed twelve months earlier, and a football team. In two hours' time, Edith was marrying Barry – a not-so-handsome football player with a thrice-broken nose and a penchant for homebrew strong enough to blind even the most seasoned of drinkers.

'Are you listening?' Edith's screech verged on delirium.

'I am absolutely listening,' I said, hearing her bridesmaids cluck away in the background. 'Aren't you supposed to be getting ready?'

'I am ready – I've been ready for hours.' She yawned. 'Is the cake still all right?'

The night before had been a last-minute panic over the cake being "too naked", and whether I couldn't "just add some more flowers". I'd been at the florist at first crack of the door lock to get extra coverage, before dashing home to fill the gaps and please the bride. A quick dozen photo messages confirmed everything was in order, even if that cake now looked like it had sprouted a pubic region somewhere towards its front.

'It's beautiful.' I smiled.

Sitting on the turntable in front of me were three layers of white chocolate and citrus mud deliciousness. A semi-nude cake, it was iced in soft lemon-gelati-flavoured meringue buttercream, and adorned with a selection of native flowers. Pink waratahs sat with golden wattle, grey-green eucalypt leaves and their gumnuts. I stood back and admired it again to the soundtrack of a grumbling tummy. Perfect.

'Do you think it's bad luck?' Edith interrupted my thoughts.

'What's bad luck?' I asked.

In my bathroom, the shower stopped running.

'The whole dead baker thing.'

Two days ago, Edith's original baker dropped dead. Just like that. I received a panicked phone call at one o'clock in the morning, asking if I could please, please, with extra money on top, resurrect my baking career to help her. It had been almost three years since I'd fashioned anything more than a birthday cake, but I was more than happy to help. So far, it was looking like a success.

'Honestly, Eds, the only person it's bad luck for is your baker, and his family. You and Barry are going to be completely fine. You'll put your dress on—'

'I've already got it on.'

'Okay, so you'll turn up, you'll say your vows.' I pulled lace curtains aside and looked out the kitchen window. 'The weather is stunning, by the way. It's a lovely Friday, with a little bit of sun and not too much wind. You're going to have an amazing day, surrounded by friends and family. It'll be one big eating, drinking lovefest.'

'You're right. Of course, you're right.' She breathed deeply into the receiver. 'Okay. I'm going for photos now. I'll see you there. Please, please don't drop it.' She hung up before I could get another word in.

I put my phone on charge, and walked into the bathroom to find Seamus buried under a cloud of shaving cream. Butcher to my baker, he'd been a trade-show find six months earlier. While I'd been wandering around, thinking I should buy a new stand mixer and considering my life path, he rounded the corner with an armful of carving knives, a headful of unruly auburn hair and bottle-green eyes. One drink had led to another, we'd discovered mutual friends, and slowly, but surely, started dating.

'Everything okay, Pet?' His Irish lilt was muffled by the soft white clouds that sputtered towards the mirror.

I pulled my blonde hair into a loose bun and leant closer to the mirror, poking at the new lines under my tired brown eyes. Baking, huh? 'Yeah, all fine. Just need to deliver it, and hark, the herald angels sing.'

'Good.' He grinned, razor gliding through foam. 'At least she'll stop calling at all hours.'

'She's allowed to call at all hours. She's my friend, she's a client, and she's stressed.' I paused, arms in the air, bobby pin poised.

'I'm just saying. Eleven o'clock on a Thursday night.'

'And it's completely fine,' I stressed, agitated. 'I need the money right now.'

As I walked away, he mumbled something just quietly enough that I couldn't hear. I ignored the call to argument and closed the bedroom door. A grey pantsuit I'd dangled from the back of the door last night now hung limply from the door handle, and had been dragged across the floor. Really? Right now? I brushed the dust and lint from the bottoms and hoped for the best.

'Oh, I got that magazine for you, too. *The Gourmet Chef*?' he asked.

'*Gourmet Traveller*?' I tugged at my shirt.

'Yeah, that might be the one.' Seamus knotted his tie. 'Something like that.'

The magazine he was talking about had already made its way to the floor of the lounge room, discarded the moment he walked through the front door. Not a moment later, as I waddled towards the front door under the weight of a cake, snapping at Seamus as I went, I kicked the magazine under the lip of the couch, and hoped for the best.

Unloading and transporting cakes is no different when they've been made for friends. In fact, it's even more nerve-racking. While I resembled something close to awake, with my suit sorted and a dab of make-up, I struggled between keeping the cake upright, and trying not to kill Seamus as he sped along Winchelsea Road towards the reception venue. The road was far from safe, one lane of dusty orange gravel or knobby bitumen most of the way, twists and bends, oncoming livestock trucks, and a driver who was hellbent on getting to his destination as if he were piloting a live-action Mario Kart game.

Edith and Barry's wedding reception was to be held in the function room of the very fancy, newly renovated Barwon Park Mansion. An 1870s bluestone building situated fifteen minutes from home, it was blessed with sweeping views of the grassy plains around it, and was the picture-perfect location for a country wedding. Perfect except for the corrugated gravel road that covered the last few hundred metres of the drive. If I could keep the cake from being smeared on the windscreen, I would die happy.

'Do you want help?' Seamus opened my door for me after we arrived.

'Not treating the drive here like a go round a rally track would have been a great help.' I huffed, sending a loose lock of hair outward in a cloud of frustration.

'Right.' He pursed his lips, eyebrows raised to the sky. 'I'll just go, then, if you're going to argue.'

I couldn't be bothered fighting, not now. 'I've got this. Go and grab some seats.'

People were already arriving, an hour before the ceremony, which would take place under a marquee in the front gardens. Workers scrambled to add finishing touches to hessian bunting, gloss-white wooden fold-back chairs, and native flowers that hung from the end of each row of chairs. Tall eucalypts, grey and white, swayed in the breeze, offering up loose leaves and gumnuts that pitter-pattered like rain as they landed on the white tarpaulin roof.

I carried the cake along the gravel driveway, sidestepping up the front stairs like a crab, and in through the heavy door with the wedge of a foot and heave of a shoulder. The foyer revealed a wide sprawling staircase covered in red velvet carpet, a sign of the original owner's wealth.

'Hello?' My voice echoed off marble statues and oil paintings of disapproving previous tenants.

No response. It seemed the building was empty, as was an

ornate frame that would soon declare: "Edith loves Barry". Every moment I stood, I became increasingly aware of the weight in my arms. Cakes were a little like babies in that the longer you held them, the heavier they felt. It was another reminder of how out of practice I was with this baking business.

A pot rattled in a far corner, so I followed the noise along a hall like Alice down the rabbit hole. Around a dark corner, a sign warned of a private function. Before I reached the kitchen, which smelt like the best roast beef I would ever eat, I was cut off by a woman who zipped past quicker than The Flash.

'Hello!' I stuttered.

'Oh, the cake. Thank the gods. I thought you'd be here earlier.' She threw her hands in the air, and a clasp of grey hair escaped her bun. She tucked it behind her ear. 'I'm Sally, and I'm running the show today.'

'Lucy Williams.' I smiled. 'Where do you want it?'

'You really want to know?' She scoffed, looking more 1800s housekeeper than event manager. Her dark pinstriped shirt was twisted and stained, and sweat patches leached from her under-arms. 'Sorry, it's been one of those days.' After more mumbling about brides, overextended budgets, ridiculous cakes, and awful caterers, she pointed me towards the next hallway. 'There's a small stand by the bridal table. I'm sure you'll see it. Just let the catering team know. They're getting the room ready now, but they're bloody late, too, aren't they?'

Without the usual throng of weekend tourists, the old halls felt empty and a little bit naughty. It reminded me of days when, as a child, I'd experienced my school devoid of other students, on nights and weekends when Mum was busy preparing teaching notes. I took a left, and a right, before I found the reception room.

Bluestone walls enclosed barn doors at the opposite end of the room, which was flooded with bright natural light, though festoon lights were strung across the room. Like the marquee, the walls were decorated with bunting, and the centrepieces matched the floral theme, making sure the room smelt like a Sunday walk in a national park.

Placing the cake by the bridal table soon became an early highlight of the day. The sweet relief on my arms coupled with a quick mental download. I'd made it, no dropping, no cracking, and no incidents. To celebrate, I snapped off some social-media-worthy photos, both to show off on my Facebook page and, also, in the odd event I felt spurred on to take up baking again. From above, below, side-on, and close-ups of the flowers, I took so many, I half expected the cake to make a duck-face at me and tell me to get a life.

Satisfied, I scrolled through my photos as I left. Reaching for the door handle, it swung open onto me, sending me scuttling backwards. That would teach me for having my head buried in a screen.

'... and make sure the napkins are folded properly, too, not like last time.' A man buzzed past me like an unwelcome memory, a mosquito on a summer night.

'Yes, chef.' Standing by a table, a teenager fiddled with silver cutlery that clattered to the ground in a display of nerves. He swore, and grabbed a fresh fork from his apron, which bore a gold "M" against the black fabric.

'We should be ready by now. You should be in the kitchen helping with prep, not going over this again.'

'Yes, chef.' With each answer, a small part of the boy's soul ebbed away. I'd been in his situation before – anyone who'd worked in hospitality had. It made me want to strangle the man responsible, the one who'd almost bowled me over. My only problem was, I recognised him – too well.

I knew his voice, and every possible incarnation it could take. The happy, the sad, the surprised, and the midnight whispers. I knew the tuft of black hair on the back of his neck and how it curled slightly to the left. The rest of his hair wound around itself like Van Gogh's 'Starry Night' when it got too long or wet. Without tiptoes, he could peer across the top of my refrigerator, and had done so many times looking for lost recipe sheets or keys.

The shape of his body had been burnt into memory, useful when trying to pick someone out in a crowd. So had his eyes, a neon blue that made it look like someone had scrawled on his face with Hi-Liter. As quickly as he made his entrance, he turned and made a beeline for the kitchen door, blustering along without so much as a glance in my direction.

'Don't just stand there,' he snapped. 'Do what you need to do and go. We're busy.'

It took me a moment to realise he was talking to me. Had he not seen me at all?

'Is this how you operate now, Oliver?'

God, he was still so beautiful, as much as it pained me to admit. He wore a black double-breasted uniform that pinched across broad shoulders, complete with the familiar "M" stitched into the breast in fine gold thread. His apron was covered in kitchen detritus. While he'd always been confident, there was added fire behind those eyes, a purpose in his soul. It was no wonder he had restaurant critics eating out of his hand. And yet, underneath it all, teenage vulnerability lapped below his concrete surface, if only you knew what to look for.

Oliver stopped, his body rigid as if on pause. He turned to me slowly, a confused frown lining his face. I felt like he'd reached into my chest and ripped out my still-beating heart. I expected that, somewhere between here and the door, he'd wave it around his head in victory, before taking a bite and spitting it out in disgust.

We hadn't seen each other in three years. We hadn't spoken in eighteen months.

'Lucy.'

I swallowed. 'Oliver.'

'Lucy,' he repeated nervously. 'How ... how are you? Are you well?'

I nodded. 'Fine, thank you. You?'

'I'm, yeah, I'm okay.' He nodded.

'This is … this is a surprise.' And one I could have strangled Edith for right now.

'You could say that, yes.' He chuckled nervously, looking over his shoulder again. This time, at my cake. 'One of yours?'

'It is.' I rubbed sweating palms on my pants. 'Issue with the original baker, so here I am.'

'Rough luck,' he said quietly, looking behind him again. 'It looks incredible, Lucy. You're still unfairly talented. What is it?' He walked across to the small distressed wood table. 'Naked is the new black, isn't it?'

'Thank you.' I'd be lying if I said the praise didn't hit me in the sweet spot, even after all this time. 'It's citrus mud with lemon icing.'

'It's gorgeous.' He leant in to look at the finer details.

I stepped forward cautiously. As proud of it as I was, I didn't think it was overly intricate, but Oliver seemed intent on inspecting it from all angles. It felt like an hour had passed before he stood back and looked at me.

'Are you … are you well?' A nervous Oliver was like Willy Wonka's Golden Ticket. You knew there was one out there some- where, but you'd be hard-pressed to find it without some serious legwork.

I felt my tongue brush against my lips, my mouth sandpaper dry. 'You've already asked that.'

'I have. Right. Of course.' He looked stuck between wanting to flee and trying to think of something else to say.

As for me, flight mode had well and truly kicked in. 'Okay. So, I'm going to go now. See you later, I guess.'

'Luce, wait.' He held out a hand. 'Stay for a drink.'

I froze on the spot, hand clutching the door handle. We watched each other silently. Seconds stretched to minutes, and Oliver looked more hopeful than he had right to.

'Why are you here?' I asked.

He shoved his hands in the pockets of his apron and rocked on the balls of his feet. 'Catering Edith and Barry's wedding.'

'And she picked you?'

I couldn't be sure, but I thought I saw the corner of his mouth twitch. 'Barry got in touch a few months ago, asked if I was going to be in town. I wanted to come back and sort a few things out, and we all know he has a bit of cash to burn through, so here we are.'

'Here we are,' I repeated, scratching my forehead. Somewhere in the back of my brain, an Oliver-shaped headache was forming. 'Are you in town long?'

'Maybe.' He brushed over my question as if in a job interview, no reaction either way.

'Right.' I turned to walk away.

'Lucy, stay. I'll make coffee.'

I remember making the same request of him once upon a time. Stay, have a pot of tea, talk. I chose not to remind him. 'Can't stop, gotta go. See you later. Wedding thing. Have a great day, chef.'

I walked so quickly I would have been disqualified from Olympic gold for having both feet off the ground. Not until I'd locked myself in the toilets and sat down on the lid did I exhale. I fired off a text to my best friend, Zoe, confident she was the only one I trusted with this information.

Help. Oliver is here.
Hey?
MY HUSBAND OLIVER.
Yes, I know who he is.
I'm currently locked in toilets.
Practising breathing.
Oh. Shit.

The next book from Belinda Missen, *Lessons in Love*,
is coming in May 2019!

DIGITAL HQ

If you enjoyed *An Impossible Thing Called Love*, then why not try another delightfully uplifting romance from HQ Digital?